THE UNRESOLVED SEVENTH

MAY   2012

THE UNRESOLVED SEVENTH

RICHARD HELMS

FIVE STAR
A part of Gale, Cengage Learning

GALE
CENGAGE Learning®

Detroit • New York • San Francisco • New Haven, Conn • Waterville, Maine • London

GALE
CENGAGE Learning®

LIBRARY OF CONGRESS CATALOGING-IN-PUBLICATION DATA

Helms, Richard W., 1955–
    The unresolved seventh / Richard Helms. — 1st ed.
      p. cm.
    ISBN 978-1-4328-2587-4 (hardcover) — ISBN 1-4328-2587-9
(hardcover) 1. Murder—Investigation—Fiction. I. Title.
PS3608.E466U57 2012
813'.6—dc23   2011047020

Published in 2012 in conjunction with Tekno Books and Ed Gorman.

Printed in Mexico
1 2 3 4 5 6 7 16 15 14 13 12

For Elaine

*Once in awhile, right in the middle of an ordinary life,
love gives us a fairy tale.*

ONE

"I'm retired," Ben Long said as he sliced a piece of grilled tuna in his salad.

"I know that," Sidney Kingsley said. "That's why you'd be perfect."

"I don't see it that way."

"Will you at least look at the files?"

"No."

"Why in hell not?"

Long took a moment to savor the tuna before swallowing.

"It's a death penalty case," he said finally.

"That never stopped you before."

"I wasn't retired before. There are plenty of young guys who'd be willing to do this evaluation. Why me?"

"Because there was a time when you were the best."

"That was a long time ago."

"Like riding a bike."

Long set his flatware down and took a sip of the chardonnay.

"There is very little similarity between forensic psychology and bicycling," he said after setting the glass back on the table. "I haven't done a competency evaluation in almost four years. What makes you think I can still hack it?"

Sid Kingsley swiped at the air.

"Four years. So what? You've been teaching. It's not as if you've been off fly-fishing."

"I teach college sophomores," Long countered. "I teach two

sections of Intro, one section of Abnormal, and a section of Developmental. It isn't exactly cutting-edge stuff. Find yourself a young eager beaver."

"What can I do to change your mind?"

Long chewed on a forkful of arugula and olive.

"Ten million dollars," he said after swallowing.

"What?"

"I'll do it for ten million dollars."

"You're joking."

"No, I'm not. I don't like to joke. I don't understand jokes. Joking would serve no purpose. Give me ten million dollars, and I'll do your competency evaluation."

"I'm a government employee," Kingsley said indignantly. "Even if I were inclined to pay such an exorbitant fee, the District Attorney's Office would go broke."

"See?" Long said, reaching for his wine glass. "You didn't want me so badly after all."

Kingsley tossed up his hands with a disgusted sigh.

"You are an insufferable son of a bitch," he said. "You always were."

"Flatter me some more. This is fun."

"Just for fucking with me, I'm going to sit here and talk about the case. You might not look at the files, but I bet you won't walk out on lunch."

"Don't be so certain. It's not that great a lunch. The wine is nice, though."

"Earl Torrence. Age twenty-six. White male. Goes about six-one. People call him *Junior*. Looks like he was born to play Lenny in *Of Mice and Men*. He's charged with murdering his brother's girlfriend, based on his own confession."

"See? Open and shut case. Gas the bastard." Long speared a piece of tomato.

"We have to convict him first. His attorney might balk at

preemptively introducing him to Mr. Needle."

"You chose your side. You knew the job was dangerous when you took it."

"They're trying to get this kid off on some incompetency bullshit, Ben."

"So prove him competent, and then gas him. Just don't involve me."

Kingsley sat and looked at his largely uneaten *petit filet.* It was a beautifully prepared piece of meat. For some reason, his appetite had evaporated.

"You're familiar with the Supreme Court's decision in *Atkins?*" he asked.

"Of course," Long said. "They held that executing the mentally retarded constitutes cruel and unusual punishment."

"His attorney says this kid is retarded, Ben."

"I didn't say I agreed with them."

"You think it's okay to execute someone who has the mind of a child?"

"I didn't say that, either. I'm saying it's a complicated matter. I'm saying that the court and legislatures' definitions of retardation have been overly broad, and poorly informed. I'm saying that it's a controversy I'd as soon leave to people who give a damn. Eat your steak, Sid. You look anemic."

Kingsley realized that he probably *did* look anemic. He had put in far too many nights and days dealing with the string of procedural challenges foisted on him by Torrence's attorney. Sometimes he wondered why this case had taken such a hold of him.

Ben Long, on the other hand, looked like the better end of a fitness club ad. Four years away from the courts, and he appeared to have carved away a decade of his life. Kingsley knew that Ben was past fifty, but anyone else would have considered him to be ten years younger. His hair, which had been conservatively razor-cut during his quarter-century of psychological practice, now hung casually down over his collar, and fell over his ears in tousled waves. His eyes were bright and clear when he made eye contact at all, which almost never happened, and his face was barely lined. Gray strands crept in surreptitiously around his temples. Otherwise, he was the picture of health.

He never touched red meat, despite the exhortations from the low-carb faddists, but instead seemed to live on a constant diet of vegetables and fish. As a result, his five-eleven frame had lost its previous paunch, and he was now flat-stomached and surprisingly sinuous for his age.

Sid Kingsley realized that he, on the other hand, probably looked like Ben Long's father.

"Okay," he said after taking a bite of the *filet*. "If you won't evaluate this kid, at least tell me how to go about getting it done correctly."

Long finished his salad and placed his silverware on the plate. He took another sip of the wine.

"I worked almost exclusively for the DA's office," he said.

"Yes."

"You know why?"

Kingsley winced. Some memories were still painful.

"Of course, Ben. It was tragic."

"No. It was criminal. Tragedy is what happens to people who have tragic flaws. Crime happens to people who don't deserve it and don't see it coming. If some criminal psychologist had done his job with Anson Mount, he never would have been released from jail. He never would have gone hunting for new prey, and we might be having an entirely more productive conversation."

"It's been almost twenty years."

"Not for me. For me it happened yesterday. Working for the previous DA, I had a chance to see to it that other predators didn't squeak by on faulty evaluations by hired gun quacks who would say anything a defense attorney asked them to for the right amount of money."

"Well, there you are! That's exactly what I'm trying to get you to do with Torrence. This kid *did* it, Ben. Like you said, it's an open and shut case. His attorney is going to keep him from paying for that."

"That's tough for you. Who is this attorney, anyway?"

Sidney placed his knife and fork on his plate. Suddenly, he had lost his appetite.

"Eli."

Ben stared at him for a moment.

"Eli Crouch?"

"Yes."

"Pass," Ben said as he folded his napkin and placed it on the table. "Thanks for the lunch. If you'd told me before we ordered that Crouch was handling the case, you could have saved the DA's office a little money. I'll see you around."

He started to get up, but Sidney stopped him.

"Don't you want to know who Crouch hired to prove Torrence incompetent to proceed?"

"No. Have a nice day, Sid."

Ben turned to leave.

"He's hired Sybil," Sid said.

Ben stopped. For a second, he looked up at the ceiling, his hands in his pockets, as if debating what he should say.

"I'm still not interested," he said finally.

"Tell me something."

"What?"

"Why aren't you still working for the DA's office? Why'd you retire?"

"Ah," Long said, as he turned for the last time to go. "That's another story."

Two

Long slid in behind the wheel of his Toyota Spyder and blipped the engine a couple of times before pulling out of the parking lot.

The road to his home wound up the side of a mountain, switching back time and again to turn the three-thousand-foot climb into four miles of rhythmic braking and shifting, which Long attacked with the mechanical precision and timing with which he approached nearly every activity. Near the crest, he pulled off the asphalt onto a gravel road and followed it deep into the trees.

His house was perched on the side of the mountain, with a clear view of the valley below and the next range of peaks five miles to the northwest. It was autumn, after a wet summer, and the hardwoods in the valley had turned into a multicolored carpet that spread out below him for miles into the distance, until it rose up to the next peak and disappeared into the bluish mists of the Smoky Mountains.

Before lunch, Long had dropped by his favorite music store in Asheville, and had purchased a new CD of Respighi's *Fountains of Rome,* conducted by Loren Maazel. He carefully hung his jacket on its designated wooden hanger in the entry hall closet, poured himself a glass of Lindeman's merlot, and slipped the CD into the changer.

He switched the amplifier to the deck speakers and walked out to sit in one of the chairs there to sip his wine and let the music transport him.

The house wasn't very large, but it included almost ten acres of heavily wooded land, so that he enjoyed absolute privacy. Except for the deck that cantilevered out over a seventy-degree drop of almost a quarter mile, the house was nestled amongst centuries-old oaks, poplars, and red spruce that provided Long's barrier from the encroaching world, and the people who lived in it.

He could crank up the stereo without having to worry about annoying the neighbors. He never had to close his back screens in pleasant weather, because you would have to be an Army Ranger with mountain-climbing expertise to break into his house from the rear.

It was fall break at his college. The students had all headed home or to the beach for one last fling before the dreaded trudge toward the semester final exams. The faculty had a few days off to ostensibly catch up with paperwork. Long's paperwork was complete, so he had nothing to do but lounge on his deck, listen to Respighi, and sip wine.

He should have been absolutely content, but something kept tugging at the corners of his mind.

As the shadows began to creep over the valley, he pulled himself from his chair and retreated to his kitchen. Before leaving for Asheville, he had taken a salmon steak from the freezer to thaw in the refrigerator. When he checked it, he found it supple and pink and ready for dinner.

He grated some fresh ginger into a bowl, to which he added teriyaki sauce and a little bit of brown soybean paste, which dissolved into a thick roux. He added a little salt and pepper, some minced shallots, and a pinch of garlic, and then poured the concoction over the salmon in a shallow baking dish. He popped this into his oven, which he had preheated, and set about making a salad and frying a few patties of sundried tomato polenta.

While the salmon finished baking, he carefully removed the Respighi CD from the changer, placed it back in the jewel case, and slid it into his bookcase between Rachmaninoff and Rimsky-Korsakov. He removed another CD, this time the *Brandenburg Concertos* conducted by Martin Pearlman, and set it to play while he ate.

After setting his place at the table—he refused to eat at the bar or, worse yet, at a television tray—he removed the salmon from the oven, slid it onto a plate, added two patties of polenta, and poured the rest of the merlot before sitting to eat.

No matter how hungry he was, Ben never hurried with his food. Even when Laura had been alive, he had always lingered over meals, savoring the *mélange* of flavors and textures, almost to the point of obsession. He ate slowly, in small bites to make the meal last, following each mouthful with a sip of the wine to clear his palate before moving on.

After eating, he rinsed his dishes and the baking dish, placed them in the dishwasher, poured a small glass of brandy, and returned to the deck to listen to the sounds of the mountain night.

He could have watched television, but he didn't feel much like it. As the dregs of the "Brandenburg Concertos" drifted out to the deck through the screened door, he found himself running the conversation with Sid Kingsley over and over in his mind.

Had he been overly curt with his old friend? He had been told he had a tendency to ignore the troubles of others. He had a hard time recognizing it, but it seemed to be a common complaint from people who knew him.

It would have been better if Sid had told him in advance why he wanted to meet for lunch. Inviting Long to meet for what he had presumed would be a reunion of some sort, and then launching into a pitch to drag him out of retirement, seemed a little devious and tacky.

On the other hand, had he become so thin-skinned after only four years away from the courts that he was irritated by a little deceit? He decided he would have to call Sid in a day or so and apologize for dismissing him so abruptly, even though he really didn't feel he had been out of line. It was one of the things Laura would have tried to remind him to do when she was alive. He and Sid were friends, after all. It was socially proper to apologize for bad behavior, he was told.

Almost without being conscious of it, he tried to recall the process of performing a good mental status examination. He hadn't done one in over four years. He recalled that, at one time, he could do it in his sleep—he even had completed one or two toward the end of his twenty-five-year career without being aware that he was noting the responses. That had frightened him a little, though not as much as the thought that he might not be able to recall exactly how to go about it now.

I'm going to say three things . . .

What is your name?

What is the date?

Why are you . . . ?

Hold out your hands.

What does it mean when I say . . . ?

How often do you . . . ?

What were the three things . . . ?

How do you feel . . . ?

At that moment, Long felt fatigued. Satisfied that, if pressed to do so, he could recall how to go about assessing mental status, he decided to call it a day.

He walked back into the house, closed the sliding door behind him, and turned off all but a couple of lamps in the living room.

He showered quickly because he had never been able to sleep properly if he felt less than completely clean.

15

Not that it mattered. The conversation with Sid Kingsley had disrupted his sense of security, and it was unlikely he would sleep for hours.

THREE

It was one in the afternoon, a week later, which was the time on Mondays, Wednesdays, and Fridays when Ben Long taught Abnormal Psychology. It was the middle of the semester, which meant that he had reached that point in his syllabus when he talked about the psychology of criminals.

"What you have to understand," he said solemnly to his class of thirty or so bright young students, "is that criminals don't think the way that you or I do."

He waited the proper, practiced number of beats before adding, "Well, at least the way *you* do."

As always, this drew a chuckle from the class. It was a guaranteed ice-breaker. After several years of delivering the line without a millisecond's deviation, Long had become bored by it.

"The criminal personality," he continued, "was the subject of an exhaustive study by Samenow and Yochelson in their three-volume work entitled—and this was a stroke of genius—*The Criminal Personality.*"

More titters from the students. Long noted the amusement of the class with a sort of detached interest.

"So, what separates the way criminals think and the way that—say—college sophomores think?" he asked.

A student in the front row, Sarah Ashburton, whom Long could always count on to respond, raised her hand.

"Yes, Sarah?"

17

"They don't have a conscience," she said.

"The criminals or the sophomores?"

Nervous laughter this time.

"The criminals," Sarah said.

"They don't?"

Sarah had looked confident as she answered. Now, she seemed less certain.

"Well," Long said. "Perhaps some don't. Most criminals, however, are capable of warmth and mutually beneficial interaction with others. On the other hand, they are able to turn off these feelings of guilt and fear of punishment, which we call *conscience*, when it suits their needs. How they are able to do this is anybody's guess. Psychopaths, on the other hand, seem to be incapable of empathetic feelings. What we need to recognize is that not all criminals are psychopaths, and not all psychopaths are criminals."

For that matter, he thought to himself as he prattled on, *not everyone who lacks empathy is a psychopath.*

"While genuine psychopaths are capable of criminal behavior, many of them simply spend their lives engaging in manipulative and self-gratifying relationships with others without ever crossing the line into illegal behavior. They might make other people's lives miserable, but they don't actually harm them, at least physically."

Sarah's hand shot up.

"Yes?" he said.

"Dr. Long, what's the difference between a sociopath and a psychopath?"

"There really isn't a difference. During the seventies, the therapy and counseling field became top-heavy with clinical social workers. Because of their training, these people tended to believe that behavior problems were the result of sociological deficits in people's upbringing. They discounted the possibility that there might be something neurologically or psychologically flawed in these individuals, because that would imply that they couldn't change. If they couldn't change, there was no point in treating them. So, they coined the word *sociopath* to apply to these individuals, which implied that if you could resocialize them correctly, they'd stop their deviant behavior.

"Some people have tried to distinguish between psychopaths and sociopaths by saying that one group—psychopaths—engage in criminal behaviors and the other group doesn't. Nowadays, we use these terms pretty much interchangeably."

Another hand went up in the back of the room. Long recognized Jake Rawleigh.

"Yes, Jake?"

"How can you tell if someone is a psychopath, Dr. Long?"

"It isn't as easy as you might think. There's a scientist in Canada named Robert Hare who's spent his entire career studying these people. He's decided that they all display two primary traits. The first is a glib, remorseless manipulation of other people to satisfy their own desires."

He noticed that several of the students were scribbling furiously, but plowed along anyway.

"The second trait is leading a chaotic, disorderly lifestyle," he continued. "Doctor Hare has developed a sort of test, called a checklist, rating twenty-two different behaviors. If an individual scores over a certain score, he is presumed to exhibit a behavioral repertoire that would be consistent with psychopathy."

"Have you worked with many psychopaths?" Jake asked.

"Oh, yes. Far too many over the years. That's why I teach now. It was good preparation for dealing with college students."

The class laughed again, less nervously this time.

"What do you think causes people to be psychopaths?" Sarah asked.

Long considered the question, then walked to the dry-erase board at the front of the room and drew a quick sketch of a side view of the human brain. He then drew a small circle near the center of the frontal lobes.

"At one time, I probably would have said that they were missing parts you can't get spares for," he said. "Recent research using magnetic resonance imaging, however, has determined that people who have been diagnosed with antisocial personality disorder—the clinical name for psychopathy—demonstrate actual differences in their brain structures compared with so-called 'normals.'

"Specifically, they have found that psychopaths have much less activity in this area," he said, pointing to the circle he had drawn, "called the limbic system. If you'll recall from our sessions on brain structure, the limbic system, one of the oldest parts of the brain—evolutionarily speaking—is also the seat of emotions. These people seem to have a very low level of activity in the structures of the limbic system, the hippocampus and the amygdaloid nucleus. You don't have to write that down, Jake. It's enough to say that there are clearly defined differences between the brain of a psychopath and the brain of Joe Average Citizen."

"But wouldn't that mean they can't change?" Sarah asked.

"That's correct. They can't. Psychopathy is hardwired into their brains. They were born psychopaths, and they will die psychopaths."

Sarah seemed troubled. Her face clouded over and her eyes narrowed. "If they can't change," she said. "What do we do with them?"

Long realized that, four years earlier, he probably would have said that you either kill them or lock them away forever.

Worse, he was acutely aware that his answer had not changed

dramatically since then.

"You stay away from them," he said.

FOUR

Long finished his lecture and crossed the campus to his office in the General Services building. As one of the newer members of the college faculty, he didn't yet rate an office in the psychology and social sciences complex.

Someday, maybe.

He signed on at his computer and quickly perused his email. At the top of the list he found Sidney Kingsley's name.

He clicked on the envelope and opened the note.

Dear Ben:

I'm sorry for bushwhacking you last week. It wasn't fair. I did enjoy seeing you again, though, and I hope your new life in academia suits you.

You never answered my question about how you would go about evaluating Earl Torrence's competence to stand trial. I am still looking for a forensic psychologist to do a report that will challenge Sybil's report for the defense. I'd appreciate it if you could jot down a few notes regarding the procedures you would use in a case like this and email them to me at the link below.

You looked great last week. Your life these days apparently agrees with you.

Don't be a stranger.

Long printed the email, tossed the note into his briefcase, and pulled a stack of term papers written by his Introductory

Psychology class from the top desk drawer. He tried to stagger the term paper due dates for each class throughout the second half of each semester, rather than face a deluge of over a hundred themes at one time. Since these were undergraduates, they only had to produce about two thousand words—roughly eight pages each plus an abstract and a bibliography—so Long was usually able to plow through a stack in a couple of afternoons.

There was a knock at his door. Long slid his office chair over to pull the door open.

Sarah Ashburton stood in the doorway.

"Ms. Ashburton," he said.

"Dr. Long, I'm sorry to interrupt."

"Not at all. I was just about to read term papers. I welcome the diversion. What can I do for you?"

"I had some questions."

"About abnormal psychology?"

"Yes."

"Perhaps it might be better to wait until class on Wednesday. Other people in the class might have the same questions."

"It isn't about the class, actually," she said.

"What, then?"

"It's . . . personal."

"Oh." He glanced apprehensively at the clock on his desk. He had another class in a little over an hour. "Well, then, perhaps you should come on in and have a seat."

He took his briefcase off the other seat in his office. She placed her book bag on the floor, sat upright in the chair, and clasped her hands together. She did not look him in the eye. He found this made him more comfortable.

"I'm not sure where to start," she said.

"Is this about you?"

"Partly. Is it unusual to read about disorders in class and

then worry that you might have them?"

"Not at all. That even has a name. They call it medical students' disease. First-year medical students read about diseases in their classes and immediately see the symptoms in themselves. Just about every kid who ever went to med school was convinced at some point in the first year that he or she was dying horribly."

"I see."

"Is this about today's lecture?"

"Sort of. You were saying that psychopaths have this part of their limbic systems that doesn't operate correctly, and for that reason they don't feel emotions the same way that normal people do."

"That's not entirely correct, but it's close enough."

"Well, sometimes I'm worried that I don't seem to feel anything. Emotionally, that is. I see someone in pain and it doesn't trigger anything in me."

"That's not necessarily a problem. We all have the ability to erect barriers to the pain of others if that pain threatens us. It's a defense mechanism called 'detachment.' "

"Well, when I feel that way, it bothers me," she said. "I . . . do things."

Long placed his pen on the desk and leaned toward her.

"I don't understand," he said.

She unclasped her hands, reached down, and grasped the hem of her skirt. Gently, she pulled the skirt up her thighs.

"Uh," Long said. "I'm not sure you should do that."

She looked up at him and then back down at her legs. He followed her gaze and saw several laser-like slashes on the skin of her inner thighs.

"It helps me to feel things," she said. "I buy disposable razors and take them apart. I never use the same razor twice."

"Yes," he said, his throat dry.

"When I cut, I feel the pain and think I'm normal. It doesn't hurt for long, unless I'm not careful and it becomes infected, but I don't even mind that, really, since then I hurt all the time and I don't feel the need to cut again."

"I see," he said.

"The fact that I sometimes don't feel . . . emotionally, that is . . . does that make me a psychopath?"

He looked again at her wounds, then forced himself to look away, but not at her face. Looking into her eyes—anybody's eyes, for that matter—was almost as difficult for him as looking at her legs.

"I think you've missed the point," he said. "What you're doing isn't a symptom of psychopathy. It is serious, though, and I really think you should see someone about it."

"Could you help me?"

"No," he said, perhaps a little too quickly. "That is, I . . . I don't practice anymore. Even when I did, I didn't work with this kind of problem. There are people much better qualified to help you."

"To help me *feel?*"

Long realized that she wasn't even focused on the dangerous nature of her self-mutilations. She didn't want to stop hurting herself. She only wanted to stop the numbness.

He also realized, at the same time, that fixing one problem could help eliminate the other.

"Are you taking any medication?" he asked.

"I'm from a Christian Science family," she said. "We don't believe in medication."

"I see." He reached into his briefcase for his address book. "Perhaps you can pull your skirt back down."

Slowly, she lifted herself from the chair and pulled her skirt back down to her knees. She smoothed it out with her palms. Then she clasped her hands again and gazed at the floor.

Long flipped through the address book until he found the person he sought.

"I'm going to give you a name and a telephone number," he told her. "This woman, Connie Fields, is very good with this sort of thing. She's a psychologist, like me, but she specializes in problems like yours."

"Is she expensive?"

"I'm sure she'll work something out with you. I'll call her after you leave and let her know I've referred you. Don't worry. I won't use your name or identify you in any way. When you see her, tell her you're the young woman Dr. Long sent."

He finished writing and handed her the piece of paper. She glanced at it, folded it twice, and placed it in the front pocket of her book bag.

Then, without saying another word, she rose, hefted her book bag to her shoulder, and left the office.

Wednesday at nine, Long walked into his Abnormal class, laden down with graded papers. He dropped them on the desk and pulled his attendance roster from his briefcase.

"Okay," he announced, "I've graded the first drafts of your term papers. Overall, they were pretty well done. Some of you chose to ignore some of the finer points of the APA Stylebook, but for the most part you made up for that by presenting good research. I'm going to hand them back. You'll note that I've made a number of comments in the margins. You should pay attention to those comments when you rewrite your papers."

He had picked up the sheaf of papers, prepared to hand them out to the class, when he noticed the empty desk in the front row.

"Has anyone seen Ms. Ashburton today?" he asked.

Karen Peters, the plump woman who usually sat next to Sarah, cleared her throat. "You didn't hear?"

"Hear what?"

"She's in the hospital," Jake Rawleigh said from the back.

"Is she ill?"

Karen Peters looked around, as if waiting for someone to respond. Nobody did.

"She tried to kill herself," Karen said.

"I didn't know. When did this happen?"

"Monday night," Jake said. "Her roommate found her in the dorm when she came home from a date. From what I heard, she slit her own throat."

"Don't be silly," Karen said. "You wouldn't survive slitting your throat. She cut her wrists."

Long thought of the disposable razors, the ones that Sarah had told him she took apart and used the blades one time. He envisioned her, holding the blade against her thigh, and suddenly changing her mind, yielding to the impulse to attack a much more lethal site.

"Does anyone know which hospital?" he asked.

"St. Joseph's," Karen said. "Her roommate told me."

Long tried to bluff his way through the class, but his mind was far away. He couldn't get the image of Sarah Ashburton from his mind. Even as he automatically droned through his lecture, which was so practiced he could have delivered it in a coma, his mind focused on whether he might have been partly responsible for her suicide attempt.

She came to me for help, he thought. *I sent her away.*

He tried to rationalize his actions, telling himself that he had referred her to a much more competent therapist. The nagging thought kept returning to him, though.

She hadn't come to him for a referral.

She had asked him to help her.

She was his student. She saw him as learned and masterful,

27

the guy with all the answers. She had steeled herself, had come to his office, and had shown him her deepest, darkest secret. He, in turn, had sent her away with nothing more than a referral.

There was no way he could have explained to her, at least no way that she could understand. He had abandoned any efforts to help people almost two decades earlier. For the rest of his professional life he had confined the boundaries of his practice to evaluations. Faced with a client in dire need of counseling or therapy, he wouldn't have known where to start.

Then there was the other problem. Even if he could have explained to Sarah why he couldn't be her therapist, he would have been hard-pressed to tell her why he couldn't be a therapist for anyone at all.

He dismissed the class fifteen minutes early and made his way to his office. The walls seemed to close in on him as he sat silently at his desk, trying to figure out what he should do. He could call the hospital, of course, but they would probably refuse to release any information to him, since he wasn't part of Sarah's immediate family. He could try to visit her, but how would that look? He could pretend to be the concerned teacher, but Sarah and he both knew the truth.

She had come to him for help.

He had sent her away.

He would send her a card. That would be the proper thing to do. He knew from watching television that people sent cards to other people when they were in the hospital. A card and maybe some flowers to cheer up her room. When she was recovered, he could sit with her after class and try to talk with her about why he had turned her away. Perhaps he could take her to see Connie Fields personally, introduce them, facilitate Sarah's passage into therapy. That kind of social interaction would be difficult for him, but he could manage it.

He slapped the top of his desk with the palm of his hand. Outside, in the hallway, a coed stopped as she walked by his door and peered in to see if he was all right. He smiled at her and slowly eased the door shut.

Cards and flowers and talks wouldn't change things. Twice in less than a week someone had approached him with a plea for help, and both times he had sent them packing, albeit with the best of intentions. As a result, Sarah was in the hospital after trying to take her life. Sid faced the potential of not trying Earl Torrence in an important capital case.

In all likelihood, Torrence deserved the needle. Sarah, though, deserved a lot better than an empty room and a sharpened razor. He couldn't help Sarah now, he reasoned, but he could do something for Sid.

He picked up the phone and dialed his friend, the District Attorney.

"Sid, this is Ben," he said.

"Ben! Always nice to hear from you."

"Yes. Send me what you have on Earl Torrence. I'll look it over. Maybe I can do something."

"Are you sure? You sounded pretty determined not to get involved last week."

"That was last week, Sid. Send them over."

"Tell you what. Why don't I assign one of our people here to bring them to you, to help you sort through all the legal mumbo-jumbo?"

"Sure. Whatever."

"You don't sound certain, Ben. Is this really what you want to do?"

"I get off at three this afternoon. You know where I live. I'll be home by four. Your associate can bring the stuff by then. I'll look over it and get back to you."

FIVE

Ben sat on his deck, sipping a glass of Australian syrah and savoring the dregs of the autumn warmth, when he heard his doorbell chime. He pulled himself from his chair and walked through the living room to his front door.

When he opened it, he saw a woman in her early forties, with hair halfway between the color of copper and gold. Of medium height, she came roughly to his chin. She looked athletic, but not mannish, and her eyes—as far as he noticed during the briefest moment in which he made contact with them—were the deepest green Ben had ever seen, like fine jade.

"Yes?" he said. "Can I help you?"

"I'm Paula Paige. Mr. Kingsley sent me."

"Oh, of course. Please, come in."

He stepped aside so that she could cross the threshold. She was carrying a square brief box by its handle.

"Thanks," she said. "This is heavy."

"So it appears. These are the Torrence documents?"

She placed the case on the table and looked at him as if he had neglected to do something, but he couldn't decide exactly what it might be.

"This is everything we had. Mr. Kingsley said you might want to do some interviews."

"I was having a glass of syrah," he said. "Would you care for some?"

"I don't know," she said. "I have to drive back to Henderson-ville."

"I'll be at least an hour looking over these papers."

"If you don't mind, then."

"It's a very nice vintage," Long said as he retrieved a glass from the kitchen. "A 1997 Stonehaven, from the Limestone Coast."

He poured a glass out for her, and then settled at the table to open the file case.

"Make yourself comfortable," he said, pointing toward the sofa. "This may take some time."

She walked over to the sliding door opening to the balcony and said, "Wow, what a view!"

"It's the reason I bought the place." Long pulled the first folder from the case. "It was at the end of a long day and I had looked at seven other houses. I walked in, and the sun was just setting over the mountain range to the left there. The light flooded in through the glass door and I felt like I had come home. I made an offer immediately. How's the wine?"

"Delicious. Would you mind if I sit on the deck?"

"No. Go ahead. I'll be a while in here. I'll find you if I have any questions."

She stepped out onto the balcony and stood at the rail, look-ing over the valley as she sipped her wine. He watched her for a few moments and then turned to the task of wading through all the papers.

The first file folder was the initial police report of the killing.

Amber Coolidge had been engaged to marry Earl Torrence's brother, Edward. The police had received a telephone call from a woman named Claudia Flatt, who lived underneath Amber's apartment in Hendersonville. She said she had heard an alarm-ing sound of clomping on the floor upstairs, and then it sounded as if a piece of furniture had been overturned. This was followed by a crash, and she heard a woman yell frantically. Seconds later, she heard a door slam and feet stamping down the inner stairwell outside her apartment.

The police took their time getting to the scene, figuring it was a domestic disturbance that had probably corrected itself, since the woman downstairs hadn't heard anything after the door and the footsteps.

When they arrived at the building, half an hour after the initial call, they were admitted to the apartment by a maintenance worker named Ernest Sachs, and found Amber Coolidge lying on her living room floor, her blood soaking into an oriental rug, her eyes fixed on the ceiling fan. She had probably been dead since before the call.

The police cordoned off the scene, called for backup, and then waited for the detectives and the crime scene investigators to show up. The chief investigator in the case, a detective named Donnelly, arrived about fifteen minutes after being called by the dispatcher. His partner, a man named Dix, showed up ten minutes after that, at the same time as the crime scene techies.

When they dusted for prints, the lab boys found four distinctive sets. They didn't identify the prints for several weeks, though, and by then Detective Donnelly had gotten a confession.

Edward Torrence showed up at the apartment, planning to take Amber to work. Instead, he found the building swarming with police, and the door sealed with yellow crime tape. He ran up the stairs, where Dix stopped him at the door. Torrence told Dix who he was and pleaded with the detective to tell him whether anything had happened to Amber.

At about that moment, Edward Torrence saw Amber, still lying on the rug and, according to Detective Dix's account, "he became extremely distraught and belligerent." Dix had to restrain *Torrence*, to keep him from barging into the apartment and spoiling the crime scene, and the EMTs had to get permission from the hospital to give Torrence a sedative.

The next folder contained the forensic results of the crime scene investigation and was written by a CSI named Charles Craig, with an addendum by the pathologist who performed the autopsy on Amber.

The arrangement of the crime scene was consistent with a struggle, Craig wrote. Furniture was overturned, a lamp was broken, and the victim showed some signs of defensive injuries to her hands. The murder weapon, which appeared to have been some kind of blade, was not found at the scene. Various fingerprints had been discovered, on the inside doorknob, various knobs around the house, on some furniture, and on the bathroom fixtures, among other locations. An addendum to the original crime scene report, dated about a week after the murder, indicated that there were four distinctive sets of prints, belonging to the people identified in Detective Donnelly's report: Amber, Edward, Earl, and the maintenance man, Sachs.

The forensic pathologist's report of the autopsy confirmed that the cause of death was exsanguinations—or bleeding out— caused by a laceration of the abdominal aorta resulting from a stab wound by a knife with a blade approximately seven inches long. Bruising around the entry wound indicated that the knife was plunged into Amber's body with some force, and went in up to the hilt. Since most kitchen knives don't have a guard between the handle and the blade, the doctor surmised that the weapon might have been some kind of hunting or fishing knife.

Ben put the folder down and ruminated over the reports. Something bothered him already. Claudia Flatt had reported that Amber cried out once, immediately before the door slammed, and didn't make any noises after that. Ben had seen the effect of an abdominal knife wound firsthand. Flatt's report suggested that Amber had perished very quickly. In reality, a laceration to the abdominal aorta should have taken a little longer to produce loss of consciousness. Unless the knife blade completely severed the aorta, and the pathologist's report didn't indicate this, there was a reasonable probability that Amber had been conscious long enough to yell more than once.

He jotted a note on the legal pad he had retrieved from the kitchen, and then looked in on Paula Paige.

"How's the wine?" he asked.

She had settled into his chair and was watching the shadows creep across the valley.

"Delicious," she said.

"It's a nice year. Not too tannic, but not as sweet as a pinot noir. Can I get you anything else?"

"No, I'm fine here. How do you ever leave this place?"

"It isn't easy. I've finished the detectives' crime reports and the forensic findings. I'm going to look over the interviews next. Let me know if you need anything."

He returned to the table and pulled another folder from the file case. This one was labeled "Detective Wade Donnelly interview with Edward Torrence."

There were several sheets in the folder. One was a photocopy of a handwritten summary prepared by Donnelly. The other was a typed transcript signed by Torrence, following the interview.

According to Donnelly, Edward Torrence had told him that Earl visited Amber on occasion. Edward reported that Earl and Amber had become close after the engagement and that Amber had developed some maternal instincts toward Edward's younger brother. Donnelly had visited Edward Torrence at his home, and found the man uncooperative and distracted. He suggested that they conduct the interview at the station, but Torrence refused. Donnelly had been forced to get a warrant— based on the presence of Torrence's fingerprints at the crime scene—compelling Torrence to come to the station.

Subject was transported to station on this date by uniformed officers, Donnelly had scrawled on the handwritten summary. *He was placed in an interview room and asked to wait several minutes until the interviewing detective was able to meet with him. After passage of about ten minutes, the interview commenced.*

Subject was moderately cooperative, but did state that he resented being brought to the station in a cruiser.

According to the subject, he last saw the victim alive around three o'clock in the afternoon of the murder, approximately eight hours before her death. When asked to characterize his relationship with the deceased, he stated that he and the deceased were planning to be married. He reported that, on the night of the murder, he was in the company of several friends, at a bar in Asheville, watching an NCAA basketball playoff game. He reports that he left the bar around midnight and returned to his home.

Subject reports that he had previously arranged to pick the deceased up to take her to work the morning after her murder and only discovered that she had been killed when he arrived that morning.

Ben set aside that report and read over the typewritten transcript signed by Edward Torrence. It repeated most of what Donnelly had written, but was written in first person. Apparently, Torrence had dictated the statement, which was typed and returned for him to sign.

Ben laid that folder with the others he had read and then picked up the one labeled "Detective Donnelly interview with Earl Torrence, Junior."

As with Edward Torrence, this folder contained two reports, one handwritten and one typed and signed by the subject. As he scanned over them, Ben noted that Earl Torrence's signature was scrawled carelessly across the line. In and of itself that didn't mean much. Ben had met a number of completely competent people with lousy handwriting.

Donnelly wrote that he had interviewed Earl Torrence at his apartment. He noted that Earl lived about a half mile from Amber's apartment. Compared with his brother, Earl looked very suspicious. He admitted that he had been to Amber's apartment on occasion, including the night of the murder, and often when Edward wasn't there. He claimed that he and Amber were "friends," but seemed embarrassed about it.

Donnelly began to suspect a possible jealousy crime, with Earl wanting a relationship with his brother's fiancée, who refused him, leading to the final confrontation between the two. He requested to be allowed to search Earl's apartment. In the course of that search, he discovered a shirt with blood on it and a cheap but heavy plastic-handled hunting knife in a box under Earl's bed. The knife at first had appeared rusty, but Donnelly quickly realized that the stains were not oxidation, but blood. Donnelly asked if he could take these items back to the laboratory for testing, and Earl gave permission.

The second part of the interview was conducted about two weeks later, after tests had been conducted on the knife and shirt. Donnelly returned to Earl's house and informed him that the blood on the shirt, and traces of embedded blood in the hilt of the knife, belonged to Amber Coolidge. He asked Earl whether he had any explanation for possessing these items. Earl clammed up. Donnelly booked him on suspicion.

Under intense interrogation at the station, according to Donnelly's report, Earl Torrence confessed that he killed Amber Coolidge and signed an affidavit. Less than a half hour later his brother arrived. Earl lawyered up and recanted his confession. It was too late, though.

Earl Torrence pled not guilty at his arraignment. The judge had set bond sufficiently high to ensure that Torrence remained in jail pending trial.

"Case closed by arrest," read the last line of Detective Donnelly's report.

Ben realized that if Earl Torrence had stuck with his confession, odds were that he wouldn't even be reading these reports. The North Carolina courts seldom condemned a murderer to death if he pled guilty, and competency to stand trial seldom became an issue.

On the other hand, he had personal knowledge of Torrence's attorney, Eli Crouch, and knew that Crouch would have advised Torrence to plead not guilty. Like most excellent defense attorneys, Crouch knew that there were many ways to skin a cat, and probably even more ways to keep a man from paying the ultimate price for murder.

Among the methods Crouch would employ would be an attempt to prove that Torrence—even if he did commit the crime—was unable to understand the nature of it, or participate in his own defense. Toward that end, Crouch had hired Sybil.

Ben realized that—had Crouch hired almost any other forensic psychologist—he probably wouldn't be involved in the case. Sybil's involvement almost begged for Sid to turn to Ben.

He picked up the transcript of Torrence's original interview, when he confessed to killing Amber Coolidge, which he had signed in his childish script. Whoever had typed it had taken great care to avoid cleaning up the grammar and syntax.

I, Earl Torrence Junior, have been told about my rights by Mr. Detective Donnelly. Mr. Donnelly has told me that I need to tell what happened on the night what Miz Amber was kilt, so I am going to tell it straight up. I used to visit Miz Amber from time to time, because she was nice to me and sometimes she made me cookies that I like to eat. Miz Amber was going to marry my brother Edward and I thought that was just fine because I liked her and I wanted to have her in the family. On the night that she was kilt, I walked over to her apartment, because I was lonely and I could not sleep. Sometimes when I can't sleep she would let me come by and watch TV with her, because she called herself a night owl, but that don't mean she was a real owl it was just an expression she said. She was at home that night that she was kilt, and she let me come inside the apartment. The TV was on and she was watching a movie about a man who was trapped in a tall building by men with guns and he was trying to kill the men with guns before they could kill his wife. She brought me some cookies and some milk because she knows I like them. We watched the movie for a while and I don't really know what happened next because I can't remember it real good, but I remember she told me I had to go home because the movie was over. I had to go to the can and I asked Amber if I could go to the can before I went home. The next thing I remember is her on the floor and blood on everything and I tried to pick her up to get her to the bathroom so she could clean herself up and get a bandage or go to the hospital but she didn't wake up. I got real scared that I might have lost my temper again like I do sometimes and kilt her without meaning to. So I picked up a knife I saw on the floor and I ran away real fast to go back to my place.

Attached to the affidavit was a transcript, apparently from a tape recording of the interview between Donnelly and Earl Torrence.

DETECTIVE DONNELLY: When did you try to have sex with her, Junior?
TORRENCE: I don't remember doing nothing like that.
DETECTIVE DONNELLY: Is it possible that you might have thought she liked you a little more than she really did?
TORRENCE: I suppose.
DETECTIVE DONNELLY: Did she ever kiss you?
TORRENCE: Sometimes.

DETECTIVE DONNELLY: Did she ever use her tongue when she kissed you?

TORRENCE: Huh? You kiss people with your lips, like this (at this point the subject pantomimed puckering his lips and smacking, as if giving a kiss).

DETECTIVE DONNELLY: Have you ever been with a girl, Junior?

TORRENCE: You mean like to do sex with her?

DETECTIVE DONNELLY: That's what I mean.

TORRENCE: Well, yeah, I suppose. I done it a few times.

DETECTIVE DONNELLY: Did you want to have sex with Amber?

TORRENCE: She was my brother's girl.

DETECTIVE DONNELLY: If she wasn't your brother's girl, is she the kind of girl you'd like to have sex with?

TORRENCE: Sure. Because of she liked me a lot. If Edward and she had broke up, I guess I would have asked her out.

DETECTIVE DONNELLY: And you'd have sex with her?

TORRENCE: Well, yeah, I guess.

DETECTIVE DONNELLY: Now, Junior, you said that she told you that you had to leave, and then you can't remember what happened next, except that the next thing you recall she was on the floor, bleeding. I'm going to give you a what-if, and you tell me if it could have happened.

TORRENCE: Okay.

DETECTIVE DONNELLY: You liked Amber Coolidge. You've already said that she kissed you sometimes, and that you wanted to have sex with her. Is it possible—and just think about this—is it possible that she said or did something that you thought meant she wanted to have sex with you, and you tried to have sex with her? And maybe when you did she told you to go away, and you became really angry, and you pulled out a knife and attacked her?

TORRENCE: I can't remem—
DETECTIVE DONNELLY: Come on, Junior. We found bloody clothes in your apartment. We found the knife that killed Amber in your apartment. You already told me you were alone with her in her apartment, and that you would like to have sex with her. You told me you saw her lying on the floor, bleeding, and that you tried to pick her up, but the only thing you don't remember is going after Amber with that knife and sticking it in her. All I'm asking you is, is it possible that you killed Amber Coolidge because she wouldn't have sex with you?
JUNIOR (after a pause of 3 seconds): I guess.
DETECTIVE DONNELLY: Okay, Junior. We're almost there. You're tired. I'm tired. Let's wrap this thing up, here and now. You've admitted that it's possible that you killed Amber Coolidge because she wouldn't have sex with you after leading you to believe that she wanted to. Having admitted that possibility, did you—in fact—kill her?
JUNIOR: I guess I did.
DETECTIVE DONNELLY: You guess you did? Or you did?
JUNIOR: I did. I kilt her. Jesus, what is Edward gonna say?
DETECTIVE DONNELLY: I've been recording this interview, Junior. I'm going to have someone type it up. Will you sign it when it's typed, so that everyone will know that we really did have this conversation?
JUNIOR: Type it up. I'll sign it. Jesus, I kilt Miz Amber. Edward is gonna be so mad at me.

Ben slipped the transcript back into the folder and placed it on the small stack of folders that had grown on his table.

He rubbed his eyes and walked to the counter to refill his wine glass. He glanced over at the deck, where Paula sat in the dimming shadows. Then he walked to the end table next to the sofa and turned on a lamp.

She turned around when the light fell across her face.

"Well?" she asked.

"If Junior had pled guilty, he might have been able to beg the charges down to voluntary manslaughter. Surely his attorney explained that to him."

"I don't know. You'd have to ask Mr. Kingsley."

"I'd rather ask Junior."

"So you're going to do the evaluation?"

"Probably. Look at the time! I didn't mean to keep you so late. I suppose you have to get home to your family."

"No," she said. "I'm at your disposal as long as you need any help with the case."

"I'm surprised Sid can spare an Assistant DA for this much time."

"It's not a problem, really. Besides, I have plenty of time to spare, at least until I pass the bar."

Ben stopped and looked down on her through the screen door. "You're not a lawyer?"

"Not yet. Law clerk. Three-L."

"I thought Sid was sending an ADA to help with the case."

"He couldn't spare anyone. Clerks are expendable."

"I see."

"Is there a problem?"

"Not as long as you can answer any questions I have about the legal process. I'm a little rusty. I haven't handled a criminal profile in years."

"Yes. That's what Mr. Kingsley said."

"Sid. Here, under my roof, you get to call him by his first name."

"I wouldn't want to get in the habit. I might slip at the office."

"You won't. It's a state dependent memory thing."

She stared at him.

"Psychology. Head stuff. You know. Are you hungry?"

"What?"

"It's late, and I haven't eaten in six hours. I was going to prepare a little bite." He picked up his wine glass, turned and crossed the kitchen to the refrigerator. Without speaking, he pulled some fresh romaine from the crisper and laid it on the cutting board. He placed a couple of large eggs and some olive oil next to it, and added a tin he pulled from the cabinet. He had a tiered set of hanging baskets suspended from underneath the cabinet on the other side of the sink, from which he pulled a large bulb of garlic.

"I suppose Sid also didn't tell you how I worked my way through college as a salad chef at *Maison Rouge* in Chapel Hill," he said. "The secret to the perfect Caesar salad, of course, is the bowl. It can't be too small and it has to be turned from fruit-wood."

He peeled two garlic cloves off the bulb with a paring knife and sliced away the tough outer leaves. Then he dropped them into the bowl and mashed them with a wooden spoon.

"Nothing metal should ever touch the salad during preparation," he said as he rubbed the garlic cloves around the inside of the bowl with a paper towel. "The acid in the dressing could leach out some of the metal in the flatware, and give the salad an off taste."

"Dr. Long . . ."

"The Caesar salad actually originated in Mexico. Not many people know that. The name has nothing to do with Rome at all. A chef named Caesar Cardini invented it in 1924. Why it wasn't called the Cardini salad, I haven't a clue."

"I should be going," she said.

"Of course. I understand. This won't take any time at all. It's as easy to make it for two as for one. Easier, actually. A little dry mustard . . . dash of Worcestershire sauce . . . some lemon juice and black pepper, and it's time to separate the eggs. Some people use whole eggs, but I prefer the yolks."

He grabbed an egg and tapped it with the wooden spoon, just hard enough to crack the shell. Then he expertly pulled the shell into two equal halves, and poured the insides back and forth from one half to another until all the albumen had drained into the sink. He dumped the yolk into the bowl and repeated the process with the second egg.

"The reason you only use the yolks is that albumen can spoil the mayonnaise mixture," he explained as he drizzled a little olive oil into the bowl and grabbed a whisk from the rack next to the range.

"Now we beat the living daylights out of it, and keep adding oil until the mayonnaise starts to form. Might take a moment or so. I haven't done this in a while. You aren't married, are you?"

"What?"

"No ring. I looked when you said you didn't have to leave. Nobody to run home to?"

"No, but I don't see where that's any of your—"

"No. Of course not. I didn't mean to offend. The fact is, I've grown tired of eating alone. If you don't have to run off to be with someone, I'd be very grateful if you'd stay for dinner. We can talk about the case."

"I don't know—"

"I'm not a creep or anything. I'm just out of practice when it comes to small talk. With women. I don't want to come off as forward, or strange."

"That's a relief," she said.

"Because that's exactly how I seem? Yes, I know. See, the mayonnaise is congealing now. You won't get a dressing like this in a bottle, Ms. Paige. This kind of salad you only get in the finest French restaurants. I do make one concession, however. I never seem to have time to make my own croutons. There's a bag of fresh ones from the deli in the cabinet next to the refrigerator. Would you be so kind as to grab it for me?"

She took out a wax paper bag and set it down next to the bowl.

"Thank you. Now the parmesan and romano. I grated some fresh this afternoon and placed it in a plastic tub on the rack inside the refrigerator door."

She retrieved the cheese and placed it next to the croutons. As she did, he began tearing the romaine into bite-sized pieces.

"You always tear the lettuce," he told her. "Never slice it. Slicing is lazy, and it removes you from the process. Tearing is personal. It's organic. It makes you one with the salad."

He dumped the torn lettuce into the bowl, poured in some of the grated cheese, and then some croutons. He began to spoon the ingredients around the edge of the bowl to mix them with the dressing.

"Would you mind getting a couple of plates from in there?" He pointed toward another cabinet.

She took out two stoneware plates. Ben grabbed a pair of walnut salad serving forks from the rack on the wall and placed some of the coated lettuce and croutons on the plates, taking care to make them equal.

"And now the finishing touch. I picked up some smoked trout filets from a shop down the mountain last night."

He opened a cabinet and took out two four-inch vacuum-sealed squares of filet and sliced through them with surgical precision to remove them from their packets. Then he sliced them into fingers, and placed them on top of the salad with the edge of the carving knife.

"*Voila*," he proclaimed, as he placed the plates on the table. "Just that easy, just that quick."

She stood, somewhat timidly, next to a chair in front of one of the plates. He pulled some flatware and a couple of napkins from a drawer next to the dishwasher, set the table, and placed a new wine glass next to each plate while she pulled out her chair and sat.

"I am having a nice Riesling," he announced. "Would you prefer water, or perhaps some tea?"

"No," she said. "A splash of wine would be nice."

"Of course."

He pulled a half-full bottle from the refrigerator, released the vacuum pump stopper, and poured some wine into each of their glasses.

"I uncorked this last night," he said. "Didn't want to kill it all in one sitting."

He sat in the chair across from her and picked up his silverware. When he looked at her, she had her head bowed and her hands clasped in front of her. Her lips were moving silently.

He waited for her to finish.

She opened her eyes, unclasped her hands, picked up her fork, and said, "It looks delicious."

"I hope you weren't praying for your safety."

"No. Just thanks for the meal."

"*I* do all the work. *He* gets all the credit. Tell me. Why did you stay?"

She took a bite of the salad, with a pinch of the smoked trout, and nodded appreciatively. "This is delicious. I didn't think you would let me leave, that's why."

"I see," he said, taking a bite from his own plate. "Yes, now I can see how you might have thought that. As I said, I sometimes have trouble . . . around people. I hope I didn't make you uncomfortable. Did Sid tell you I originally refused to help him with this Torrence case?"

"Yes."

"Did he tell you why?"

"No."

"Shall I tell you why I changed my mind?"

"If you like."

"I have a student who came to me for help. I didn't help her and something terrible happened. She was the second person to ask me for help in a week. I thought it would be bad karma for me to ignore the other request—Sid's request."

"Karma."

"Yes."

"That's it?"

"Yes. You seem somewhat old to be a law student."

"That was diplomatic."

"I don't understand."

"It's generally considered impolite to remark about a woman's age."

"Oh, yes. I see. I think that, at this point, I'm supposed to apologize. Please forgive me. I'm not always insensitive, Ms. Paige. No, that's not true at all. I don't know why I said that. I'm almost always insensitive, but it's completely unintentional."

"It's all right. And you're right. I'm a little more mature than the average law student. It's a midlife thing. Change of career. I worked in advertising for twenty years, and decided I was tired of shilling crap for multinational corporations. It seemed dead-end."

"Why law?"

"Why not? Maybe I thought my karma needed a little mending itself."

"And yet you were married until a couple of years ago."

"How in hell can you know that?"

"Old psychologist's trick. I'm right, though?"

"Yes. You were fishing!"

"A little. I risked being wrong. Not much at stake there. I'm wrong a lot."

"Well, you're right, in this case. He's a doctor."

"Specialist?"

"Yes. Nephrology."

"I see. It was a difficult divorce, I would imagine. I suppose you didn't get much out of him."

"More tricks?"

"Lucky guess. You supported him all through med school, an internship, a residency, and his kidney training, and then he decided to take off."

"It's an old story."

"I'll bet he had one hell of a divorce attorney."

"No, just better than mine. Someone told Hal—that was my husband's name—that if he consulted with all the best attorneys in town before filing for divorce, they wouldn't be able to work for me. Conflict of interest. I had to take the dregs. You were right. The wine is very tasty."

"I like it. What I can't figure out is why you're working for the District Attorney's office and not a civil firm."

"Beg pardon?"

"You want to see to it that none of your clients ever get shafted the way you were. I'd have thought that you'd try to get on with a firm that handles civil suits and divorces."

"It's a tight market," she said. "You take what you can get."

"How true. Did you know there are more students in law schools in this country than there have ever been lawyers in this country?"

"You're joking."

"I don't joke, Ms. Paige. I'm quite certain of that statistic. It would explain why your choice of firms was so limited. So what's your take on this Junior Torrence case?"

"I don't know much about it. I think Mr. Kingsley wanted me to advise you in general terms."

"I'm going to ask you to read over the files before we meet again. I would like your views on how the case was conducted. How do you feel about the death penalty?"

"I think it's a great idea, especially for nephrologists."

"What about the *Atkins* decision?"

"Do I agree with it? I don't know."

He took a sip of the wine, savored it as it flowed over his tongue, and for the tangy after-bite.

"The real question, as I see it," he said, "is whether mental retardation implies an absence of responsibility."

"Doesn't it?"

"We spend a lot of time trying to empower the mentally disabled. Vocational Rehabilitation forms sheltered workshops to provide the less handicapped with marketable job skills, and then they are asked to join the regular work world. The social service agencies in general, especially in the last ten years, have de-emphasized the idea of disability and have preferred to build on strengths."

"Okay."

"Yet, in this one area—criminal culpability—it is presumed that an IQ under seventy precludes any chance that you might actually understand the nature of your acts, or that you act with genuine intent."

"Doesn't it?"

"I have doubts. If you take every person in the United States and give him or her the most popular intelligence test, fifty percent will score over a hundred and fifty percent will score below a hundred. One hundred is both the mean and the median IQ among adults in this country."

"How fascinating," she said as she stifled a yawn.

He ignored the yawn and said, "What that means, of course, is that half of the people in America can't produce a triple-digit IQ. There's a little wine left. Would you like some more?"

"Please."

He poured roughly half the remaining Riesling into her glass and emptied the bottle into his own.

"In this case, however, you have to look at IQ more or less the same way you look at eyesight. What is the qualitative difference between having twenty/twenty eyesight, as opposed to twenty/twenty-five?"

"I don't know," she said. "I wear contacts."

"And without them, what is your vision?"

"About twenty/two hundred."

"Then you get to sample both ends of the visual spectrum. Vision of twenty/two hundred would be the eyesight equivalent of having an IQ of approximately fifty, which would put you in the mentally retarded category."

"I have retarded eyes," she said, sipping her wine.

"But the deepest green I have ever seen. Back to our problem. If you had natural twenty/twenty-five vision, and put on glasses that gave you twenty/twenty vision, you might notice a difference. Most of the time, you would accommodate to that slight difference and think you were seeing the world in perfect clarity. It's only when you are shown the difference that it becomes apparent."

"I see. Has anyone ever told you that you tend to lecture?"

"Frequently. So, is there a qualitative difference in ability between a person with an IQ of seventy-three, and one with an IQ of sixty-eight?"

"One would not think so."

"In fact, you're right. When you measure IQ using tests, you arrive at a reported IQ number, and everyone thinks that's your score. In fact, they neglect to consider that every IQ score includes a slop factor called the 'standard error of measurement.'"

"Slop factor," she said, raising the glass to her lips.

"It's a statistical thing. It accounts for the fact that you can give the same test to the same person on two separate days and arrive at two different scores. I could test Junior Torrence today and find an IQ score of sixty-eight, which would qualify under the state's definition of mental retardation, but test him next week and get a score of seventy-five, which doesn't."

"And that's the difference between living and dying?"

"Pretty much, under the state's interpretation of the *Atkins* ruling. When you do an evaluation for educational or disability purposes, you have to take other factors into account, such as the subject's adaptive skills. The state is primarily interested in numbers, though. That was another reason I didn't want to take the case."

"You don't agree with *Atkins.*"

"I don't agree with the way the state interprets *Atkins,*" he corrected. "As for the death penalty . . ." He shrugged and finished eating his salad.

"The real problem, as I see it," he continued, "isn't *Atkins* at all. I'm sure the swine representing Torrence has it in the back of his mind somewhere, of course, but I have a feeling what he really wants is to avoid the entire trial process completely. That's why we're dealing with competency before we've barely gotten past arraignment. It's rather shrewd of him. If Torrence were to be found competent, he could always withdraw the not guilty plea and make a deal with Sid to reduce the charges. Are you done?" He gestured toward her empty plate.

"Yes. Thank you. It was quite nice."

He cleared her place and put the dinner plates in the sink. Then he picked the file case up from next to the sofa and put it back on the table.

"Tell Sid I'll do the evaluation," he said. "I want to interview Junior Torrence before I test him. I also need to set up some appointments to look at some educational records, and I'd like to talk with Junior's brother, Edward. We might need a couple of court orders to access the records. I'm going to ask you to set up some meetings. I'll email a list to Sid."

"I'm not sure he will want me to continue working this case," she said.

"He will if I ask him."

A cloud crossed her face. "Why would you do that?"

"Maybe because you didn't run screaming from the slightly creepy but ultimately harmless psychology professor. Thank you for coming out. I'd appreciate it if you'd read over the files before our next meeting. Sid will show you how to set up the meetings I need. When I email the list, I'll also include a list of dates when I'm available. I can't take time away from teaching, so we'll have to work around the college's schedule. Oh, and I'll need a copy of all those reports for my own files. I use them when I do my evaluations and when I prepare my reports for the court."

He walked her to the door. She walked outside, took several steps, and turned around. "Mr. Kingsley did tell me you would be a little quirky," she said. "I think, though, that maybe you aren't really completely harmless."

"Time will tell," he said.

"I do think you're a little sad."

He managed a smile. "Oh, if I had a nickel for every time I've heard that."

Six

"He kind of creeped me out," Paula told Sid Kingsley the next day.

Kingsley walked around his desk and quietly shut the door to his office. "What did he say?"

"It wasn't exactly what he said, it was the way he acted. He had this—I don't know—sense of *entitlement* about him. He presumed that I'd stay to eat with him, without so much as seeking my permission."

"He let you stay for dinner?"

"Yes."

"My, my. How interesting. Tell me, how did he do that?"

"He asked me if I was hungry, and then he started making a salad."

"Caesar salad."

"Yes. How did you know?"

"It's his specialty. He used to be a salad chef."

"In Chapel Hill. He told me."

"Did he actually ask you to stay for dinner?"

"Well, yes, but only later."

"How did he do it?"

"I don't see how—"

"Please, Paula. This is kind of important."

"He said something about being tired of eating alone; that he was out of practice at making small talk with women."

"I see."

"What is he, some kind of monk?"

"You could say that."

"And then there's the eye thing."

"Eye thing?"

"He didn't look me in the eye once after I walked into the room. It was as if he completely avoided eye contact."

"Yes. I've noticed. What else did he say?"

"He was very inquisitive. He wanted to know about my divorce. He talked about the *Atkins* decision and the plan to find Torrence incompetent to proceed."

"And he agreed to evaluate Junior Torrence?"

"Yes."

"Good. Very good."

Kingsley retreated to his desk chair. He steepled his fingers and stared off into space.

"He wants me to work with him on the case," Paula said after a moment.

"How do you feel about that?"

"Like I said, he sort of creeped me out."

"To the point that you feel you can't work with him?"

"No, not that badly."

"Good..I'm a little torn when it comes to discussing Ben. I've known him for over a quarter century, and I sometimes think I don't have a clue how he works. You needn't worry about him. Ben *is* strange. I've never met anyone as objective or incisive when it comes to evaluating a psychological subject."

He paused for a moment, as if deliberating with himself.

"I love Ben as if I were his brother. A protective big brother. Ben isn't like the rest of us. For a long time, I had no idea that there was a real name for what's different about him. He can talk your head off all day long, but doesn't seem to know the first thing about social interactions. Did you notice that he completely avoids abstractions and metaphors in his speech?"

"Now that you mention it."

"It's fascinating. He's brilliant, of course. There's no question about that. Put him in a room full of people, though, and he disappears. He's deathly afraid of crowds, especially crowds of strangers, and even more if he's expected to talk about virtually anything but work. One on one, he eventually reverts to making observations, as if he were doing some kind of psychological investigation. He is one of the most socially inept people I've ever met."

"He seemed very lonely and sad."

"Sad, perhaps, but never lonely. That's part of the problem. Ben was diagnosed some time back with Asperger's disorder, a sort of atypical autism."

"He's autistic? I don't think so. I've seen autistics before and he doesn't look like them at all."

"I said *atypical* autism. People with Asperger's look and act for all the world like you and me, until they open their mouths. I suppose he lectured you."

"Yes. I pointed it out to him."

"You aren't the first. Most people with his disorder have extremely refined verbal skills, but their speech tends to be formal, almost distant."

"The lack of metaphors and abstractions you mentioned."

"He doesn't mean anything by it. It isn't intentional. At rare moments, I even see a hint of humor peeking around the wall of formality he throws up to protect himself. For the most part, he comes off as . . . well, *aloof.*"

"Because of his Asperger's."

"Yes. It's the way he's wired, you see. On the other hand, the very disorder that makes him cold and distant also contributes to his gift for observation and analysis. People with Asperger's are extremely analytical. They love to take things apart to see how they work. They become obsessed with specific subjects."

"Like *idiots savants?*"

"Not exactly, but I can see the similarities. Ben, for instance, became obsessed with psychology when he was still in his teens. He entered graduate school with a breadth of knowledge that outstripped that of most of his professors. They had to develop an entire curriculum for him."

"Which, of course, separated him from his classmates."

"Yes. Asperger's gives and it takes away. I think you could be an excellent match for him. How would you like to continue working with him on the Torrence case?"

"What do you mean, an excellent match?"

"Ben is one of the best people I've ever seen with a criminal subject, or testifying on the stand. Sometimes he needs a little reminder that he's pissing people off. He isn't aware of being irritating, or he doesn't care. It helps if someone nudges him once in a while to remind him that other people have feelings."

"I think you want a babysitter, not a lawyer."

"Which is convenient, because you aren't a lawyer yet. You will be one someday, though, and being exposed to the kind of work Ben Long does could be of incredible benefit to you. You may learn more working with Ben than you would ever pick up here in the office drafting briefs and subpoenas. And there's another thing. I knew when I asked Ben to help us what it would mean to him. I need someone working with him who can keep me apprised of how he's holding up."

"I don't understand."

Kingsley drummed his fingers on the desk as he deliberated what to say next.

"What I'm about to tell you isn't exactly a secret, but it is sensitive. I'd appreciate it if you'd treat it that way. Ben lived with his mother until he was in his middle thirties."

"Really."

"Yes. Laura has been dead for almost twenty years. That's

what Ben called her. *Laura.* She was never *Mom* or *Mother.* He always called her by her given name, at least since I've known him. He was totally devoted to her. Sometimes I think she was the only person with whom he could have a genuinely emotional relationship.

"Laura knew early on that Ben was different. I guess she felt she had to protect him from the world. Ben never left home. Laura was the center of his life. She understood him, and he loved her as much as he was capable of loving. At the very least, he was devoted to her. More than that, though, she was his barrier against the outside world. She was a sort of buffer against the inevitable conflicts and knocks that Ben couldn't handle.

"About twenty years ago, a career criminal named Anson Mount was arrested after beating an elderly woman into a coma to steal her purse. At his arraignment, his defense attorney hired a psychologist to tell the court that Mount would be safe on bond. You haven't attended arraignment court yet?"

"No."

"It's a cattle call. They empty the jail and parade each and every prisoner arrested since the last arraignment court before the judge, who decides whether to grant bail. Each case takes about two minutes. There are always attorneys swarming about and the room is filled with victims who don't understand the process and mistakenly believe that they are going to see a little justice done, so it amounts to one huge chaotic scene.

"Anson Mount's attorney brought in this hired gun shrink, who said he'd evaluated Mount and found him safe for release pending trial. The judge released Mount on a ten thousand dollar bond. Mount's brother, another low-life, posted the fifteen hundred dollar minimum, and Mount walked.

"Two nights later, Ben and Laura parked their car in Laura's driveway after going to dinner and a movie. When they got out, Anson Mount walked up to them and demanded their money and jewelry. They didn't move fast enough, and he knifed both of them."

"Jesus."

"It was totally random. Mount was going to rob the first people he saw, and Ben and Laura had the bad luck to be in the wrong place at the wrong time. Laura died at the scene, in Ben's arms. The paramedics took him to the hospital and took her to the morgue. He was laid up for several weeks—lost a lot of blood. It was touch and go for a while."

"How awful."

"When Ben was released, he went home and didn't come out for weeks. I visited him a lot during that time. He was a wreck. He couldn't attend Laura's funeral because he was in Intensive Care. He wouldn't go to the gravesite because that would mean having to say goodbye."

"No wonder he's so strange."

"Oh, he was *always* strange," Kingsley corrected. "In some ways, Laura's killing may have saved his career. He never did very well as a therapist. He was outstanding at figuring out what was wrong with his clients, but he never could connect with them in any intimate way. After the murder, he changed course. From that point on, he specialized in forensic work."

"With criminals."

"*Only* criminals. No divorce work, no custody evaluations, no mental health commitment hearings. The only thing he did was evaluate criminals to determine their risk of reoffending and their fitness to stand trial. It was like a crusade for him."

"And then he quit."

"Just like *that,*" Kingsley snapped his fingers. "One day he walked into the DA's office and said he was leaving. It broke my predecessor's heart. Having Ben on the team had jacked his sentencing rate through the roof, and allowed him to win every election on a law and order platform. Ben had applied for a teaching job and said he didn't want to deal with criminals or the courts anymore."

"People change," Paula noted.

"I suppose they do. When this Torrence case came up, I knew that Ben was the right psychologist to handle it. I figured he'd blow me off. In fact, he did at first."

"You didn't expect him to take the case?"

"I was cautiously optimistic," he said, smiling. "I thought there might be . . . *hooks* in this case that would draw him in. Mostly, I was worried about what Ben was doing to himself. Ever since he took that college position, it's like he's completely retreated from life—to the extent that he was engaged in it before. He goes to work in the morning, then goes home at night and sits on his deck, drinking wine and listening to that damned classical music. He has no life at all outside his classroom. I was hoping this case might help . . . I don't know. Maybe attract him, if only a little, back toward the land of the living."

"I see," she said. "Whatever happened to Anson Mount?"

"He's still alive. He's doing a life sentence at Central Prison in Raleigh."

"He didn't get the death penalty?"

"No. He had a very good attorney."

"Who?"

"My former partner, Eli Crouch. Mount's case was the one that led to our split. He's in Charlotte now."

"Torrence's attorney."

"Yes. One of those *hooks* I mentioned. Eli and I had a private law practice. I tried to talk Eli out of taking Mount's case because of my friendship with Ben and Laura. I thought it might be a conflict of interest. He told me to ram it and represented Mount. I couldn't be part of that, so I took off and went solo. After Ben recovered from his injuries and started working for the DA's office, I sort of tagged along. I became a public servant. Eli got rich. I'd like to think I sleep better at night. Paula, will you help Ben with this case?"

She clasped her hands and looked at them. Something about Ben Long had troubled her. At one point she had been torn between staying in the house and running out to her car. Kingsley's reassurances that Long was quirky but harmless had comforted her, but she was still wary.

"Asperger's is a mental disorder, right?"

"Yes. But not the way you probably mean. Ben presents absolutely no danger to anyone else. The only person he harms is himself, and then it's only socially. I'd consider it a great favor if you would help him with this case. It could also be an important boost to your marketability once you pass the bar."

"I'll give it a try," she said. "Let's see how things work out."

SEVEN

Ben parked his car in the visitors' lot at St. Joseph's Medical Center in Asheville and made his way to the central lobby.

"Excuse me," he said as he walked up to the reception desk. "I'm looking for a patient named Sarah Ashburton."

The receptionist checked the computer.

"She's in the psychiatric unit. It's on the—"

"Thanks. I'm a psychologist. I'm on the staff here. I know where it is."

He walked to the elevator. When it opened, he was followed inside by a family of five. Ben was crowded to the back corner of the car, where he stood stiffly and tried very hard not to touch anyone.

He was carrying a potted plant. He had absolutely no idea what kind of plant it was, except that it was green and had some purplish flowers. He had dropped by a florist's shop and had asked the clerk what he might take to a woman who was in the hospital. The clerk had taken things from there, to Ben's relief.

The family exited the car on the third floor. Ben was going on to the sixth. As the doors closed, leaving him alone in the car, he finally dared to breathe.

The door opened on the sixth floor. Ben stepped out into the hallway, facing a sign that said CHILDREN'S MEDICAL/ SURGICAL WING.

He looked to his right, and then to his left. He didn't see any signs for the psychiatric unit.

He was puzzled for a moment. The last time he had conducted an evaluation on the St. Joseph's psychiatric unit, he could have sworn it was on the sixth floor.

Then he realized that five years had gone by. Things change. They had probably moved the unit.

He walked up to the nurses' station and cleared his throat.

"Yes," a woman behind the counter said.

"I'm sorry, but I seem to be lost. I thought the psychiatric unit was on this floor."

"Oh, honey, you *are* lost. They moved that unit to the eighth floor *years* ago."

"Thank you," he said and turned to go back to the elevator.

Moments later, he walked into the alcove of the psychiatric unit. Unlike other parts of the hospital, where the hallways were open and access to rooms was relatively effortless, the psychiatric unit was barred by electronically operated security doors. He walked to a small window next to the doors and pressed a buzzer. A few moments later, a thin woman in a starched white jacket appeared at the window.

"I'm Dr. Long," Ben said, sliding his identification through the opening at the bottom of the window. "I'm on the adjunct staff here at the hospital. I'd like to see Sarah Ashburton."

The woman looked at the ID card.

"This card is out of date," she said. "It expired over a year ago."

"I haven't been here for a while. You can check it, though. I'm still listed on the adjunct staff."

"Just a moment," she said.

She walked over to a desk and dialed a number on the telephone. She spoke to someone on the other end. There was a short wait and she replaced the receiver.

"I'm sorry, Dr. Long, but the personnel office says that you need to have a new card made before you can be admitted to the unit. Visiting hours haven't begun yet, and only hospital staff can be admitted."

"They didn't have me listed as an adjunct staff member?"

"She said you were on the list. You still have to get a new ID badge. It's a security regulation."

"Where is the personnel office? I suppose they've moved it, too."

"I wouldn't know about that. I've only been here a few weeks myself. It's on the first floor, though. You can ask the reception desk down there."

"I see. Could you do me a favor? I brought a plant for Ms. Ashburton. It's pretty heavy and my arms are getting tired. Could you place it in the office there while I get a new card made?"

"I'm really sorry, Doctor, but I'm not allowed to do that."

"Yes. I see. All right then. I'll be back in a bit."

He hoisted the plant and retreated to the elevator. It was empty. He liked that, until he hit the fifth floor and it filled with half a tour group of pregnant women doing a prenatal tour of the maternity unit. Again, he found himself squeezed to the back corner, barely able to breathe. His heart hammered and he felt sweat pop out at his temples.

This visit hadn't gone at all the way he had planned.

The doors opened on the first floor and the gaggle of expectant mothers waddled out into the main lobby. Ben followed them and made his way to the reception desk.

"Personnel office?" he asked from behind the blooms of Sarah's plant.

"Down the hall, third door on the right. It's marked *Human Resources*," the woman behind the desk said. She pointed the way to him, and he walked off in that direction, forgetting to thank her.

Nobody was in the Human Resources waiting room. He placed the plant on a table and walked over to the desk.

There was a long hallway leading off to his right. He peered down it, looking for any sign of human habitation.

"Hello?" he asked in what seemed to him a small, timid voice. Nobody answered.

"Hello?" he said again, this time putting a little more effort into it.

"Just a moment," someone said at the back of the long hallway. "Be right with you."

Ben stood at the desk, waiting. A couple of minutes later, a woman in her middle twenties walked up from the end of the hallway.

"Sorry, sir, I was on the telephone. Can I help you?"

"I'm Dr. Long," he said, holding out his badge. "The nurse up on the psychiatric unit—"

"Oh, yes, she called a few minutes ago. Certainly. Can I see your badge for a second?"

He handed it to her.

"Been a while since you've visited us, Dr. Long?"

"A few years, yes."

"I can tell. We haven't used these for almost two years. I checked the hospital records when the nurse called. You're still listed as an adjunct staff, so we should be able to take care of you fairly quickly. If you'll step back here . . ."

She walked down the hallway. Long followed her into a cubicle.

"Just have a seat there," she said.

It took about ten minutes to finish the new badge. "Don't be a stranger for so long next time," she said, smiling, as she handed it to him.

"No," he said. "Can I go now?"

"Sure."

Ben got up and walked back out to the elevator. This time it went straight to the eighth floor. He stepped out of the car and walked to the window. The nurse who had sent him downstairs was sitting at a desk behind the glass. When she saw him, she stood and walked over.

Ben held out his new badge.

"They updated me."

"Wonderful, Dr. Long. I can buzz you through now."

He heard the electronic lock on the door click. He turned the handle and walked onto the unit.

"Have you forgotten something?" the nurse asked as he signed in at the front desk.

"Beg pardon?"

"Your plant. You had a plant when you were here before."

Ben felt his face and ears heat up. "I must have left it in the Human Resources Office. I'll be right back."

The nurse buzzed him back through the electronic door. He punched the button on the elevator call and waited for three minutes as the car made its way from the lobby back up to the eighth floor.

When he finally arrived in the lobby, he made his way to the Human Resources Office. There was a sign on the door indicating that the office was closed for lunch and that the staff would be back at two o'clock. The door was locked.

Ben could see his plant sitting on the table on the other side of the room from the door.

He had a class to teach at two o'clock.

He couldn't see Sarah without bringing something, after the way he had treated her when she came to him for help. He wasn't completely certain what the social protocol was in such a situation, but he was relatively clear on the need to bring a gift of some kind.

He stood at the door for a minute or two, trying to figure out what to do next.

Finally, he turned and walked out the front door of the hospital, back to his car.

Eight

A FedEx truck had delivered a box of documents to Ben's house while he was teaching the last class of the week on Friday. He arrived back at his house to find the package on his front porch.

He left it on the kitchen table, in no hurry to open it since he had already looked the material over once. Instead, he changed into crisply pressed jeans and a flannel shirt, popped a CD of Vivaldi's *Four Seasons* in the player, and sat on the back deck with a glass of Wild Horse cabernet sauvignon to contemplate what to make for dinner.

He was still mulling it over when his telephone rang an hour later.

"Dr. Long, this is Paula Paige. Did you receive the package we sent?"

"Yes. It arrived this afternoon."

"Have you had a chance to look at it?"

"I read most of it the other night. I got home only a little while ago. I was relaxing."

"You might want to take a look over the weekend."

"Thank you."

"Are you . . . all right?"

"Of course. Why do you ask?"

"You sound a little, well, melancholy."

"No. I'm perfectly fine. I was just thinking about what to make for dinner."

"I see. Ah, I'd like to give you my cell phone number so you can get in touch with me over the weekend if you run across anything in the files you don't understand."

"That's very kind of you, but totally unnecessary. I've been around the courts for a long time."

"Mr. Kingsley wanted me to provide you with whatever assistance you need. I'm just a clerk and I don't want to make any mistakes. I'll leave the number with you, if you don't mind."

She waited for him to jot it down.

"Thank you," he said. "I'll call you if I need any help."

After dinner, Long slipped a CD of Haydn masses into the player and settled on the sofa to look over the additional materials Paula had sent. After reading for a quarter hour, he grabbed a legal pad from his desk and started jotting notes.

Paula Paige was in the middle of an unpleasant dream involving skiing down an endless snowy slope at the Olympics in her bikini bottoms when her cell phone chirped on her bedside table.

She glanced at the clock through sleep-leaden eyes.

Three-thirty in the morning.

"What in hell?" she mumbled as she flipped the phone open. "Hello?"

"This is Ben Long."

"Dr. Long? It's three-thirty in the morning."

"Yes. I've been looking over the materials you've sent me and I think we need to expand our list of people to interview."

"I see. Do you want to interview them right *now?*"

There was a pause on the other end.

"No," he said tentatively.

"Is it possible, then, that you could have waited until *later* in the morning to call? Say, after I get to the office?"

"I . . . uh. I suppose I could. Would you like me to call you then?"

"I would appreciate it. I'll get into the office around eight-thirty."

"All right, then."

He hung up without saying goodbye.

She folded the phone and placed it back on her bedside table, then slipped back down under the covers.

She didn't sleep, though.

At first she was furious. After a few minutes, she remembered what Sidney Kingsley had told her about Long's condition, and realized that he probably had absolutely no idea he might be inconveniencing her by calling at such an ungodly hour. She began to relax again.

Still, she didn't sleep.

After the anger departed, she began to wonder what he had found.

She glanced at the clock. *Three-fifty.*

It would serve him right.

She picked up the telephone and dialed his number.

"Hello," he answered.

"I'm awake now. Mission accomplished. Tell me who you want to interview."

"I thought you wanted me to call you at the office at eight-thirty."

"*I* thought I wanted to go back to sleep. Now I can't. What did you find?"

"I was reading through the reports from the police interviews with Torrence, and I thought there were some things there that indicated potential problems with Torrence's adaptive skills."

"I don't understand."

"Adaptive skills are the abilities we use every day to survive, such as feeding ourselves, dressing ourselves, doing the laundry, writing checks, washing up—"

"I get the idea. What about the reports bothered you?"

"Do you really want to get into this at this late hour?"

"I'm wide awake now."

"I see. Of course. I was reading the interview between Detective Donnelly and Torrence again, and noted that Donnelly seemed to be leading Torrence's responses. Also, the way Torrence expressed himself led me to believe that his account of the events on the night of the murder might be . . . well, open to suggestion."

"I don't follow."

"It seems to me that Torrence might have believed that he killed Amber Coolidge, but only because Detective Donnelly was so insistent that he had done so."

"You think Donnelly talked Torrence into confessing to a murder he didn't commit?"

"Whether he committed the murder or not is still a matter of conjecture."

"Not to the DA's office."

"Be that as it may, Detective Donnelly's questions assumed events that are not necessarily documented in the forensic reports, but Torrence apparently readily agreed to them."

"And your point is?"

"Well, this is very common in low-functioning people, such as retarded subjects."

"Let me get this straight. You reviewed the materials from the police interrogations and want to expand your list of interviewees because you think that Torrence behaved in a way that makes him look mentally handicapped."

"That's about it. Yes."

"And how does this help our case? According to my understanding, we're trying to prove that Junior Torrence is competent to stand trial. Proving that he has mental retardation could lead to him being ruled *incompetent*."

"Yes."

"Does that not strike you as something that would help the *other* side in this case?"

There was a long silence.

"We need to talk," he said finally. "I'd like to meet you for lunch tomorrow."

"My date book is out in the car and I'm in bed. I'm not crazy about dressing just to run out and check my lunch schedule. Call me at the office tomorrow morning."

"I thought you couldn't sleep."

"I was sleeping fine until you called me at half past three in the morning. Don't you ever go to bed?"

"Of course."

"Then I suggest you do so. Call me at the office. I'll check my lunch schedule then."

This time, *she* rang off without saying goodbye. It was vaguely satisfying, almost empowering.

She still couldn't sleep, but the drone of late-night television was infinitely preferable to dealing with Ben Long's eccentricities.

Paula sat at her desk and began compiling a list of telephone calls to make that morning. As she reached for the receiver to make the first one, the phone rang.

"Paula Paige," she said.

"This is Ben Long."

"Yes, Dr. Long," she said, trying not to let her frustration beacon through in her voice.

"It's eight-thirty."

"And what's the temperature?"

"I don't know." He sounded puzzled. "I can check."

"Don't bother. I was putting together the list of people to call to set up interview appointments. What can I do for you?"

"You were going to check your date book about lunch today."

"Just a moment." She pulled a thick, leather-bound ring binder from her briefcase. "I appear to be available at twelve-thirty."

"Excellent. There's a bistro about a block from your office. They have a wonderful *salade nicoise.*"

"I know the place. Mona Lisa. I can meet you there."

"I'll see you at twelve-thirty."

Since it was Saturday, things were a little slow at the office. Sidney Kingsley was playing in a North Carolina Legal Aid golf tournament in Banner Elk, and many of the ADAs were working away behind closed doors on briefs for Monday court hearings.

Paula busied herself trying to reach people on the phone and managed to set four appointments for Long's interviews by ten o'clock.

Kingsley had left her several briefs to proof, and she was about halfway through the second one when one of the office doors opened behind her and an ADA named Carl Young stepped out into the cube farm.

"Going to lunch, Paula?"

She glanced at her desk clock. It was twelve-fifteen. "I have an engagement," she said.

"Okay. I'm probably gone for the day. I heard Sampson saying that he would be here most of the afternoon, so you shouldn't be working alone."

"Thanks."

Young collected his jacket and his briefcase and walked into the hallway. As soon as she heard the elevator door close, Paula put away the contracts, freshened her makeup—though she wasn't certain why—then followed Young into the hall.

She found Ben Long waiting in the doorway of Mona Lisa, a

block from the office.

"You could have gone inside, gotten us a table," she said.

"It's Saturday. It shouldn't be too crowded."

"Just crowded enough to make you uncomfortable," she said. "Mr. Kingsley told me you don't like rooms filled with strangers."

"I don't know what you're talking about. Shall we?"

He opened the door and stepped inside. She followed close on his heel, just as he released the door and let it close on her.

"Dr. Long!"

He turned to her.

"Yes?"

"You let the door go in my face!"

"Did I? I wasn't aware. I suppose this is one of those points where I am expected to apologize. I'm sorry."

"You don't sound sorry," she said as the hostess walked up to them.

"I didn't mean to hit you with the door. It was unintentional. I thought that you would catch it."

"*I* thought you were holding it open for me."

"Yes. I see. Courtesy. I do apologize."

The hostess seated them quickly in a booth toward the back of the room. The walls were polished fumed white oak, and the coffered ceiling featured stamped tin panels between the crisscrossed beams segmenting its surface. The tables were made of oak with a heavily lacquered lacewood veneer. Ben sat quietly, watching her as she surveyed the room.

"Have you eaten here before?" he asked.

"No. Some of the associates have. I've heard them talk about it. What is a *salade nicoise?*"

"Ah," he said, smiling. She figured that this meant he was now on familiar turf. "It's a bed of green beans and red-skinned potatoes with tomato wedges, sliced eggs, bell peppers, and grilled tuna, served with a basil anchovy dressing."

"Sounds yummy."

"It's one of my favorites."

The waitress appeared at their table to take their orders.

"I'll have the Bistro Burger, all the way, and an iced tea," she said.

She could see Long wince slightly. She enjoyed it, which surprised her.

"I'll have the *salade nicoise* and a glass of your house *pinot grigio*," he said.

"You have something against hamburgers?" Paula asked after the waitress retreated to put in their orders.

"For other people? No. I don't eat red meat."

"Is that on religious, ethical, or simply health grounds?"

"A little of each, I suppose. Mostly, I don't like food made from animals with legs and fur. Have I done something to offend you?"

"Besides slamming the door on me?"

"I have observed that you don't appear to like me much."

"You've *observed* that."

"Yes. I'm quite certain of it."

"I wasn't aware that you were going out of your way to be likable. Is it important to you that I like you?"

"Under normal circumstances, no. However, I think it would help us work together more effectively."

"So I should like you in the interest of this case?"

"I think it would make things work more smoothly."

"Okay," she said, placing her date book on the table. "In that case, I would like to suggest that we lay down some basic ground rules. I'm no longer in my twenties. In fact, in a very short time I'll no longer be in my thirties. I need my beauty sleep. When strange men call in the middle of the night, I have a hard time getting back to sleep. I would respectfully request that you not do that again."

"I'm sorry," he said. "I thought when you gave me your cell phone number you meant I should call when I needed assistance."

"I did. However, you did not *need* assistance at three this morning. Next, you seemed to presume when we met last week that I would stay for dinner, without asking whether that was all right with me."

"You told me you didn't need to rush home. I had deduced already that you weren't married. And I did ask."

"You did *not* ask. You asked whether I was hungry, and then you began assembling a Caesar salad before I could answer. That's called a sense of entitlement. As a psychologist, you've heard the term. If you want people to like you, I suggest you first learn to understand them."

"This isn't going well," he said as the waitress returned with their drinks.

"What isn't going well? Did you have some ulterior motive for asking me to lunch?"

"Yes."

For a moment she was speechless. It occurred to her that if this data processor of a human being made a pass at her, she would slap him across the face—very hard—and walk out of the restaurant. Then she would have to spend the rest of the afternoon cleaning out her desk at the DA's office.

"It's like this," he said. "When you called me this morning—I mean, *early* this morning—you asked whether I understood that our goal in evaluating Junior Torrence was to find him competent so he could stand trial for Amber Coolidge's murder."

"That's right."

"I'm not so sure we share the same goals."

He reached for his glass and took a sip of the *pinot* as he

74

waited for this to sink in.

"I think you had better explain that," she said finally.

"You've heard the term 'hired gun'?"

"Of course."

Everyone in the legal profession was familiar with the term. Whenever a law firm needed a professional opinion to bolster its arguments in court, it tended to turn to a list of contracted doctors, psychologists, and social workers who could provide the court with an impressive *curriculum vitae* and a convincing canned report. This was all provided for a fee, of course—usually a very handsome one.

Most hired guns were retired from active practice. They had worked for years, often in the worst of conditions for obscenely modest pay, and had decided late in life to cash in on their considerable expertise. Their testimony, therefore, was now available to the highest bidder, and was as likely to change at the whims of the firm who hired them.

"I'm not one of those guys," Long said. "I refuse to be one. I didn't sign on to this project with the intent of finding Torrence competent, whether he is or isn't."

"Then why are you doing it?"

"Because Sid Kingsley needed me. We've already discussed this."

"Your student. The 'terrible thing' that happened to her."

"That she did to herself." He took another sip of the wine.

"Does this have anything to do with what happened to your mother?" she asked.

"Sid told you about that?"

"Yes."

"It has *everything* to do with my mother. Anson Mount was released from jail pending his trial because his attorney—Eli Crouch, the very attorney representing Junior Torrence—placed a hired gun on the stand to say whatever he was told to say. It was the same as setting a wild animal loose in the streets."

"We aren't talking about cutting Junior Torrence loose. We're only trying to get to trial without having to dance through Crouch's procedural minefield."

"By hiring me, you've already started that dance. On the one hand, I agree with you completely. If Torrence committed this crime, he should die."

"What you mean is, Anson Mount should die?"

"Don't put words in my mouth."

"I don't have to, Dr. Long. They're written all over your face."

"I have no particular interest in seeing Junior Torrence either executed or spared. I only want to know the truth. Somehow, from my observations of your behavior and Sid's in this case, I think perhaps you have other motivations."

The waitress returned with their orders. Long stared at his plate as he tried to calm his nerves. When he looked up, Paula was praying again.

She unclasped her hands and opened her eyes. The first thing she saw was Long staring at her.

"If it makes you feel any better, I gave thanks for the chef," she said.

She poured some catsup on her burger and folded the sandwich together. Then she cut it in half with a heavy wooden-handled steak knife, poured a little more catsup onto the plate for her onion rings, and dipped one of them before munching on it.

He picked at his salad.

"I told Sid I'd help him with this case," he said between bites. "That means I'll do the very best evaluation on Torrence that I can do. I won't report false findings. If he tests as retarded or otherwise incompetent to stand trial, well, good for him. If he doesn't, then he doesn't, and he gets what he probably deserves."

"That sounds fair enough."

"Besides, if my findings aren't of any help to Sid, I imagine he'll simply find another person to support his argument."

"I think you may be underestimating your friend."

"He's a lawyer, Ms. Paige."

"Call me Paula."

"I'm not comfortable calling you Paula. I'm comfortable calling you Ms. Paige."

She had been raising half her burger to her mouth, but she stopped midway. "Give it a try. If we have to work together, we can't keep calling each other Ms. and Doctor."

"Why is that?"

"It's clumsy and unwieldy. It's inefficient."

"I can't say I agree."

"Push yourself. What would happen if you don't find Torrence retarded, and Mr. Kingsley brings in another psychologist? Wouldn't your report still be on file?"

"Yes. I suppose that I'd eventually be approached by someone from Eli Crouch's office to support their argument for inability to proceed."

"Would you do it?"

"I imagine I'd have to. There would almost certainly be a subpoena involved."

She took several bites of her sandwich while she thought this over. He finally managed to make a healthy dent in his salad.

"You were right," he said when he was about half finished.

"About what?"

"When you walked up to me in front of the restaurant today. You were right about why I hadn't gone inside."

"You said you didn't know what I was talking about."

"Yes. Sometimes it's hard to admit a weakness."

"So why are you telling me now?"

"Because it gives you an advantage over me."

She swallowed an onion ring and looked over her hamburger at him. "What do you mean?"

"By telling you that I am afraid of enclosed spaces with people I don't know, I'm giving you something you could use against me."

"I don't *want* anything to use against you. What a strange thing to say."

"It's a peace offering. When cavemen first began to live in communal settings, one caveman would greet another by holding out his club-wielding hand. It put him at a great disadvantage to the other person, but also demonstrated that he presented no threat and that he believed that the other caveman wouldn't brain him."

"And?"

"It was a gesture of trust. By allowing that you were right about me, and by confirming that I am afraid of enclosed spaces filled with strangers, I am basically showing you that I trust you not to use this knowledge against me."

"You're beginning to creep me out again."

"Didn't mean to. Shall I apologize again?"

"Don't bother."

He attacked his salad with renewed vigor.

"Good salad, huh?" she said.

"Excellent. Would you like to try a bite of the tuna? It's yellowfin, sashimi grade, seared and sliced after marinating for over six hours. Delicious."

"Maybe a taste," she said.

She reached across the table with her fork and speared a piece of fish the size of a nickel. After chewing on it, she nodded approvingly. "It's very nice. Quite tasty."

"Thank you. I thought you would like it."

"Would you like a bite of the other half of my burger?"

He smiled as he shook his head. "Red meat? Oh, good Lord, no."

NINE

The County Jail was a depressing facility, all painted cinder-block and boilerplate steel. Sounds of clanging doors, ringing telephones, country music, and the random pointless argument echoed off the walls incessantly, creating a din similar to that commonly only found in a Las Vegas casino.

Paula Paige and Ben Long had arrived a half hour earlier. After being forced to relinquish the articles in their pockets, and Paula's entire purse, they had been escorted to the control room of the third floor where the most dangerous inmates were housed. The control room occupied the center of a ring of corridors. It had thick acrylic windows on each of its four sides, so that Paula could see down each corridor as Long reviewed Junior Torrence's jail record.

As Paula watched, a uniformed guard walked down one of the corridors, opened a cell door, and escorted a young black man out. He walked the man to the day room area, where he stepped through an open door and into a glass-enclosed, tiled room. There, he slowly took off his clothes and laid them on a bench. He turned on the water and began showering.

As he turned, he saw Paula in the control room. His gaze locked on hers. Paula was aware suddenly that she had been staring.

The young man's eyes were sadly empty. They seemed to be asking her for a little privacy. Then he blew her a kiss.

She turned away.

"You get used to it," the officer said to her. "It's tough the first several times. It's a fact of jail life. These guys give up a lot, being here. Privacy is the first thing to go."

"I'd imagine dignity can't be far behind," Paula said.

"That boy there," the guard said, pointing toward the naked man in the shower, "is relatively new. He was admitted to the unit two weeks ago after being charged with gunning down a couple of illegal Mexican immigrants in a drive-by shooting. His own mother is afraid to make his bail. I reckon he'll stay here until his trial. I'll likely retire before that happens."

Paula looked over at Ben Long. He was flipping through the file he had been given by the second uniformed officer in the control room.

"This doesn't bother you?" she asked him.

"No," he said casually without looking up. "Like the officer said, you get used to it."

He closed the chart and handed it back to the officer.

"I will need to see Mr. Torrence in a conference room," he told the officer. "It's okay if he's cuffed and shackled."

"I'll escort you to the conference room now."

The officer walked to the steel blast door of the control room and inserted a heavy key. At the same time, the first officer flipped a switch releasing the magnetic lock that would have held the door fast even if the key lock had been left open.

"Dual lock system," the second officer said as he held the door open. "Nobody's getting in here unless we want them to."

Long started to walk through, but then stopped.

"Ms. Paige?" he said, gesturing toward the doorway.

"You want me to be in on the interview?"

"I need someone to take notes," he said.

They were led to a space that was the complete antithesis of any definition Paula had ever heard of a *conference room*. It was a ten-by-ten-foot cell with a metal table screwed into the floor and two steel chairs screwed into the floor on either side. The walls were painted cinderblock. The ceiling was plaster. The floor was concrete. The atmosphere was cold and oppressive. The entire room was relentlessly lit by the banks of fluorescent bulbs set into the plaster and covered with a thick-gauge wire. The light was so pervasive that there weren't any shadows.

A thick sheet of lexan polycarbonate glass was embedded in one well, beyond which she could see a smaller observation room. No attempt was made to disguise the window. Two solid steel blast doors were set into opposite walls. They had entered through one. Junior Torrence would enter through the other. Nobody would leave through either door until an officer on the other side allowed them to do so. For a moment Paula felt the helplessness of a trapped animal, even as she realized that this was the day-to-day reality for the men in the County Jail.

Again, Ben Long appeared to be immune to the claustrophobic effect of the room.

"Don't you feel the walls closing in?" she asked him in a voice not much louder than a whisper.

"Not at all," he said, his voice echoing off the concrete walls. "This isn't so bad. They usually don't allow visitors to see prisoners without a sheet of bulletproof glass between them. If this bothers you, you really don't want to deal with the typical visitors' chambers."

There was a loud rap against the door to the chamber, then the sound of a lock being sprung. The door hissed open and an officer led Junior Torrence into the room.

He blinked once or twice, seemingly surprised that there wasn't a partition between him and his visitors.

Torrence was a little over six feet. What struck Paula immediately was his youthful face. His cheeks were puffy, his forehead clear, his nose slightly turned up. He had full lips and a slightly receding chin. His eyes were a watery blue. They were flat and empty. He looked much younger than his files showed him to be. He might have been athletic once, but time spent indolently in his prison cell had turned him to suet. He must have weighed easily two hundred fifty pounds or more.

He had handcuffs on, which had been strung through a steel loop attached to a heavy leather belt around his waist so that he couldn't raise his hands any higher than his chest. His legs were manacled at the ankles, with another chain that led up to the belt. It made him hobble as he made his way to the seat across from them. He stood next to the chair.

"You can sit," Long said, gesturing toward the seat across from him without looking up.

Torrence eased himself down into the chair and waited.

"You're Earl Torrence, Junior?" Long asked.

"Yeah. Who are you?"

His voice was a hoarse tenor, out of place with his size, but completely in keeping with his baby face. He had a heavy southern accent and he tended to mumble. Paula couldn't put her finger on why, but he didn't sound very intelligent.

"My name is Ben Long. I'm a psychologist. I was hired by the District Attorney trying your case to do an assessment with you."

Torrence nodded toward Paula. "What about her? She a psychologist?"

"I'm Paula Paige," she said, stopping herself as she almost impulsively raised her hand to shake with him. "I work for the DA's office as a law clerk. I'm assisting Dr. Long with your case."

"Haven't seen a real woman in months," he said.

She couldn't think of anything to say to that, so she stayed uncomfortably quiet.

"Treating you all right, are they?" Long asked.

"Can't complain. Except sooner or later they'll get around to killing me."

"Excuse me?"

"Why. What did you do?"

Long blinked for a moment, as if replaying the conversation to figure out where it had gone wrong.

"Oh, I see," he said. "Yes. Let me rephrase my question. Why do you think someone is going to kill you?"

"That's what the other guys in here say. They say I killed Amber and after I go to court the judge is going to send me to Central Prison in Raleigh to be killed. They said I'm gonna get sent to Raleigh and the warden there is gonna knock the fire out of my ass. I don't know what that means, but it sounds like it would hurt."

"I don't doubt it. However, I think that there is a lot that needs to be done before we should worry about that. Do you know what today's date is?"

"Sometime in November. We don't have no use for calendars around here."

Long turned to Paula. "I need you to write down his responses," he said. "No need to do it completely verbatim and don't worry about my questions."

"Okay," she said a little uncertainly.

He settled in his chair and placed his hands on the table, palms down. "I'm sorry I didn't have a chance to call you in advance," he said. "I would have preferred to let you know we were coming."

"That's okay," Torrence said. "I was just watching TV. I hope this don't take long. *Gilligan's Island* comes on in a half hour."

"Do you know why you are here?"

"Sure. I got charged because I killed Amber."

"You admit killing her?"

"That's what I told the cop. But my lawyer said I didn't do it and I shouldn't tell anyone else I did."

"Were you in the apartment with Amber the night she died?"

"I already told the cop I was there, but my lawyer told me to make sure I told anyone who asked that it don't mean I killed her."

"Wise advice, I'd imagine. Tell me, do you recall everything that happened that night?"

"Not real good. But I can recollect most of it."

"Tell me what happened."

"Well, it was like this. I used to go over to Amber's on account of she was going to marry my brother, and she was real nice to me. I didn't get the idea she was being nice to me on account of him, but she really liked me, you know? So I went over to her house one night and we watched TV and I had to go to the can. The next thing I know I'm standing over Amber with my pants down and I have a knife in my hand and—"

"Wait," Long interrupted. "Your pants were down?"

"Yeah."

"You didn't say that in your interview with Detective Donnelly or in your confession statement."

"I didn't? I don't recollect."

"Why were your pants down?"

"I reckon it was because I wanted to do sex with Amanda."

"Do you recall wanting that?"

"I can recollect thinking about it once or twice. But I think that about a lot of girls."

Torrence glanced a little self-consciously at Paula. She was embarrassed as she realized that—as the only woman he had seen in the flesh in months—she would probably occupy his masturbatory fantasies for some time to come.

Long seemed unaware of the interaction between them.

"Have you ever tried to force one of those girls to have sex with you?" he asked.

"Geez, no. That's wrong."

"Why is it wrong?"

"On account of you can get in trouble for that. Bad trouble. Edward always told me I had to be careful around girls and not to make them do stuff because they might say I was bad to them."

Paula scribbled feverishly to transcribe Torrence's side of the conversation. She wished she had been able to bring her laptop computer. She could type much faster than she could write by hand.

"So if you think it's wrong to force a girl to have sex with you, why do you think you might have tried to force Amanda to have sex with you? Would it be wrong with her, too?"

"Well, sure. She was gonna marry my brother."

"I see. So you found yourself leaning over Amanda, your pants down, with a knife in your hand. What did you do next?"

"I tried to get her to wake up so she could get cleaned up. There was a lot of blood. So much blood. She looked like a ghost."

"And you ran away."

"I left her on the floor and I ran home."

"With the knife."

"I didn't know I had the knife until later, when the police come to my place. They found it."

"Did you kill Amanda Coolidge?"

Torrence blinked twice, very quickly. "I ain't supposed to talk about that."

"You watch much television here?"

"Sure. Not much else to do. I like TV."

"You like sports?"

"Yeah."

"Which is your favorite sport?"

"I like baseball. I like stock car racing. Pro football."

"Who won the World Series last year?"

"That's easy. Red Sox."

"Who is the President of the United States?"

"George . . ."

"George who?"

"George . . . Washington?"

"How far is it from New York to London?"

"I don't know nothin' about them places. I couldn't tell you where they are."

"Count down from one hundred for me by sevens."

"Huh?"

"Start at one hundred and count down by sevens. I'll get you started. One hundred, ninety-three, Eighty-six."

"Uh, seventy . . . seventy-nine. Uh, seventy . . . seventy-one. Uh, sixty-seven. Uh, fifty-seven. Uh, forty-seven."

"That's fine," Long said. "I'm going to say three things, and I'd like you to repeat them after me. Yellow, key, thirty-three Park Avenue."

"Yaller, key . . . uh, thirty-three Park Street."

"Very good. What's the capital of North Carolina?"

"I don't know."

"Okay. How does your brother feel about you being charged with killing Amanda?"

Torrence's face contorted briefly, as if changing gears in his head. "My brother loves me."

"Even though you killed his fiancée?"

"My lawyer told me that I shouldn't say I did that. Edward, he was angry, but he talked to me before I come to the jail, and he said he loved me and he would try to help me any way he could. He even said that everything turns to shit—that's what he said. I ain't cussin' or nothin'—and they send me to Raleigh to let the warden knock the fire outa my ass, he's going to be there when they kill me so I won't be alone."

87

"If you stand trial, you could be given the death penalty. What does that mean?"

"It means that the state can kill me."

"Do you know what it means to die?"

"That's when they kill you."

"What happens when you die, Junior?"

"If you're a soldier, they shoot you and you fall down and stop moving and breathing."

"What happened when Amber died?"

"She stopped moving and breathing."

"Did she get better?"

Paula stopped writing and turned sharply to face Long.

"I don't think so," Junior said after glancing at her, distracted. "I don't think it's like with soldiers in the movies. I think maybe she stayed dead."

"Do you think you will stay dead if they send you to Raleigh and kill you?"

It was as if the thought had never occurred to Torrence. He squinted his eyes and considered it for a moment.

"I hope not," he finally said. "That would suck."

As she and Ben Long walked out the front door of the Henderson County Jail, Paula saw a man sprinting up the steps toward them. He was in his middle-fifties, with thick wavy brunette hair graying at the temples, and he wore a suit, obviously hand-tailored for him. He carried a Tumi briefcase in his hand, and walked with the self-assured confidence that only came with success and wealth.

Even as she saw the man, Paula realized that Ben had frozen in his steps. She turned to him.

"Dr. Long?" she asked. "Are you all right?"

He could only shake his head as the man approached them.

"Well," the man said. "As I live and breathe, I do believe I behold a ghost!"

He stepped up to them and extended his hand. "Dr. Long, I can't recall the last time we met. Must have been years ago."

Long ignored the hand, which the man held out for an uncomfortable moment before pivoting to face Paula. "Eli Crouch. I'm Earl Torrence's attorney."

Almost instinctively, Paula grasped his hand. It was warm and dry, like the skin of a molting snake.

"Paula Paige. I'm a clerk with the Henderson County DA's office."

"Ah, yes. And how is Sidney Kingsley?"

"Overworked and underpaid, like all civil servants."

"He made his bed, as they say. I am *so* glad I ran into the two of you. I was told Dr. Long had been retained by the DA's office to evaluate my client, and I had hoped to get here to advise him before you saw him. It seems I missed the boat, as it were."

"We're not finished," Long said. "I haven't really started my evaluation."

"So, no conclusions yet?"

"Hardly."

"I don't suppose you tried any of those famous Ben Long tricks on him?" Crouch's conspiratorial grin froze on his face as if chiseled there. "I'd hate to hear that you had cajoled some kind of confession out of Earl by confusing him. He is—as I'm sure you've noticed—easily led."

"Is that the thrust of the evaluation Sybil is conducting on him for your office? That Torrence was convinced to admit to a murder he didn't commit?"

"Among other issues. Well, I am sorry I wasn't able to be there for the meeting, but as long as I'm here I might as well pop in and spend a few minutes with my client. I do hope you'll do me the favor of informing me ahead of time the next time you schedule an evaluation with him. I'd love to see what he tells you."

"I'd imagine so," Long said. "We must be going."

"Before you do," Crouch said as he snapped the catch on his fancy leather case, "I think I have something for you. One of my clients gave me a letter to pass along if I ever ran into you."

He pulled a shopworn envelope from his briefcase and handed it to Long, almost as if serving a subpoena.

"Do have a nice day," he said, his even, well-tended teeth glistening like fine ivory in the sunlight. Then, in a burst of energy, he was gone, bounding up the steps toward the jail entrance.

Long stared at the envelope, then opened it cautiously. As he read over the letter inside, Paula watched his face cloud over and the color start to rise in his cheeks. Finally, he stuffed the letter back in the envelope and placed the envelope in his jacket pocket.

"He had no right," Long said as he walked toward the car, ignoring Paula entirely as she worked to keep up with him.

"What was that all about?" she asked after they cleared the downtown area and began the short trip to Asheville.

Without saying a word, he pulled the envelope from his jacket pocket and handed it to her.

The note inside was scrawled in grade school handwriting, all printing.

"Docter Long," it read. "I have binn told by my therappist that it is importent for me too make amens for what I have done. I have binn in this plase for twenny years so far and I rekon I will be hear for the rest of my life. What I done to you and youre mama was very bad, and I no that now. Prison does things to a man that I wuld not wish on a dawg, and after a wile you begin to think about what you have done and start to regret it. I dont especk that I will ever git a shot at parole, and may be I dont deserve one anyhow. I aint going to aks you to forgiv me, becuz my therappist says that it aint right for me to do that. He tells me that all I can do is tell you how sorry I am about what I done and leve the rest to god. Sense I have binn put in prison I have come to exept Jesus as my lord and saveyer, and I can tell you from the bottum of my hart that I am a saved man and that I repint all the bad stuff I have done in my life. I no that dont mean nothing to the state and it wont get me out of prison or nothing, but for the ferst time in my life I have peace in my hart. I rekon thats about all I had to say. I wish you a happy life in spite of what I done, and hope you will find some peace from the fact that I am so sorry for my crime aganst you and your mama. Sincerely Anson Mount."

"Oh," she said.

Long didn't say anything. He gripped the steering wheel and stared straight ahead.

"Do you want me to drive?" she asked.

"That might be a good idea."

He pulled the car into the breakdown lane at the side of the highway, unhooked his seat belt and opened the driver's-side door. She met him halfway around the back of the car. His face was stony and ruddy. He met her eyes for a second, then looked down at the ground as they passed.

She was past the Asheville city limits before he spoke.

"He had no right," he said again.

"To write the letter?"

"To contact me at all. Isn't that why they put people in prisons? To keep them from infringing on the lives of decent people?"

"I suppose that's one reason."

"And for punishment. What in hell kind of punishment is it that allows a man to feel at peace with himself when his victims can't sleep at night?"

"It doesn't seem right."

"It isn't right."

She drove for a short distance, the air in the car increasingly tense between them. She decided to change the subject. "Tell me what you saw in your interview with Junior Torrence."

"What?"

"The evaluation. Did you see anything important?"

"I haven't really started the evaluation. All I did today was a brief mental status examination. I wanted to look at the man, see if anything registered."

"Did it?"

"A little."

"He didn't seem to understand what death means."

"Is that what you heard?"

"He said staying dead would suck."

"Yes."

"Doesn't that indicate a lack of understanding?"

"Not necessarily. Consider all the different religions of the world that believe death isn't final. Yours included."

She thought about it. "You think he meant if he died and didn't go . . . *wherever,* that would suck?"

"Not at all. I didn't try to read anything into what he said. Maybe Junior Torrence doesn't understand death, or maybe he thinks he will go to some sort of eternal reward after he dies, or maybe he really believes that nobody actually dies at all, just falls down and shows up again the next week, playing a different role. I can't say what he thinks yet. This interview wasn't about understanding Torrence. It was about *seeing* him."

"We drove all this way just to see him?"

"And for him to see us. The next time we show up, we won't be strangers. He'll be more at ease around us. He'll be more likely to open up. Today was an introduction."

She waited for him to continue. After a moment, he did.

"How can Edward Torrence deal with it?" he asked.

"I don't understand."

"Earl killed Edward's fiancée. He told Detective Donnelly he did it because he wanted to have sex with her. Yet Edward has stood beside Earl throughout the arrest and pre-trial hearings, and visits him every other week. How does he get past the grief?"

"Blood is thicker, I suppose. Maybe if Anson Mount had been your brother—"

"Not a chance. Never. Laura was everything to me. If my own grandmother had killed her, I'd have cut her off without a word. I don't understand how Edward can handle it."

"Maybe when you talk with him, you can ask him."

"Do you think he would mind?" Long asked absently.

"Yes," she said. "I think he would. But I don't think that will stop you."

Ten

"I left my plant in here a few days ago," Long said as he stood in front of the secretary's desk in the Human Resources office at St. Joseph's hospital.

"Oh, yes, the iris. We wondered where it came from," she told him.

"It's an iris?"

"Yes, and a beautiful one, too. We put it in the lounge."

She rose from her desk and walked back down the narrow hallway, disappearing around the corner for a moment. When she reappeared, she carried the pot.

"I left it here accidentally," Long said as she set it down on the desk. "I was here to visit a student, and they told me I needed a new identification badge."

"You're on staff here?"

"Adjunct staff. I haven't worked here for a few years, so I needed to update my ID." He fingered the badge clipped to his sweater.

"Well, Doctor, thank you for allowing us to enjoy your iris. I hope your student is better."

"Yes," Long said as he hefted the pot. "So do I."

He made his way to the elevator and was thankful that, for once, it wasn't packed with people. Hospitals were terrible places for crowds of people, he mused as he pushed the button for the eighth floor. He was all too aware that some of your nastiest opportunistic bacteria loitered in hospitals, just waiting

94

for some compromised immune system to drift their way. The very thought made him itch.

The elevator door opened on eight and he stepped up to the nurses' window. He pressed the call button and the same nurse who had greeted him the other day appeared shortly.

"Oh," she said. "It's you, Dr. Long. We weren't certain what had become of you."

"I left my plant downstairs. When I went back, they were closed. I had to go teach a class."

"Yes," she said. "I see. Please, come on through."

She pressed a button and he walked through into the hallway.

"I haven't been here since they moved the unit," he said. "I've come to see Sarah Ashburton."

"She's in Room 821. Down the hall, turn right at the end, and it will be the third door on your left. She should be in her room. She just finished lunch and she doesn't have group until two."

"Thank you," he said.

He found Room 821 on the first try and cradled the plant with his left arm so he could rap on the door.

"Come in," someone said.

He pushed on the door, enough to open it halfway. "Sarah? It's Dr. Long. Is it all right to come in?"

"Of course," she said.

"I brought you a plant."

He allowed the door to close behind him and peered at her over the iris.

"Oh, my," she said as she rolled off the bed. "It's lovely." She walked over to him and took the plant.

"They tell me it's an iris," he said.

"You didn't need to do this."

"I wanted to. When I heard what had happened, I felt as if I should do . . . something."

She settled the plant on a table next to the window.

"What did you hear?" she asked as she pointed toward a chair and plopped onto the bed.

"The other students weren't exactly clear on what happened, but from what I could gather you attempted to kill yourself."

"Attempted. Right. Damned near did it, too."

She held out her wrists. Both were bandaged. "I don't know what I was thinking. I must have been in a really bad place."

"I think you were very upset the last time I saw you."

"You noticed."

He hadn't, not really, but he nodded because he thought it was probably the right thing to do.

"I think I might not have been very helpful," he said.

"No, you were great. You didn't judge me or anything. I called that doctor you referred me to, but she couldn't see me for a week. That night I had a fight with my mother and I started to cut on myself again, on my thigh like I usually do, but something came over me. I felt like I had nothing to live for. So I used the razor on my wrists."

"Was it painful?"

"It stung. The razor was very sharp. I hear the sharper the razor, the less the pain."

"Is that so?"

"Take it from me. If you ever plan to kill yourself, make sure you use a very sharp blade."

Long didn't know what to say to that, so he nodded.

"Do you know how long you're going to be here?" he asked after several uncomfortable moments of silence.

"A few more days. They have me on meds and they want to give them some time to start working."

"I thought you couldn't take medications. You said you were a Christian Scientist."

"My parents are Scientists. I couldn't take meds because they wouldn't have approved. When I got here, though, the doctor put me on the medication. My parents argued with him, but he reminded them that, legally, I'm an adult and can make my own decisions. He asked me if I wanted to get better and said if I did, the meds could help."

"So you're taking them."

"Yes."

"Are they helping?"

"Can't tell yet. I still feel down a lot. The group therapy helps."

"That's good."

"I can't believe you came up here to visit me," she said, smiling.

"I felt partially responsible for what happened."

"I don't understand."

"You came to me asking for help, and I sent you to someone else. I thought maybe I hadn't done enough."

"You did plenty. I'm sorry you felt that way. I must have been pretty messed up."

"I think you must have been. I'm glad that you're going to be better. What medicine are they giving you?"

She told him.

Long had never heard of it. He recalled that he had been out of active practice for over four years. It was likely that a lot of developments had passed him by. He was more out of touch than he had realized.

"Well," he said, placing his hands on his knees. "It's good to see you're doing so well. When you get out, come by my office and we'll figure out what to do about your classes."

"That would be great. I was afraid that I'd have to take Incompletes for all my courses this semester."

"Don't worry about that. For now, you should concentrate on your treatment."

He stood and clasped his hands together. "I have a class to teach. I just wanted to check in on you."

"Will you come back?"

"Do you want me to come back?"

"I wouldn't ask if I didn't," she said.

"Then I'll come back. You get better, okay?"

He started to open the door and she jumped up from the bed and rushed over to him. Before he could do anything, she put her arms around him and hugged him tightly.

"Thank you for coming," she said. "Besides my parents, nobody else has come to see me. I thought nobody cared."

She held him so tightly, Long began to feel panicky. He carefully put his arms around her and patted her back uneasily.

"That's all right," he said, not really certain what he meant.

Eleven

Edward Torrence looked much like his brother Earl might have looked, had Earl been bestowed a better set of genes. Like Earl, he was tall, with a youthful, open face, blue eyes, and straw-colored hair. Long noted when he shook Edward's hand that it was slightly limp.

Unlike his brother, Edward Torrence's eyes betrayed the depth of his soul and intelligence. They also conveyed an intractable sadness that Paula thought might never be erased.

"So you've met Junior," he said.

"Yes," Paula and Long said at the same time.

Edward smiled briefly. "So, what do you think?"

"I don't think anything yet," Long said. "I do have some questions."

"Shoot." Edward shrugged a little, as if to make it clear he had done little but answer questions since the day Amber had been murdered.

"Your brother admitted killing your fiancée and then retracted that confession. Do you believe he did it?"

"Of course not. Junior couldn't have killed Amber."

"Even if he did change his story after his first interrogation and pled not guilty, one could infer that he did so only because his attorney told him to."

"It *was* his attorney's suggestion, but Junior has never come right out and told *me* he did it. I think his original confession was forced."

"If you don't mind me asking, how do you deal with it?" Long asked.

Paula glanced over at Long. She wasn't certain whether he was asking a professional question or a personal one.

"Day by day," Edward said. "I get up in the morning and go minute by minute through the day until it's time to go to bed. The next day I get up and do it again."

"You've stood by your brother throughout the arrest and the arraignment and all the pre-trial motions."

"What would you have me do, Dr. Long?"

"I'm curious. This man may have killed the woman you loved, and yet you support him implicitly."

"*This man* is my brother," Edward said. "Beyond that, he's practically helpless. He has the mind of a child and the needs of a child. I can't bring Amanda back to life. If I were to abandon Earl, I'd lose both of them."

"You were responsible for much of Earl's upbringing."

"Yes. My parents both worked. When they were out of the house, I was responsible for Earl's safety. It wasn't easy. He was a demanding child, and I wasn't all that much older. After our parents died, I was his sole support."

"You say he has the mind of a child. Has he ever been evaluated for retardation?"

"I can't say. Our parents might have taken him to a psychologist once or twice when he was younger. They didn't talk to me about that. When they died, I went through all their papers—I was only twenty-one, but I was the executor of the estate—but I didn't see any testing results. If he was tested, they didn't keep the reports. You've met Junior. You can see he isn't . . . right."

"I think that remains to be seen. Did you know that Earl was visiting Amanda before she was murdered?"

"She mentioned he had been over a number of times. Amanda loved Junior. In a way, he was more like a stepchild to her than a brother-in-law. *To be,* that is. I think she figured when she married me, he would come along as part of the package. She thought the world of Junior."

"Junior seems to have thought of her in a different way."

"You can't convince me of that," Edward said. "I know Junior like I know myself. Sure, he's a grown man. He has impulses and feelings like the rest of us. On the other hand, I know he never would have tried to do anything with Amanda."

"Why?"

"Because he knew she was going to marry me. Junior would never do anything to harm me or make me angry, if he could help it. He might have been aroused by women from time to time, maybe even by Amanda, but he never would have done anything with or to her because he knew I'd be upset. Junior would cut off his right hand before he'd make me upset."

"What about . . ." Paula started.

Long turned to her. Paula blushed slightly.

"It's all right," he said. "You had a question?"

"I was thinking. What would Earl do if he thought Amanda was doing something that would upset Edward?"

Long turned to Edward, his eyebrow raised.

"I never thought of that," Long said.

"Impossible," Edward said. "Junior loved Amanda the way he would a big sister or a mother."

"But did he love her as much as he does you?" Long asked.

"What are you implying?"

"Suppose Amanda did something that would make you angry? If Earl found out, what would he do to protect you?"

"I can't imagine what you could be thinking. *If* Junior killed Amanda, and you can't convince me he did, then he couldn't have known what he was doing. He didn't understand the consequences, for her or for himself. Isn't that part of being incompetent, Dr. Long?"

Long didn't reply.

"Isn't it?" Edward asked again.

"I'm sorry," Paula said as they drove back to her office.

"About what?"

"I didn't mean to butt in like that."

"You did the right thing. In fact, you made me look at this situation from an angle I hadn't considered. Very insightful."

"How so?"

"It had always been my opinion, based on the police reports, that Earl Torrence killed Amanda because she wouldn't yield to his sexual advances. It never occurred to me that he might have attacked her to defend himself against *her* advances. A very interesting possibility, wouldn't you say?"

"I'm not sure that's what I—"

"Of course it was. Think about Earl's statement to us at the jail. He found himself standing over Amanda's body with his pants down. He never said he pulled them down himself."

"Don't you think he would remember?"

"What I think or don't think is immaterial. Earl says he doesn't recall why his pants were down. Memory is strange. It's about the strangest thing we do in our heads. It's also subject to the most amazing feats of magic. When memory finds a hole, it tries to fill it. Sometimes it manufactures memories to fill gaps. We call these manufactured memories 'confabulations.' Looking back on the police report, I seem to recall that Earl couldn't remember much about the murder, until Detective Donnelly suggested to him that he might have committed it because Amanda rebuffed his sexual advances."

"Right."

"So maybe it was the other way around. Maybe he killed her to rebuff *her* sexual advances."

"That's a pretty extreme response."

"Maybe not for Junior. As you observed, he appears to have a very immature concept of death. Also, he knew that having sex with Amanda would be wrong. He said so. What if *she* came on to *him,* and his primitive sense of right and wrong led him to kill her? He might not have thought she was going to *stay* dead. He just wanted her to stop."

"Does it matter?"

"Of course it does. At least, in regard to his culpability. One reason for killing is pretty much as good as another. On the other hand, if he can articulate a specific reason for killing her, it would indicate a level of reasoning inconsistent with mental retardation or incompetence."

"Meaning it would help our case."

"Exactly. Do you have Detective Donnelly's address handy? I'd like to talk with him about his interview with Junior."

Wade Donnelly was a tall, gangly man with an Adam's apple that looked like a tumor. He looked like someone who had a glandular disorder, from his protruding eyes to the way his pants gathered where he had cinched them to his waist with his belt. His fellow detectives called him "Wade the Blade."

He sat in his office sipping coffee as Long and Paula Paige went over the arrest and interrogation reports with him.

"We appreciate you seeing us on such short notice," Paula said while Long reviewed his notes.

"Uh, yes," Long said without looking up. "Very kind of you."

"Not at all," Donnelly said. "It's part of my job. In this case, though, I'm not sure why you want to talk about Junior Torrence. That boy's been tagged, bagged, and delivered."

"Yes," Long said. "His attorney, though, is trying to get a ruling that he isn't fit to stand trial, due to incompetence."

"Can't say I'm unhappy to hear that. Torrence killed that poor girl as sure as I'm sitting here, but I swear I'd hate to see that boy get the needle."

"Why?"

"He's a simp. If brains was pudding, that poor boy would flat starve to death. Don't seem right, somehow, to kill someone like that. Be like killing a puppy or something. Some kind of dumb animal."

"Is it your impression he didn't understand what he was doing?"

"Don't know if I'd go that far. It's like this. People wind up dead and somebody has to clean up the mess. It won't do to allow killers to walk around free. Upsets the natural order, know what I mean? Like this case I'm workin' on right now. Some guy picks locks and sneaks into women's bedrooms at night, holds a knife to their throats and makes them do what he wants. Sicko like that needs to be taken off the streets. So when Amber got killed, I had to do my job. I found the guy who killed her, and I arrested him. The rest is up to the courts. Except for reciting to the court what I found, my part in the story is over. I could tell from the first moment I met him he wasn't right."

"Interesting," Long said.

"What?"

"That's exactly what his brother said about him a little while ago. He said Junior isn't right."

"Have you met Earl Torrence?"

"We visited him at the jail," Paula said.

"You talked with the boy?"

"We did," Long said.

"Did he seem right?"

"The term is a little broad," Long replied.

"Okay. How about retarded? Did he seem retarded?"

"That's what we're trying to determine. Did he seem retarded to you when you interviewed him?"

"Man, it was like shooting fish in a barrel, interrogating that boy. I knew, almost from the moment I found the bloody shirt in his room, that he killed that girl. All I had to do was get him to admit to it."

"How do you go about that, exactly?"

"Interrogations?"

"Getting people to admit to things."

"Well, there are some tricks involved. There are things you can do and things you can't, you understand. You can't tell someone you have their mother in the next room and you're going to shoot her if he don't talk. You *can* tell him you have a witness who saw him commit the crime, and can identify him, hoping he'll confess."

"I don't understand the difference. Both statements are lies."

"It comes down to whether what you tell the guy would make an innocent man confess. If you threaten to cap his mom, well, maybe an innocent man would admit to a killing to save her life. If you tell him he's been ratted out, there's no penalty for lying and a reasonable man will only admit to the crime if he's guilty."

"A reasonable man," Long said. "Yes. However, as you already stated, Junior Torrence wasn't right. Am I correct?"

"I said that, yes."

"But he was reasonable?"

"I don't follow."

"We'll get back to it. What other kinds of ways do you have to get people to admit things?"

"I carry a clipboard."

"A clipboard? What do you do with it?"

"A clipboard is a symbol of authority. You can go anywhere you want and do anything you please if you carry a clipboard. Nobody questions you. It's a barrier between you and the guy you're questioning. The best thing is, it's opaque."

"Opaque," Long repeated.

"You can't see through it."

"I understand the word. I just don't see how it helps in the interrogation."

"It's like this. You walk into the interview room, and your suspect is sitting there sweating it out. He knows he's in deep shit—pardon my French, ma'am—but he don't know how deep. Then you walk in with a clipboard that has fifty or sixty sheets of paper on it. You let him see how thick the pile of paper is, but you don't let him see what's on it."

"Ah," Long said. "I see. He doesn't know how much *you* know."

"Yeah. You sit down, and you give him a taste to start out with. Take Torrence, for instance. I told him I'd found a knife and a bloody shirt in his room and we knew the blood belonged to Amber Coolidge. He admitted right away that he had been at her place the night before, and he admitted he was there around the time she was killed."

"But he never volunteered that he tried to have sex with her."

"Come again?"

"He never mentioned trying to seduce Amber until you asked him *when* he tried to have sex with her."

"I don't follow."

"It's right here, in the dictation. Torrence described watching the movie with Amber, and then she told him it was time for him to go home. The next thing he knew, she was dead on the floor. You then asked, 'When did you try to have sex with her?' He denied any memory of that, but you kept questioning him about it."

"And he finally admitted it. Look, Dr. Long, there's only a few reasons people kill other people. They do it for money, or for revenge, or out of rage. Sometimes they do it to avoid being caught at something else they're ashamed of. Once in a very long while you run up against some character who kills because he thinks it's the merciful thing to do. That about covers it."

"So you considered all the reasons that Earl Torrence might have killed Amber and the most reasonable one was sexual?"

"I'm a cop. I got this cop brain thing going on all the time. You spend twenty years busting criminals and it can make you a little cynical. I know that. Another thing you learn along the way is motivation. You've seen pictures of Amber. She was a beautiful girl, a real knockout. She was a catch. I see a guy like Torrence, I know he's not right in the head. I can see he's a little dim. I've seen a lot of dim guys in my time, and they always seem to be driven by their glands, know what I mean?"

"You made an inference."

"Huh?"

"An assumption."

"A correct one, as it happened."

"Are you certain about that?"

"Beg pardon?"

"Let's say you're right about Torrence. We're going to presume—for the sake of argument, and recognizing it hampers the DA's case—that he is mentally handicapped. Without any evidence, you suggested to him that he had attempted to have sex with Amanda, right?"

"Right."

"And he denied it."

"At first, right."

"And you pressed on. You presented him with a scenario in which he attempted to seduce Amanda, in which she rebuffed him, and in which he then killed her."

"Correct."

"You made this suggestion to a possibly mentally handicapped man who had previously told you he couldn't recall what had happened between the time Amanda let him use her bathroom and the moment he saw her lying dead on the floor."

"What are you implying?"

"Marlene Sinclair, Detective."

"Who in the hell is Marlene Sinclair."

"She was a social worker in Nebraska. She specialized in working with children who had been physically and sexually abused. She was regarded as the foremost national authority on child sexual abuse. She was as close to famous as someone gets in that business."

"I never heard of her."

"That's okay. I'm going to tell you about her. There was this case involving the owner of a private school for young girls around four or five years of age. Kindergarten age. One of these girls accused a man working for the school of taking indecent liberties with her. After a few days, another girl came forward. The police sensed a possible pedophile, and arrested the worker, a man named Henry Beech. The local Department of Child Protection called in Marleen Sinclair to do the evaluations on the victims. She interviewed the two girls who made the allegations, who told her that several other girls had also been abused by Beech. So she interviewed those girls, too."

"Good, standard police work. Woman would have made a good cop."

"Maybe. We'll never know. Sinclair made a critical error—two, actually. First, she videotaped her interviews with the children. Second, instead of letting the children tell their stories, she gave them scenarios and asked them whether they could have happened. Before she knew it, almost every girl in the school said that Beech had tried to molest them."

"And?"

"And Marleen Sinclair was destroyed on the witness stand. The defense attorney brought in an expert on memory, who demonstrated how you could implant a memory in the mind of an impressionable young child. He cited the exact same techniques that Marleen Sinclair had used to extract the children's testimony against Henry Beech."

"And Beech got off?"

"He got off. Then he sued Sinclair for defamation. He claimed she manufactured the evidence by implanting memories of his abuse in the children's minds. He was awarded several million dollars."

"A bad break."

"Especially for her. Suddenly, nobody in the child abuse treatment field wanted to have anything to do with her. She was fired from her job. She couldn't get onto any panels at conferences. No reputable journal would publish her articles. The entire world turned its back on her. Beech filed a complaint and she was stripped of her license to practice."

"What became of her?"

"I haven't a clue. Nobody in the field has heard from her in years. She might be working somewhere, but not as a social worker."

"What's your point, Doctor?"

"Earl Torrence admitted being in Amanda's apartment. He admitted seeing her lying on the floor dead. He probably killed her. However, he never mentioned trying to have sex with her until you convinced him that he could have. If you're right, and he *is* mentally retarded, then he was as open to suggestion as Marlene Sinclair's five-year-old clients."

"You're saying he only admitted trying to have sex with her because I told him so?"

"It's a possibility we have to consider."

"What difference does it make? He admitted killing her."

"Not exactly," Long countered. "He thought he might have killed her because he was there when she died. He had no direct memory of plunging the knife into her body. Then you gave him a motive. It became part of his memory. It filled the gaps in his mind surrounding the murder and it gave him a justification for having killed his brother's fiancée."

"You don't think he killed her?"

"Actually, I think he probably did. If you discount the sexual motive, I still don't know *why*. Thank you for your time, Detective."

Twelve

Long and Paula sat in Sidney Kingsley's office. Paula sat very erect in her leather-upholstered chair. Long slouched, his fingers steepled in front of his face as he tried to pull together all the pieces of his interviews to that point.

Kingsley sat behind his desk. He waited patiently, as his lengthy association with Ben Long had taught him to do. He had learned years earlier that—sometimes—Long had to let the ideas in his head cook for a while before speaking.

Without moving, Long took a deep breath. "Crouch didn't plead Junior out," he said.

"No," Kingsley said. "I was wondering when you would get around to that."

"It's curious. Torrence admitted to Detective Donnelly that he killed Amanda Coolidge."

"No, he didn't. I saw through that interrogation as easily as you did, Ben. Junior said he *might* have killed Amanda, but he never admitted it until coaxed by Donnelly."

"It doesn't matter when the admission took place. It was on the record. If Crouch convinced Junior to plead guilty, he could strike a deal with you. He could beg the charge down to—say—involuntary manslaughter."

"Torrence would still be convicted of killing her."

"But he wouldn't go to Death Row. That's what I can't figure out, Sid. Cutting a deal would be the logical thing to do, in light of the admission. How did Crouch convince Junior to go

111

along with a not guilty plea?"

Kingsley shut his eyes and leaned his head back on the chair.

"Edward," Long said. "It had to be Edward."

"I don't understand," Kingsley said.

"Junior Torrence has lived under the direction of his older brother for all his life. He wouldn't listen to Crouch if it meant possibly going to prison, but he might listen to Edward."

"I don't know. Eli can be very convincing."

"It had to be Edward," Long said again after a moment or so. "What I don't understand is why Crouch didn't approach you first, maybe test the waters for a reduced plea."

"He did," Kingsley said. His face betrayed his immediate regret for saying it.

"He suggested a plea bargain, and you turned it down?"

"He wanted too much."

"A conviction is a conviction, Sid."

"Not always."

Long thought for a moment. "It's an election year," he said finally. "I forgot about that."

"It isn't germane, Ben. Earl Torrence is guilty. He will be sentenced to death. I'm not interested in taking any plea bargains, and I'm not interested in talking about deals. Focus on the job at hand."

"This *is* the job at hand. I wouldn't be sitting here if you had simply pled Junior out. If you'd accepted Eli Crouch's offer, there'd be no talk about competency!"

"What difference would it make?"

"Crouch came to you with a plea offer. You rejected it. You backed him against the wall, knowing it's where he's most dangerous. He had no choice but to pursue an incompetence plea. None of this is necessary, Sid. You had a conviction in the palm of your hand, and you threw it all away."

"It wouldn't be a capital conviction."

"Who cares?"

"*I* care!" Kingsley said. "The *voters* care. All those Bible Belt conservatives in all those stone churches in the hollows and mountain ranges care."

"This is politics. This isn't about the truth. It's about pandering to a bunch of eye-for-an-eye constituents."

Kingsley slapped his palm down on his walnut desktop.

"Do the evaluation!" he said, his voice brittle and spiked. "Do what you were hired to do. Give me some proof that Earl Torrence isn't mentally retarded so that he can go to the death chamber. Is that too much to ask?"

Long shook his head slowly. "I think maybe it is. I'll bill you for my time spent on this case, but I think you need to find another hired gun."

He pulled himself from his chair and walked out the door without saying goodbye to either Kingsley or Paula.

"I knew he was going to do that," Kingsley said.

"You could have stopped it, then."

"No. Not with Ben. This had to happen sooner or later. There was no way he was going to miss a point as important as Torrence's plea. I know the way his mind works."

"What do we do now?"

"Give him a day or two to think things over. I've seen that look in his eyes before. He's pissed off at me for holding out on him, but that won't stop him from working on the case in the long run. He's hooked by the puzzle now. In a couple of days, I'll send you out to that mountainside perch of his to pull him back into the fold. He'll bite. Bet on it."

"Why me?"

"You've established a relationship with him. He's beginning to trust you. If you ask him to continue working the Torrence case, he'll do it."

"Why do I get the idea you're pimping me out?"

"Not the way you mean. I'd never do that. For that matter, the relationship you have with Ben is probably as deep as it will ever get. He's way too well defended for anything more substantial."

"You're so certain?"

"It's the nature of his disorder as it's manifested in his case. Everyone is different. He's incapable of forming deep emotional bonds the way you or I might. Whatever obligation he feels toward other people is held together by other concepts, like responsibility, or simply the desire not to let things change. He listens to you, though. He thinks you have a good mind. He respects that. If you ask him to stay, he'll stay."

"There are other psychologists."

"Not like Ben. I *need* him on this case. I can't explain why, beyond what I've already told you. There are things you can't know, things that would place me in a position of violating privilege. All I can say is that Ben is the man for this case, as much as this case is Ben's last hope for salvation."

She stared him down. "I can't let that one pass. Salvation from what?"

"From himself. His grief. His isolation. When I recruited him, Ben was inches from becoming lost in himself. Surely you can see a difference in him since he's started working on the Torrence case."

"This isn't about Dr. Long," she said. "This is about you. I think you still blame yourself because you couldn't talk Eli Crouch out of defending Anson Mount. You think everything that has happened to Dr. Long is a result of your failure to protect him from the best efforts of your own partner."

"Does it matter? Does it really matter why? Ben is my friend. I've known him for more than half my life. When you see a friend drowning, you throw him a life preserver."

She crossed her arms and tapped her toe on the deep pile carpet.

"As long as the life preserver is the Torrence case and not me," she said.

THIRTEEN

Paula parked her car in the gravel driveway of Long's mountainside home and walked up to the front door. She could hear music coming from inside the house and recognized it as Grieg's piano concerto.

Tentatively, she rang the doorbell.

Moments later, the door opened.

Long wore a soft plaid flannel work shirt and a pair of jeans. His sneakers looked as if he had worn them for years. It was as dressed-down as Paula had ever seen him. He wore reading glasses and held a sheaf of papers.

"Did Sid send you?" he asked.

"May I come in?"

"Oh. Ah . . . of course."

He unlatched the screen door and held it open for her. She squeezed between him and the jamb and walked into the living room.

"I've been grading term papers. Please excuse the mess."

She looked around. She saw a well-stacked pile of stapled papers sitting on the kitchen table, alongside an open bottle of Chilean merlot. A half-full wine glass sat on the end table next to the sofa. Otherwise, the house looked as clinically sanitary as she recalled it from her earlier visits.

"Would you like a glass of wine?" he asked, almost as an afterthought.

"No, but thank you for offering."

"Please, sit down."

She sat in the chair across from the sofa and crossed her legs. She wasn't certain why. She knew she had good legs, especially attractive when crossed, and she wondered whether she had subconsciously arranged herself in a way to get his attention and approval.

She dismissed the thought as ridiculous. She was simply more comfortable with her legs crossed.

He did not sit. Instead, he picked up his wine glass and walked over to the sliding glass door to the deck. He gazed out over the valley.

"You didn't say whether Sid sent you."

"Yes, he did."

"He wants you to convince me to continue working on the Torrence case."

"That's right."

"You wouldn't have come on your own."

"No. I don't think so."

"Because I creep you out."

"Well, not so much anymore, now that I've gotten to know you a little better. I probably wouldn't have come out on my own because we have a working relationship, and if you aren't working for the DA's office that relationship is nonexistent."

"My God, you are going to be a good lawyer," he said without looking at her. "Okay, pitch me."

"I'm sorry. What?"

"Give me the pitch. Tell me why I should finish evaluating Junior Torrence."

"I can think of a number of reasons. Besides the obvious, that Torrence may go free if he's found mentally handicapped, you should return to the case because you don't know all the answers yet."

"You think that's important to me."

"It seems to be. You could have done a perfunctory assessment of Junior at the jail. You could have run a few tests, crunched the numbers, and written your report. Instead, you've insisted on talking with Junior's brother, the detective who interrogated him, and a whole list of people we haven't even met yet."

"I'm thorough."

"You want to be certain."

"Isn't it the same thing?"

"It implies that you aren't certain now."

"That's your lawyer brain talking again."

"All right. Let's put it on the table. Is Junior Torrence mentally retarded?"

Long took a sip of the merlot. "I don't know."

"Do you care?"

"About whether he's retarded? Not particularly. About whether he dies? If he killed that girl, I'd be perfectly content to see them execute him."

"So, what is it then? Why are you talking to all these people?"

He placed the glass on the end table and sat on the sofa. She noticed that he sat very carefully, with a hand flat on each thigh, completely different than the slouch he had adopted in Kingsley's office.

"It doesn't *feel* right," he said. "The pieces aren't falling together the way they should if the case was cut and dried. There are complications. Jagged edges."

She realized that he was describing the way the case looked inside his own head.

"I shouldn't have come," she said, standing. "This isn't right."

"What?"

"We really aren't after the same things. We're using you for our own purposes, but your goals aren't our goals."

"I thought I explained that over lunch the other day."

118

"I think you did. I just don't know whether I heard you."

"Sometimes I can be a little murky."

She stopped halfway between him and the front door. She looked back at him. He was still sitting on the sofa. His hands hadn't moved.

"Is that an apology?" she asked.

He smiled a little, as if it embarrassed him to do it. "An explanation."

"Do you want to continue working the Torrence case?"

He shrugged. "I don't know."

"If you were to return to the case, why would you do it?"

"To finish."

"The evaluation?"

"The case. I don't think it's finished."

"Why do you say that?"

"Because if it were, it would *look* finished." He tapped the side of his head. "In here."

"Are you saying that maybe Torrence didn't kill Amber?"

"No. I think he probably did."

"Then what isn't finished?"

Long's face darkened and lines appeared on his forehead. It was almost as if formulating the response was painful.

"I'm going to try to explain this," he said. "I'll probably fail horribly because I really have a hard time with metaphors, but there you are. When a case is *right*, when all the pieces fit together properly and it's all finished, it's as if a knot inside my head is loosened. The tension flows away. I perceive a color more like green than like brown. None of this is real, you understand. I can see you don't understand. Okay, I think I can demonstrate."

He walked over to the stereo and turned off the Grieg concerto. Then he crossed the room to the piano and sat. "Tell me how this makes you feel," he said.

He played a scale and sang along, in a strong, melodic voice that Paula found slightly surprising.

"Do-re-mi-fa-so-la-ti . . ." and then he stopped.

"You didn't finish the scale."

"That is factually correct, but nonresponsive. You understand the legal term 'nonresponsive,' right?"

"Of course."

"Now, this time, answer my question. Don't tell me what I did. Tell me how it makes you *feel*. Do-re-mi-fa-so-la-ti . . ." He stopped again.

"It makes me feel incomplete. Something is lacking."

"Exactly. The octave scale I played ended in something called an 'unresolved seventh.' If I were to play a complete scale, you wouldn't remember it. It would simply be something you experienced that resolved itself satisfactorily, allowing you to move on with your life. The unresolved seventh, though, sticks with you. You walk around waiting for it to finish. It's waiting for that last note to complete the scale. It's maddening."

"For you."

"For anyone. We are a species that thrives on resolution. Resolution is calming. We crave an ending, closure, finality. When something is unfinished—like the unresolved seventh—we feel disjointed. We are irritated. We want to find that major eighth and put it in its rightful place so we can move on."

"And until you find that eighth, you can't move on? You're stuck?"

He nodded slowly.

"How does this apply to Earl Torrence?"

"I don't know," he said. "There's something missing. I am uncomfortable with the way the case stands right now."

"Is that enough to make you continue the evaluation?"

"I have to think about it. I just don't know yet."

She turned and walked all the way to the front door.

"I'll tell Mr. Kingsley I spoke with you. I'll tell him your concerns. Before I go, I'd like to add one more reason for you to finish the assessment. Sidney Kingsley is the closest thing you have to a friend in this entire world. Of all the people who have passed through your life since your mother was murdered, he's the one who has stood by your side whenever you needed him there. Now he needs you. Not only that, but he thinks you need this case. He'd have to tell you why. You want to know how I *feel*? I feel like you owe that man a favor or two, and you ought to follow through with your agreement to examine Junior Torrence. It's human decency."

She opened the door and started out to her car.

"Wait," Long said from the piano.

She stopped and looked back at him.

"When you get back to the office, tell Sid Kingsley that he's a son of a bitch."

"That last bit was from me, not him."

"Then you're a son of a bitch, too."

"Takes one to know one," she said, and closed the door.

She stomped across the gravel drive to her car, jerked open the door, and slid in behind the wheel. She opened her purse and fumbled for her keys. As she searched, she became aware of Long's shadow falling across her window. She rolled down the window.

"What *now?*" she almost yelled at him.

"I don't have any classes next Friday," he told her. "Could you arrange for me to meet with Torrence again?"

She gripped the steering wheel so hard that she thought she might leave indentations.

"Edward or Junior?"

"Junior."

"I'll see to it as soon as I get back to the office."

"Thank you."

121

"No need to thank me. It's my job."

"Well, thank you anyway."

Then, without saying goodbye, he turned around and walked back into the house.

Fourteen

The next Friday they were back in the conference room at the County Jail. The room still gave Paula the willies. Long sat quietly in his chair at the table, seemingly oblivious to the surroundings. He almost seemed to be meditating.

Probably is, she thought.

The blast door opened, and a prison guard led Junior Torrence into the room. As he had been on the previous visit, he was cuffed and shackled, with his wrists constrained by a tight belt around his waist to which the cuffs were chained. His face was flat and vacuous. His eyes were blank. He looked heavily medicated.

"I'll need the cuffs off," Long told the guard without looking up from his notes. "You can stay in the room in case he becomes disruptive."

"I'll need backup," the guard said.

"No you won't, but if protocol dictates backup I'm fine with that."

The guard punched an intercom set into the wall and requested another officer to assist him.

Moments later, Torrence sat across from Long, his hands free, rubbing his wrists.

"Thanks, mister," he said. "I don't much like them things."

"Do you remember me?" Long asked.

"I don't know. You look familiar."

"I was here several days ago."

123

"Yeah. I recall you now. I recall her, too," he said, nodding toward Paula. "She's a pretty lady."

"I hope I didn't interrupt anything for you," Long said.

"Naw. I was just watching TV."

"What do you do all day?"

"Not much to do. I get up. I wash my face. I get dressed. I eat. I watch TV. I eat lunch. I watch TV until supper, and then I go to bed when it gets dark."

"What about books?"

"Don't read 'em."

"I want you to do something for me. I want you to touch your ear and pat your head."

"At the same time?"

"No. Touch your ear and then pat your head."

Torrence seemed to think about it for a moment. Then he touched his ear, and placed his hand back on the table.

"You didn't pat your head," Long said.

"Oh. I forgot. Sorry."

He reached up and patted his head.

"You didn't touch your ear first."

"Huh?"

"You were supposed to touch your ear and then pat your head. Can you do that?"

"I reckon."

He reached up and touched his ear and placed his hand back on the table.

Long turned to Paula.

"Receptive language disorder," he said. "He could only store part of the direction in his memory."

If Torrence understood what Long was saying, his facial expression didn't indicate it.

Long wrote something on his legal pad and placed his pen back on the table.

"I'd like to talk with you about the night Amanda died," Long said. "Is that all right?"

"I reckon.."

"I met with Detective Donnelly, who interviewed you at the police station. Do you remember that conversation?"

"Kind of. He was a real skinny guy."

"When you spoke with Detective Donnelly, you told him that you watched a movie with Amanda, and when the movie was over she told you that it was time for you to go home. According to your story, you asked to use the bathroom. You said the next thing you knew, you were standing over Amanda and she was on the floor bleeding."

"That's the way it happened."

"You didn't tell Detective Donnelly your pants were pulled down."

"I didn't?"

"No. You only told him you were standing over her. You never mentioned your pants. When I met with you last time, you said your pants were down."

"Okay."

"What I'm wondering is whether there are other things you don't remember."

"Like what?"

"Well, how about the other man in the apartment?"

"Just a moment!" Paula interrupted. She leaned over and whispered, "What in hell are you doing?"

"I'm going to demonstrate that Torrence's memory of the events surrounding Amanda's death may have been manipulated," Long whispered back.

"For what purpose?"

"I want to see how easily he can be convinced of an alternate story."

"What will that prove?"

"It supports his suggestibility. Believe me, Eli Crouch's psychologist will follow up on this. We don't want to get blind-sided."

"What if he starts to doubt he killed her?"

"What difference does that make? He's already entered a not guilty plea. Crouch isn't going to let him retract it, whatever doubts Torrence might have."

"I'm uncomfortable with this."

"You can fire me at any time."

Then he addressed Torrence again. "The other man in the apartment?"

"I don't really recollect another man in the apartment."

"You didn't recall trying to have sex with Amanda either until Detective Donnelly brought it up, did you?"

"I don't suppose."

"Well, what if I were to tell you that the police found fingerprints on the front door of Amanda's apartment, and they found the exact same fingerprints inside her apartment?"

"I don't know."

"Could that mean that someone came into the apartment through the door?"

"I reckon."

"After the movie was over, Amanda said you had to go home, right?"

"Yeah. She said it was late, and I had to go home."

"What did you do then?"

"I don't rightly remember."

"You don't have to remember everything, Earl. All you have to do is remember the first thing you did after she told you to go home. The very first thing."

"Well . . ."

"Didn't you tell Detective Donnelly you had to go to the bathroom?"

126

"Yeah. That's right. I had to go to the bathroom."

"When you went to the bathroom, did you stand up or sit down?"

"I don't rightly know."

"You said the next thing you knew, you were standing over Amanda's body and your pants were down."

"Right."

"Do you take your pants down when you stand up in the bathroom?"

"No. That's what kids do. I'm a grown-up."

"So, if your pants were down, did you stand up or sit down in the bathroom?"

"I reckon I . . . sat down?"

"Fine, Earl. You're doing fine. When you sit down in the bathroom, do you always pull your pants up right away when you're finished, or do you walk around with your pants down?"

"I pull them up right away. Don't you?"

"We'll put that aside for the moment. When you sit down in the bathroom, how long does it usually take?"

"I don't know. A few minutes. More if I'm backed up."

"Great. If you were in the bathroom for a few minutes, would that give someone time to come in the front door of Amanda's apartment and leave his fingerprints there?"

"Sure."

"Did you like Amanda, Earl?"

"Yeah. She was very nice to me."

"Did you love her? Like a sister, I mean."

"I don't know. I reckon I did."

"Do you love Edward?"

"Of course. Edward's always took care of me."

"And you would never want anything bad to happen to Edward, right?"

"Right."

"Suppose you were to find out that someone was doing something that would hurt Edward? How would you feel about that?"

"I'd be pissed off."

"And you liked Amanda? Maybe even loved her?"

"Yeah. She was nice."

"Did you love her more than Edward?"

"No."

"Okay, Earl. We're getting down to it here. Isn't that what Detective Donnelly said to you in the interview? I want to tell a story, and I want you to tell me whether there is any chance whatsoever that this story is true. Do you follow me?"

"I guess."

"Here's what I think happened, Earl. I think you went to the bathroom for a few minutes to sit down, and then you heard a noise. I think you forgot to pull your pants up and you looked out the bathroom door and you saw something that made you very angry."

"What?"

"I think you saw Amanda kissing another man who wasn't Edward. I think you realized she was cheating on Edward."

"You mean I didn't try to have sex with her?"

"Not in this story, Earl. In this story you saw someone else try to have sex with her. You got very angry and you told them to stop. You pulled your pants up, but didn't have time to button them. The man who was with Amanda ran out, but Amanda stayed. You realized Edward would be very hurt if he found out Amanda was kissing another man and you were so angry she would hurt Edward that you grabbed a knife and stabbed her to make her stop. To do that, you had to let go of your pants and they fell back down."

Torrence nodded a little, but his eyes were clouded.

"Now," Long said. "I want to ask you a question. Is there any possibility whatsoever that the story I just told you is true?"

Torrence reached up and rubbed his jaw. His eyes seemed to be searching the past for any clue the story might be true. "It could be true," he said. "That could have happened."

"Great. We're almost finished. I have one more question. The story I told you. Is it, in fact, the truth? Did you kill Amanda because she was kissing another man and you didn't want her to hurt Edward?"

Torrence looked at Long and then Paula. He seemed confused, his forehead ridged and his face tight. He looked as if he were dredging the bottom-most regions of his memory for something he could hold for support.

"Yeah," he said. "Yeah, I remember now. That's what happened."

"Earl?" Paula asked.

"Yes'm?"

"Why didn't you tell the police this story?"

"I reckon I didn't remember it right. Like I told the police, all I could remember was finding Amanda dead. Now, I guess it was because I didn't want her to hurt Edward."

"And you never told Edward because?"

"He loved Amanda something awful. Edward's always took good care of me. I couldn't tell him I found his girl kissing on another man. He'd be hurt bad if he learned that."

"So you let him think you killed her because she wouldn't have sex with you?"

"I reckon I did. Did I do a bad thing, ma'am?"

FIFTEEN

After collecting their items held by the front gate security, Long led Paula to the car. She held her tongue until they were both inside and belted.

"I think you have some explaining to do," she said, exiting the grounds.

"I don't doubt it."

"Does the word *ethics* mean anything to you?"

"Of course. Ethics: A noun. 'A system of accepted beliefs that control behavior, especially such a system based on morals.' Shall I use it in a sentence?"

"Jesus, sometimes you can be such an asshole."

"Would you like me to define *hostility* next?"

"What did you think you were doing back there with Junior Torrence? Is that the way you operate with all your patients?"

"Torrence isn't a patient. I haven't seen patients in almost twenty years. He is the subject of an evaluation. The rules are a little different."

"So you think you're allowed to fuck with their heads whenever it pleases you?"

"No. I'm only allowed to fuck with their heads when it serves a diagnostic purpose."

"What was your diagnostic purpose in filling Torrence's head with lies?"

"Actually, I did nothing of the kind. Detective Donnelly, in his zeal to pin Amanda's murder on Torrence, convinced the poor boy that he had attempted to rape her."

"And that's not true?"

"Probably not. I suspect Junior would rather kill himself than do anything to distress his brother. He worships Edward. It is evident to me that Junior would never have attempted to have sex with Amanda."

"So you invented this story of a mystery man in Amanda's apartment."

"Yes. You just ran a stop sign, you know."

"Damn! And now Junior thinks he killed Amanda to protect his brother Edward?"

"Best thing for him, actually. Can you imagine how he must have felt, knowing not only that he killed Edward's fiancée, but also that he had done it in the course of cuckolding his brother? By replacing that memory with this new one, he not only protected his brother from finding out about Amanda's lover, he also prevented his brother from being betrayed by her after marriage."

"And this isn't a lie?"

"It's an alternate explanation. A working hypothesis, you might say. I have no idea whether it's true or not. In my version, Junior gets to be something of a hero."

"By killing Edward's fiancée?"

"I didn't say he was a *perfect* hero. You must admit that he does come off in a somewhat better light now."

"And what did this prove?"

"First, that Torrence is easily manipulated. His receptive language disorder apparently extends to other regions of his brain, leaving memory gaps that are easily filled with all sorts of factitious nonsense."

"You mean fictitious, don't you?"

"Ms. Paige, have you ever heard me misstate myself? The term 'factitious' refers to a contrived or manufactured *version* of the truth, which may be almost completely but not quite totally incorrect. In this case, we start with a known *fact*, that Earl Torrence killed Amber Coolidge. He doesn't know why. *We* don't know why. Detective Donnelly proposed one possible set of reasons for the murder, which cast Earl as a cuckolding sex fiend. I proposed a different explanation that cast him as an imperfect protector of his brother. It is very likely that neither is completely—or even partially—true. For that reason, they are *factitious.*"

"I give up," she said. "But I still think what you did was unethical."

"Fortunately, if you are correct, it is a cross that I alone shall have to bear. Would you please slow down? I don't wish to be killed on the highway before I can finish this evaluation. I think we should visit Amber's apartment now."

"Thank you, Captain Random."

"Who is Captain Random?"

"You are. It's what you're doing. Changing the subject without warning."

"Oh. Sorry. I had been thinking about visiting the scene of the murder for some time. I forgot you weren't aware of that. Perhaps, before we stop for a bite to eat, we could drop by there and look around."

"Why?"

"Because I haven't seen it."

"You think there's something there that could prove Junior is competent to stand trial?"

"I haven't any idea. Why? Do you?"

Paula didn't answer. Instead, she gripped the wheel and calculated the shortest possible route for a detour by Amber Coolidge's apartment.

The apartment in which Amber Coolidge had been murdered

hadn't been rented since the murder. For a matter of months it had been cordoned off for continuing investigation by Detective Donnelly's crime scene investigators. After that, its reputation as the scene of a grisly and unexpected death had deterred any would-be lessees.

The building had been built during the Depression, as a Works Progress Administration project. It was a fourplex, two apartments downstairs and two upstairs. Each apartment had a balcony and an interior entrance door opening into a central staircase.

The building maintenance man, Ernest Sachs, was working on a broken lamp over the entrance when they drove up. Paula introduced herself and Ben, and told Sachs what they wanted to do. Sachs escorted Paula and Ben up the stairs to the apartment.

"You let the police into the apartment on the night the Coolidge girl was murdered, didn't you?" Ben asked.

"Yeah. That was me."

"Did you know Amber Coolidge?"

"Only as one of the tenants. I don't get close to the people who live here. I just keep the place in shape. Otherwise I keep to myself. Besides, I'd only been working here for a few weeks when she was killed."

"New to the area?" Ben asked.

"You could say that. You know how it is. People come, and people go. I imagine I won't be workin' here a year or so from now. Sooner or later, I'll wake up with the wanderlust, and head off down the road. That's what makes this kind of job so attractive. Wherever you go, there're jobs available."

He unlocked the front door of the apartment and held it open for them as they walked inside.

"She was over there," Sachs said, pointing toward the middle of the room. "There was a sofa there at the time and some kind of hook rug. She was lying on the floor, half on the rug and half on the hardwoods. There was a lot of blood."

"Do you live in the building?" Ben asked.

"No. But I was here when the police arrived."

"How's that?"

"Mr. Holmes, in 1A. He complained that his satellite dish was misaligned and he asked me to re-aim it for him."

"When was this?"

"Oh, about nine o'clock that night, I reckon. I really shouldn't have done it. Satellite dishes aren't included in the rent. If someone has one, it's because they've contracted for it themselves. Really, I should have told him to call the satellite people, but you know how hard it is to get them to come out to the house for a service call. Mr. Holmes, he's pretty old, and you sure wouldn't want him scrabblin' around on the roof, so I told him I'd take care of it."

"So you were here when the murder took place."

"Lessee. I got here around nine-thirty. Mr. Holmes called me around nine, like I said, and it took me about a half-hour to get here. The police got here before midnight, I know that. I was gettin' ready to head back to my place when they pulled in the drive."

"Where do you live?"

"I got an apartment five, six blocks from here. All the tenants, they got this button on their telephones. If they need service, they push that button, and it rings me up direct. I can usually be here in less than a half-hour, dependin' on what I'm doin' at my place."

"You didn't see Junior Torrence in the building the night of the murder, did you?"

"No. When I got here, I went straight to the roof and worked on Mr. Holmes's satellite dish. It took a while, on account of the mount was real finicky. I called Mr. Holmes on my cell phone each time I made an adjustment, and he'd tell me if it was better or worse. Finally, he said it was okay, so I climbed back down, stowed the ladder under the building, and was about to pull out of the drive when the police drove up."

"The police found your prints in the apartment," Long observed.

"I s'pose they would. I reckon my prints are all over this building. I work on about everything here. It's an old building. Things break. Someone's gotta fix them."

"When the police got here, the door was locked."

"That's right," Sachs said.

"Ms. Flatt told the police she heard a scream and a sound like something being dropped on the floor. Several seconds later she heard the door slam shut and someone ran down the stairs, according to the police report."

"Yeah?"

"What I can't figure," Ben said, "was why the door was locked. Who murders a girl and then takes care to lock the door on the way out?"

Sachs grinned. "Oh, heck, that's easy. The door is locked from the inside. The main door lock catches automatically when you close the door, like in a hotel room. Can't tell you how many times I've had to drive over here because one tenant or another's locked hisself out in pajamas. It's worth a laugh, I'll tell you. Listen, you guys look around here all you want. Just let the door close when you leave. I'll get the deadbolt later."

Paula listened as he clomped down the stairs.

The apartment was small, just a living room with a kitchen, the two rooms separated by a bar, and a bedroom with an attached bath off the back of the living room. It was on the right side of the building, if you were facing the front. The floors were solid red oak, the walls plaster over lath, and the ceilings were ten feet high, with heavy solid wood crown moldings.

"Okay, Sherlock," Paula said. "What are you looking for?"

"Nothing. I need to see the place, so it isn't a concept. I sometimes have a difficult time imagining spatial relationships."

"It takes me back," she said. "When my husband and I were first married, he was still in medical school. We lived in married students' housing provided by the college. Our place was about this size."

Long seemed to ignore her. He walked to the kitchen, and noted a door just on the other side of the bar. He reached out and grasped the handle. It wouldn't budge.

"Locked. Thought it might be a pantry."

"I think if this place had a space large enough for a pantry, they'd advertise it as a two-bedroom."

Long stood in the center of the living room and looked around.

"The sofa must have been here," he said, drawing a long line in the air with his index finger.

"What makes you say that?"

"It's the most likely place. See the television cable outlet against the wall? Most people place their televisions against the wall with the cable outlet, with the television facing out from it. The best place to locate the sofa would be right here, facing the television."

"Okay."

"That means Amber would have had her back to the bedroom when she was sitting on the sofa."

He crossed the living room to the bedroom. "In order for Earl to use the bathroom, as he said he did after the movie, he had to go through Amber's bedroom."

"Right. What does that mean?"

"I have no idea." Long peered through the bathroom door. "Tiny. Hardly enough room to turn around in here."

"It wasn't permanent."

"What?"

"She was planning to marry Edward. She knew she was going to move in with him after the wedding. She didn't need a large apartment because this was only temporary."

"A good inference. And an interesting one. How often, these days, do you see people who plan to marry living in separate homes?"

"Not often enough, I'd imagine."

"What can we determine from the fact that Amber kept her own residence?"

"She was a good girl. She was the kind of girl who wouldn't be likely to smooch another man while her fiancé's brother was in the next room."

"I never intended that story to be reasonable. It was merely an alternative. We could, if we were determined to be cynical, also imagine she would live away from Edward if she weren't completely convinced they would be married."

"She kept this apartment as an ace in the hole."

He looked puzzled for a moment and then his face relaxed. "Oh, poker. Yes. Or, you could have been right the first time. Maybe she was a good girl. I think it's time to speak with Claudia Flatt."

Claudia Flatt was in her early sixties. She had retired after thirty-five years working at the local telephone company, to a two-bedroom apartment that she shared with a cat and a nervous parakeet.

The apartment was cluttered with antiques, giving it a claustrophobic atmosphere that was not relieved by Ms. Flatt's intolerance to cold. She had turned the thermostat up high and seemed perfectly content in the swelter. The cat lounged, almost comatose, on the hearth.

"Thank you for seeing us," Paula said as she sat next to Long on the settee. Flatt sat in a wing chair near the fireplace. "As I explained on the phone, Dr. Long has been contracted by the DA's office to evaluate the man who's been charged with killing Amber Coolidge. Dr. Long has some questions he'd like to ask."

"Of course. But I am a little confused. I was under the impression the Torrence fellow confessed."

"Yes," Long said. "He retracted that confession. That means we will be going to trial, and it's also possible that Earl Torrence may not be eligible for execution. His attorney's firm would like to avoid a trial altogether. Wouldn't it be terrible if Torrence wasn't punished for killing that nice girl?"

"Oh, yes," Flatt said.

"Well, if the DA's office made critical errors of their own, they might be found to have engaged in an incompetent prosecution of the defendant, which could lead to the conviction being overturned."

He ignored the warning look that Paula gave him.

"Oh, my," Flatt said. "That would be just awful."

"I presume that you knew Ms. Coolidge well?" Long asked.

"Such a sweet girl. And so lovely. She moved in about a year after I retired. She was a perfect upstairs neighbor—hardly ever knew she was there. That's why I was so surprised when I heard the noise from her apartment on the night she died."

"Could you tell us exactly what you heard?"

"It's been a while. As I recall, I had just fed Mr. Simpkins and I was getting ready for bed."

"Excuse me," Paula said. "Who is Mr. Simpkins? Is he another neighbor?"

"Oh, no," Flatt said, chuckling. "Mr. Simpkins is my cat. He prefers to eat at night. Cats are nocturnal, you know. That's why they sleep all day. They like to roam at night. It's a hunting thing, I believe, a holdover from their days in the wild."

"Yes," Long said. "And you were preparing for bed after feeding, uh, Mr. Simpkins."

"I had finished washing my face and had placed my night-gown on the bed. I heard footsteps upstairs and the sound of things being tossed to the floor, as if there was an argument of some kind. I heard a scream, followed by a terrible thump, like someone dropping a piece of furniture. My first thought was that Amber had been moving a couch and had dropped it on her foot, but that wouldn't make sense, now would it? I mean, why would she scream *before* she dropped the couch?"

"Indeed," Long said. "And what else did you hear?"

"Not a great deal, I'm afraid. I heard someone walking around upstairs, and I heard the door to the apartment slam, and someone ran down the stairs outside my apartment."

"Then you called the police."

"Yes. The more I thought about it, the more I realized the scream was much worse than someone should have made if she simply dropped a couch on her foot. She sounded absolutely terrified."

"And you called the police as soon as you heard the footsteps outside your door."

"Yes. I thought maybe Amber and the young man she had been seeing had gotten into a fight. I was worried she might have been injured."

"But you didn't go upstairs to check on her."

"Oh, no. I wouldn't want to get involved."

"Of course not. Tell me, Ms. Flatt, did you get to know Edward Torrence at all?"

"Who is Edward Torrence?"

"He was Amber's fiancé."

"The young man? I only spoke with him a couple of times. I saw him the morning the police were here. He was terribly upset."

"Do you recall seeing his brother Earl in the building?"

"You mean the man who killed Amber? Of course. He visited from time to time. I got the impression he wasn't a bright young man, and he seemed rather clumsy. And he stared."

"Stared?"

"You know. Like he was ogling. I walked out the front door one evening and found him standing on the sidewalk, staring at the front door. I said hello, but he just kept staring. It made me very nervous."

"Did this happen often?"

"Only that one time. I didn't like it, though, not one bit."

"He visited Amber often?"

"Every several days. I would hear his boots clomping on the stairs and he'd always knock on her door the same way."

"You said he didn't seem bright. Why would you think that?"

"Oh, you know. I'd try to pass the time of day with him when we'd meet on the stairs. He never had a lot to say. I'd ask him about the news, or the weather. Sometimes he'd nod."

"So, it was difficult to carry on a conversation with Earl?"

"Like skinning eels. I didn't know at the time he was her fiancé's brother. I thought he was some unfortunate young man who she liked to help out."

Long decided to change the subject. "On the night Amber was murdered, you said you heard a scream and some furniture being moved about, but you didn't say anything about voices. Did you hear anyone speak?"

"No. But that wasn't unusual. This is a very solid building. The walls and ceilings are plaster over wood lath. These apartments are extremely quiet. I never hear the television in the apartment next to me, or upstairs. A sound has to be quite loud to get through."

"Like a scream," Long said.

"Yes."

"Or something falling to the floor."

She nodded.

"But you could hear someone knocking on Amber's door one flight up?"

"Yes. Sound echoes up and down the stairwell. I can hear things on the stairs, but not in the apartments."

"You said Edward was upset the morning after Amber was murdered. Did you have a chance to talk with him?"

"Only briefly. I was on the way out to the market—I like to do my grocery shopping in the morning, because the crowds are lighter—and I saw him sitting on the bench outside the apartment with his head in his hands. I knew Amber had been killed by then, of course, because the police had been tramping in and out all night. I barely got a moment's sleep that night."

"What did Edward tell you?"

"I patted him on the shoulder and told him how sorry I was about Amber being killed. He thanked me for my concern. He was very tearful and said he wished he could have been here before she was killed, that perhaps he could have prevented it."

"You mean he thought he could have kept his brother from killing Amber?"

"I suppose. Isn't it awful, hindsight? So many things in our lives we'd change if only we could go back in time."

"Yes," Long said, his eyes focused on a point very far away. "A great many things."

Sixteen

"Maybe you should leave the legal stuff to me," Paula said as Long drove her back to his home to pick up her car.

"Beg pardon?"

"You told Ms. Flatt that if the DA's office made critical errors, it could be found to have provided an incompetent prosecution and it could overturn Junior's conviction."

"Yes."

"That's not true. The DA's office gets one shot at Torrence. If we botch the job, he goes free. There wouldn't be any appeals."

"I know."

"Then why did you tell her that?"

"Because Claudia Flatt isn't ignorant. I knew she would be suspicious, so I tossed some gobbledygook at her, to cloud the issue. None of it made sense, but it sounded good. The important part was to sound like I knew what I was talking about and to be sincere."

"Sincere."

"Of course. Sincere authorities are instantaneously trustworthy. Doesn't matter what they say, actually."

"Something you learned from some of your criminal clients over the years, I'd imagine."

"Actually, I learned it from watching politics. It's hard for me, of course, because it requires a certain . . . imprecision in language. That sort of thing does not come naturally to me."

"But lying does."

"Not really. I provide a different version of the truth. It's double-talk."

"You manipulated her."

"I engaged in social engineering. I set the stage to motivate her cooperation."

"You conned her."

"If you like. I suspect that con men are the ultimate social engineers. In this case, it worked. She was placed temporarily off balance, her defenses were broken, and she told us more than she probably would have otherwise."

"I think I'm beginning to figure out how you work."

"Really."

"There are no boundaries for you, are there? To get a subject to cooperate you'll say anything, *do* anything, whether it's ethical or not."

"There are things I won't do."

"Such as?"

"I won't promise a subject anything I can't deliver. I won't make threats I can't back up. I won't divulge a confidential statement by a client. There are others."

"But you'll lie."

"Never. I do, however, feel free to manipulate the truth. Perhaps I don't tell all of it, or perhaps I augment it with additional but irrelevant truths. Deception is a very common tactic in psychological research. I may lead a subject to think I know something I don't. I may want him to think I don't know something I do. I may tell him I'm looking for one thing when I'm actually looking for something else."

"And you can sleep at night?"

"Sometimes. When I can't, it has nothing to do with the tactics I use with my subjects."

"This is scientific?"

"Parts of it are. Human behavior is largely predictable, Ms. Paige. There are rules people follow, patterns that can be predicted. The brain works more or less the same in every person on earth—even for people like me. The biochemical processes and electrical conduits are the same. When things go very wrong, they tend to go wrong the same way in one person as they do in another, as long as the basic underlying pathology is the same. That's the scientific component to what I do. The rest is art."

"Art."

"Or maybe a craft. I've never been really certain."

"Is this what I was supposed to learn from you?"

"I don't understand."

"When Mr. Kingsley assigned this case to me, he told me I'd learn more working with you than I'd ever pick up in the office drafting briefs and subpoenas."

"How flattering."

"Is this what he meant? That I'd learn to lie and manipulate?"

"I can't say. I don't know what Sid had in mind. I only know what works for me, what has worked for me for almost twenty years. I just do what I do. I didn't sign on to serve as some kind of tutor. Are you hungry?"

"Thought you'd never ask. Where would you like to eat?"

"You choose."

"This looks nice," Paula said as she pulled into a restaurant parking lot. "I'll buy. Sid gave me a company credit card."

"Did you realize that you just called him Sid?" Long asked as he closed his car door.

"Did I? Funny. I've never done that before."

"I would imagine it has something to do with all the time you and he have spent talking about me."

He opened the front door of the restaurant, walked through,

and immediately let go of the door. Forewarned, but exasperated, she caught it before it could slam shut on her.

"You did it again," she said.

He turned to her.

"Did what?"

"Let the door slam on me. That's twice."

"It is? I wasn't aware. Is this one of those times when I'm supposed to say I'm sorry?"

"I'd say so."

"Well, in that case, I'm sorry. Does that help?"

"No, but thank you anyway. Do you imagine Mr. Kingsley and I talk about you a lot?"

"I don't imagine a thing. I know Sid. I've known him for a long time. I understand how his mind works."

He stopped at the greeter's lectern at the front of the restaurant and looked around. The motif was rustic, with exposed beams and rough-hewn columns. The walls and ceiling were decorated with license plates from all over the country, mounted animal heads, and the occasional bluegrass musical instrument. Country-western music played in the background.

"Good God, woman, you've brought us to a steak house," he muttered.

"Yes."

"A *steak* house?"

"That's right."

"But, you know that I don't—"

"Eat red meat? I'd heard that."

"Then why on earth—"

"I'm a law clerk. I don't make much money. I do eat red meat and I wanted a steak. I'm eating on the firm's nickel. You like puzzles. You fill in the blanks." She smiled. "You said I could choose, right?"

"Well, of course, but I never thought you'd choose, well, a

steak house."

"Surprise," she said as the greeter came up to escort them to their table.

Paula slid into one side of the high-backed booth and Long slid tentatively into the other.

"Have you ever eaten steak?" she asked as he gingerly opened the menu.

"Of course I have. Years ago. From what I understand, there may still be fragments of it floating around my colon."

"Don't believe everything you read. Do you think it would look greedy if I ordered the filet?"

"If you can get away with calling your boss Sid, I don't think it would matter one way or the other."

He started reading the menu. "Porterhouse . . . ranch steak . . . ribeye . . . Delmonico . . . steak and ribs. I don't see any fish here."

"Next time, you can take us to a fish camp."

"What will I eat?"

"Have a salad. There's chicken. That's not red meat."

"I don't eat any meat, red or otherwise. Just fish."

"Sounds like a salad, then. Oh, look, they have a fried shrimp Caesar salad. Perhaps you could order that and then teach them how to make it correctly."

"Hmmm," he said, and turned back to the menu.

The waiter arrived at their booth a couple of minutes later to take their order.

"Are you drinking alcohol?" Paula asked Long.

"No."

"Good. You can drive."

She placed her menu on the table and looked at the waiter. "What do you have on tap?"

He rattled off a list of brands.

"I'll have that last one. And I'll have the filet grilled medium-rare, with a baked potato and the house salad. Load the potato, please, and could I have some béarnaise sauce on the side?"

"You bet, ma'am. And for you, sir?"

"Ah," Long said, making one last furtive survey of the menu. "I suppose I'll have the fried shrimp Caesar salad and sweet tea."

"Excellent. Would either of you like an appetizer?"

"Yes," Paula said. "We'd love one of those onion things."

"One Bronco Blossom coming up. I'll bring it with your drinks in a moment."

He hustled off to the kitchen. Long folded the menu and placed it behind the condiments.

"I hope you won't mind my observation that this is somewhat passive-aggressive on your part."

"Why would I mind?" she said as she peeled the shell from a peanut she'd picked from the bucket next to the condiments. "Nut?"

"No."

"Could have fooled me. There was nothing passive at all about the aggression I used picking this place. I don't think you completely understand what a control freak you are. Besides the fact that I will deeply, truly, almost erotically enjoy this steak, I thought it might be nice to give you a dose of your own medicine."

"Nice for whom?"

"For me. It wouldn't hurt you, either, to see how your behavior affects others."

"Don't be silly. I'm perfectly content."

"Now who's lying? I can feel the waves of your discomfort all the way across the table."

"I wasn't talking about the restaurant."

"What, then?"

The waiter returned with their drinks—her beer in a tankard

that might have been invented by Vikings, and his tea in a glass he suspected might require both hands—and a multi-legged battered and fried concoction Long had never seen in his life.

"What's this?" he said, pointing at the plate in the middle of the table.

"They call it a Bronco Blossom," Paula said. "Think of it as a huge onion ring, just not in a ring. Here. You pick off a piece and dip it."

She demonstrated and chewed rapturously on the treat.

He stared at her and then at the Blossom.

"Oh, come on," she said. "Please don't tell me you've never had onion rings."

"Well, yes. Many years ago. I try to avoid fried foods."

"Treat yourself."

He reached out and meticulously pulled a piece of the onion away from the blossom. He dipped it in the sauce, popped it into his mouth, and chewed.

It took a moment, but Paula saw a smile start at the corners of his mouth.

"Like it?"

"I think I do."

He pulled another sliver and dipped it. Within moments, he was working deftly on his side of the blossom.

"This is delightful," he said. "What do you suppose is in that sauce? I can taste the horseradish, but the other flavors evade me."

"I'm not surprised. I think it's mostly catsup and mayonnaise. I have a hard time imagining you eating a lot of catsup."

"This is a surprise. I hadn't imagined I'd find anything interesting in a steak house, of all places."

"Still think I was passive-aggressive picking out this place?"

"Absolutely. On the other hand, I'm glad you did. Tell me, what exactly do you and Sid talk about when you discuss me?"

Her hand stopped midway to her mouth. She cocked her head at him. "Oh, I'm sorry. I let the conversation drift away from *you* for a moment."

"Beg pardon?" he said as he dipped another onion finger.

"The term *self-absorbed* comes to mind."

"Regarding me?"

"Of course. How long have you been perched in that house on the mountainside?"

"Thirteen or fourteen years."

"What's the name of your nearest neighbor?"

"How would I know? The nearest neighbors are half a mile away, both horizontally and vertically. I don't think I've ever seen them."

"Besides Mr. Kingsley and me, how many visitors have you had since you moved there?"

"I couldn't say. Not many."

"No girlfriends? No dates?"

"I don't date, Ms. Paige."

"You don't see anything pathological about that?"

"No."

She took a sip of her beer.

"Wait," she said. "You mean you've never had a date with a woman?"

"No. I always say exactly what I mean, Ms. Paige. I said I don't date. I didn't claim to never have been on a date."

"How long?"

"I beg your pardon?"

"How long since you last had a date with a woman?"

"Define date."

"An assignation. A prearranged meeting for nothing other than social purposes. An overture to sex. You know. A date."

He nodded. "That would be five years, seven months and twelve days ago."

149

"You keep track of it?"

"Not consciously."

"Then how could you recall the time so precisely?"

"I just know, that's all. I know I graduated from college thirty-one years, six months and four days ago. I received my doctorate twenty-six years, six months and eight days ago. I know this as certainly as I know you dragged me into a steak house this evening, knowing I don't eat meat."

"I didn't drag you."

"You didn't tell me it was a steak house before we entered the building. You engaged in subterfuge."

"Hold on a minute," she said. "You haven't dated in over five years?"

"That's right. I recall it vividly. It was not a pleasant experience."

"Five years. Wow. That's a long time without . . . you know . . ."

"What?"

"Um, release?"

"Why don't you ask what you want to know?" he said. "You have a troublesome tendency to dance around things."

"Okay, if you don't date, what do you do about sex?"

"Oh," he said, nodding. "I see. Yes. Well, I masturbate."

She leaned back against the rear of the booth. "I don't think I wanted to know that."

"Then why did you ask?"

"I mean, I was curious, but most people wouldn't just come out and say something like that."

"Yes. I know. It's sad. People rarely say what they mean. The fact is, Ms. Paige, I do not enjoy the physical closeness of others. Part of my . . . the way I am. I've only willingly allowed one woman to so much as hug me in years."

"Your mother."

"No, and that's about as much as I prefer to say about it. Do you think we might order one of these Bronco Blossoms to take home?"

"They don't travel well. Admit it, Dr. Long, your entire life is built around your own neurotic needs."

Long cleaned his fingers with the heavy cloth napkin and took a sip of his tea. "I'm a psychologist. I've been a psychologist for over a quarter century. I'm intimately familiar with my own neuroses and have grown comfortable with them. I am also completely conversant in all the diagnostic aspects of Asperger's disorder, which I'm certain Sid told you I have. For the most part, it does not inconvenience me. It does, however, seem to be a matter of some concern to a lot of other people."

"People like Mr. Kingsley."

"Yes."

"Your friend, who cares about you."

"And I care about him, in my way, but I don't choose to make his life my personal hobby."

"Because that would distract you from yourself."

"Because it's none of my business. I am completely content with how my behavior affects others. To be otherwise would imply that I am acting in a neurotypical manner."

"A *what* manner?"

"Neurotypical. I am entirely aware of my disorder, Ms. Paige. I would be nonplussed, however, to discover that you are aware of yours."

"My disorder?"

"I would invite you, for one moment, to look at the world from my perspective. You say I should see how my behavior affects others, implying that I am the one with a problem. For people like me—"

"People with Asperger's disorder?"

"Precisely. For people with Asperger's disorder, it is the neu-

151

rotypicals who appear strange."

"You just used that word again."

"I think it should be self-explanatory. 'Neuro,' referring to the brain, and 'typical,' meaning perceived to be normal, or the status quo."

"You mean everyone except for people with Asperger's."

"Not precisely, but I would expect such a generalization from a neurotypical. You might be interested to hear that fifty years ago, when autism was first described clinically, it was estimated that only sixty in ten thousand were born with it. New estimates now place that number at one in one-hundred-sixty. In other words, we are gaining on you."

"You make it sound like some kind of competition."

"That would be unintentional. Competition is a neurotypical phenomenon. People like me don't need to feel superior to others. In fact, it's rather anxiety-producing. I would invite you to consider neurotypical behavior as if it were a disorder, the way you see my way of thinking as atypical.

"If I were to seriously consider diagnosing you, I'd note that you have a very difficult time establishing your own individuality. Your identity, as you call it, is bound to the opinions of others. This is why neurotypicals engage in fad behavior, jumping on whatever bandwagon seems most popular at the moment. Neurotypicals feel uncomfortable if they are dressed differently than the masses, or openly express unpopular opinions."

"Do not," she said.

"Do so. Look around you, if you don't believe me. Worse, neurotypicals can't seem to engage in frank, direct dialogue. They have to couch their meanings in murky subtext. They don't say what they mean because they are afraid their words might bruise another person's delicate neurotypical ego. You don't explain things in sufficient detail because you don't want to give other people the impression you think they are stupid."

"It's called consideration."

"It leads to miscommunication. But it's understandable. After all, your speech only reflects your thought, which is chaotic and disorganized. Facts get all bound up with emotions, until you can't tell one from the other. You don't ask questions because you fear others will think you an imbecile. You form your opinion based on emotion rather than what you know to be true, most often because your fellow neurotypicals have the same opinion. Everything is about other people. Neurotypicals are obsessed with being social, even with people they can't stand."

"That's called manners."

"Oh, balderdash. It's called lying to yourself. Let's say you're invited to somebody's home, and you really don't like that person but you agree to go anyway, even though you'd really prefer to stay home and read a book. You tell yourself it's better to do what you don't want to do because otherwise people you don't like may think you are a recluse and not invite you to visit their houses again, even though you'd rather not go there in the first place. How absurd is that?"

"But man is a social animal."

"No, neurotypicals are social animals. Seems a waste of time to me."

"So you'd rather spend your time sitting around your house listening to the music of dead composers and drinking wine."

"I think that should be obvious."

"And there's nothing pathological about that?"

"Not in the least. It is how I prefer to live my life. I am responding to my own desires, not the urges of the herd. That seems much more logical and much less stressful. That, Ms. Paige, is the definition of stability."

"Doesn't make sense to me."

"I'm certain it doesn't. Look, let's try this another way. Suppose, one day, you were to come across a Martian who had just landed on this planet. Miraculously, he speaks English, so you at least share a common tongue. In every other respect, you have no shared experiences, no shared history, no shared culture, and no shared ideas or concepts. You are completely alien to him, as he is to you. Would you immediately try to make him behave exactly the way you do?"

"No, of course not."

"I should hope you wouldn't. On the other hand, you—and all neurotypicals for that matter—are all too willing to attempt to change people like me, to make us more social, to require us to adhere to rules of social convention that make no sense whatsoever."

"You're saying you're a Martian."

"In the view of most neurotypicals, I might as well be, and I would invite you to show me the respect you'd show any extra-terrestrial you might encounter. As a popular cartoon character says, I am what I am. I am content to be the way I am and I see no need to change. Please do not attempt to make me conform to your disordered way of thinking and behaving."

"You really see me—all of us—as being the ones with the problem?"

"I know I would not want to live the way you do."

"But there are a lot more of us than there are of you."

"That's the herd mentality talking again. Simply because you are in the majority doesn't mean you are right or, for that matter, healthy."

The waiter arrived at the table with their meals. He set the sizzling platter with Paula's steak and baked potato in front of her, and a small ramekin bowl of béarnaise next to it. Then he slid a salad in front of Long.

"Will there be anything else?" he asked.

"Everything's fine," Paula said.

Long picked at his salad while Paula took a bite of her baked potato.

"Heaven," she said, closing her eyes as she chewed.

"They used a bottled dressing," Long said.

"All right," she said, opening her eyes. "Here's a new rule. For the next half-hour, we will discuss anything that is not specifically about you or your finicky eating habits. Okay?"

"Bottled dressings are nothing but preservatives bound by a smidgen of mass-produced mayonnaise. I don't know whether I can eat this."

"Force yourself. I don't want you passing out behind the wheel from hunger before we get home."

He speared a shrimp and a limp piece of lettuce and held them an inch over the plate for a moment to allow the dressing to drip off a little. He eyed it suspiciously, then put it in his mouth. He chewed carefully, as if waiting to hit a pit or bone.

Paula sliced off a sliver of the beef, charred on the outside and purplish in the middle, and placed a small amount of béarnaise on it.

"Do you have any idea," she asked after swallowing, "how long it's been since I had a filet mignon?"

"No."

"Well, it's been a long time. I can tell you that."

"You didn't have children."

"No."

"You and your nephrologist husband were married for—what?—ten years or more?"

"That's right. Eleven years, to be exact."

He nodded as he speared another shrimp. "Interesting."

She tried to ignore him as she worked on her potato and filet. After a couple of slices, her curiosity got the better of her, to her dismay.

"Okay. I'll bite. Why is that interesting?"

"Did you and he agree not to have children?"

"Not explicitly."

"That's an attorney response. You never had children, but you never agreed not to have children."

"Sure."

"Yet you were married during those years when your imperative for parenthood must have been at its greatest. At least that's what I've heard. All those middle-thirties hormones raging. Your biological clock ticking, ticking, ticking."

"There was that," she said, trying to remain nonchalant.

"The subject never came up?"

"I never said that. I said we never agreed on it."

He took a sip of tea. "How old was the woman he left you for?"

"Are we seeking some kind of *aha* moment here? I figured this one out a long time ago. I'll save you a lot of painful exploration. Yes, we didn't have children because I didn't want children. Yes, I arranged—surreptitiously—the circumstances so having children was unlikely. Yes, he became irritated at my seeming lack of fertility. Yes, he tossed me over for a younger woman and they now have a darling two-year-old monster who puts anything smaller than a Volkswagen into his mouth. May I get back to my steak now?"

"Of course. I wouldn't think of intruding on your meal."

"Good."

She sliced off another piece of meat and dipped it in the béarnaise, ignoring the ghost of Emily Post who chastised her from deep inside her head.

"Yet," he said after choking down another bite of his salad, "my actual interest wasn't in your refusal to have children against your will. I was really interested in what you have against having children at all."

"Why? Are you one of those people who believe every woman

156

should go through the physiological equivalent of shitting a watermelon to feel completely fulfilled in life? I don't buy it."

"Because your own childhood . . ." he tailed off.

"Leave my childhood out of this. Better yet, let's just drop this entire line of inquiry before I get indigestion."

"As you wish."

"In fact, I'd appreciate it if you'd extend me the same courtesy you do for Mr. Kingsley, and not take any particular interest in my life. As you said, it's none of your business."

"Absolutely. I'll drop it."

"Good."

They were a half hour out of Asheville when Paula turned to Long in the bluish glow of the dashboard instruments.

"I *did* have a good childhood."

"I'm happy to hear it. It's rarer than you might think," he said, keeping his eyes on the road.

"Mr. Kingsley says he thinks I'm good for you."

"In which respect?"

"He says he thinks you respect the way my mind works, and you'll listen to me."

"Does he?"

"Do you? Respect my mind, I mean?"

"Is that important to you?"

"More shrink talk. As soon as I get home, I'm phoning the Pope and putting your mother up for sainthood."

She almost had to grab for the door handle as Long swerved to the breakdown lane and jumped on the brakes. The car skidded to a stop and Long stared ahead, both hands on the steering wheel.

"That was over the line," he said quietly. The menace in his voice was unmistakable.

"Sorry."

"No, I don't think you are. I think you're still angry about the way I dealt with Torrence and Claudia Flatt this afternoon, and you're taking it out on me deliberately. The steak house. That crack just now."

"Grow a skin, Dr. Long. You've done your share of sniping too. I think maybe you're great at flinging it, but you don't like it flung back at you."

"Are you purposefully trying to anger me?"

"No. It just comes naturally in your case."

He twisted his hands on the steering wheel and sighed heavily.

"This isn't any good," he said. "This isn't useful. I have a suggestion."

"Fire away."

"I think we should constrain our discussions to the Torrence case. I'll tell you what I need and you'll arrange it. If you have a problem with that . . ."

"No problem," she said. "No problem at all."

SEVENTEEN

"I think I pushed him over the edge," Paula told Kingsley over lunch on Saturday.

"How?"

"I made a crack about his mother."

"Oh. May I ask what it was?"

"He was pulling all this psychologist crap on me, and I'd had enough. I told him I was going to call the Pope and nominate Laura for canonization."

"That would do it. Not that she wouldn't have deserved it, you understand. Ben wasn't always as severely self-absorbed as he is now, but it would be safe to say that Laura had her work cut out for her. What did Ben say?"

"He suggested that we only talk about the case."

"Too bad. You managed to get under his skin. Strange as it may seem, that's quite a feat. You intend to agree to his suggestion?"

"Of course. The man is insufferable. I spent a large portion of last night debating whether to request assignment to a different case."

"And?"

"I'll see it through, don't worry."

"That's good. I wouldn't reassign you anyway."

"Why not?"

"Because you are a clerk, which means that you are little more than my indentured servant and I have the right to tell you what to do. Someday, if you are lucky, you will enjoy this power over others, but for the moment you are required to submit to my directions. Beyond that, you're doing a good job with the Torrence case and I'm not interested in backing up while some other clerk gets up to speed."

"Nice to know I'm appreciated."

"My pleasure to accommodate you. Now, tell me what Ben learned about Torrence."

She related the findings from their visit with Junior Torrence.

"That's intriguing," Kingsley said. "I'm not certain it helps us, though."

"Dr. Long doesn't seem terribly concerned about being helpful."

"He's working on a puzzle."

"It seems that way. He says the picture isn't complete in his head. It's missing pieces."

"Ben likes puzzles, Paula."

"Oh, I've figured that one out already."

"He's also very good at solving them. It's one of the primary symptoms of Asperger's disorder and it's served him well over the years. I'm happy to let him run with this one, for the time being. Ben is as aware of the deadlines we face as we are. He may take his time getting around to the evaluation, but in the end he'll deliver the goods right on schedule. Let's allow him to pull the strings on this case for a while longer. He might unravel something interesting."

Paula returned to her desk after lunch to find a message from Long. She dialed his number.

"You left a message for me?"

"Yes," he told her. "First, I wish to apologize for my behavior in the car yesterday. I have been thinking about it and I think it might have been rude."

"Okay. I suppose I shouldn't have made the comment about your mother."

"No. But it's over. I thought a lot about the case last night. I'm about ready to test Torrence."

"I'll set it up."

"I want to get hold of Torrence's school records, especially any confidential files."

"The confidential files are usually sealed after graduation. It will take a court order."

"That's why they keep your office so close to the courthouse. I'd like you to schedule the testing for Torrence for next Saturday. I have classes every day this week."

"I'll get right on it. Do you want me . . . am I going to the jail with you for the testing?"

There was a pause on the other end.

"I don't understand. Is there some reason you wouldn't go?"

She stifled a sigh. "No. None that matters, I suppose. I'll set everything up and get back with you when it's done. Is there anything else?"

Another pause.

"No. I don't think so. I'll look forward to your call."

EIGHTEEN

Junior Torrence sat across from Ben and Paula, slack-jawed, vacant-eyed, waiting for instructions.

"How are you feeling today, Earl?" Long asked.

"Okay. Will this take long? My story is on TV soon."

"What story is that?"

"*The Silver Lining.* I watch it every day."

"What else do you watch?"

"Sports sometimes. Cartoons. I like cartoons."

"Do you know what we're going to do today?"

"No."

"I'm going to give you a test."

"I didn't study or nothing."

"That's okay. It isn't the kind of test you can study for. I'm going to begin by asking you some questions, and then I'll have you write some things for me, and maybe I'll have you work with a couple of puzzles and some blocks."

"Sounds easy enough."

"Then let's begin, shall we? I'll need his hands uncuffed," Ben said without looking up from his testing kit.

The jailer attending Torrence unlocked the cuffs. Torrence reflexively rubbed his wrists.

"Are we going to be here a long time? I don't want to miss my show on TV."

Long looked up from the testing materials he was arranging on the tabletop. "Yes, so you said."

"I did?"

"Yes. Don't you remember?"

"No."

Long took a moment to scribble something on the legal pad. "We won't be here too terribly long," he said, not looking up.

"Okay."

Ben pulled a sheet of paper from his briefcase. Printed across the top of the paper was a single sentence: "The quick brown fox jumped over the lazy dog."

He placed the paper on the table in front of Torrence and handed him a pencil. "I'd like you to write this sentence for me four times. Twice printing, and twice in cursive."

A cloud crossed Torrence's face. "I don't know how to write cursive. I never learned it."

"Just do your best."

Torrence grasped the pencil in one fleshy paw and began writing on the paper. The first sentence took him almost a minute and a half to complete. His handwriting looked like that of a seven-year-old. After completing it, he immediately launched into the second sentence. It took him a little over six minutes to write all four sentences.

Ben looked at the paper and showed it to Paula.

"The average is between two and three minutes," he said without revealing to Torrence exactly how long he had taken. "This sentence contains every letter in the alphabet. Anyone can write it accurately once. By the fourth try, especially in people with expressive writing disorders, you start to see the real product show through. Look at this."

He pointed to a "q" that looked like a "g" and to a backwards "b." In the first sentence Torrence had written, the lines were relatively even and straight. In the fourth, the lines started to arc toward the lower right-hand corner of the sheet. None of the sentences were in cursive script.

"This is a point for Crouch's side," Ben said. "Writing disorders are common among the M.R. population."

He pulled an envelope from the briefcase and handed it to Torrence.

"Earl, I'd like you to address this envelope to your brother Edward, as if you were sending him a letter."

Torrence stared at the envelope. He picked up the pencil and placed the point on the paper, but didn't write. After a few moments, he sighed and lifted the pencil.

"I ain't gonna lie to you," he said. "I don't rightly know how to do this. I ain't never sent a letter by myself. I sent off for some stuff from cereal boxes from time to time, but Edward always wrote the envelopes for me."

"That's all right." Long took the envelope and pencil. "Let's play a game."

He retrieved a couple of dollar bills and some loose change from an envelope in his briefcase.

"I'm going to give you this change, Earl."

He slid the money across the table: several quarters, five dimes, eight nickels, and four pennies.

"Now," Long said. "Let's pretend you're working in a store and I want to buy a candy bar. The candy bar costs seventy-five cents. With me so far?"

Torrence nodded.

"Terrific. Now, I'm going to give you a dollar for the candy bar."

Torrence watched as Ben slid the bill across the table.

"I ain't got no candy bar," he said.

"Let's pretend you do."

"But I don't. This is a hard game."

Ben reached into his briefcase and pulled out a Three Musketeers bar. He slid it across the table.

"Now you do."

"That was cool. You had that candy bar all the time."

"I came prepared. Okay, let's play. You have the candy bar and I want to buy it. It costs seventy-five cents. I just gave you a dollar."

"But the candy bar is only seventy-five cents."

"That means you have to give me change. So, you figure out how much money I get back and give it to me with the candy bar."

Torrence stared at the change, then at the dollar bill and the candy bar. After a few moments he handed Ben the candy and a quarter.

"Excellent. Now, let's try it again."

He returned the candy bar and the quarter and took back his dollar bill.

"This time we'll say I want to buy the candy bar, but it costs a dollar and fifteen cents."

"I thought it cost seventy-five cents."

"It did. Now it costs a dollar and fifteen cents."

"Why does it cost more now?"

"In this game the price can change. This time the candy bar costs a dollar and fifteen cents. I'll give you two dollars and you make the change and give it to me with the candy bar."

He handed the bills to Torrence, who stared at the items in front of him in consternation, his brow furrowed. Paula could make out small beads of sweat forming at his hairline. Finally, he slowly picked out two quarters and a nickel and slid them back to Ben, along with the candy bar.

"I don't think that's right," he said.

Ben slid the money and the candy bar back to him.

"Then let's do it again, and make it right. Don't worry if it takes a while. I'm not timing you."

Torrence fiddled with the money for a few moments. Paula saw him counting silently but moving his lips. Slowly, he picked out three quarters and a dime and slid them across. Then he picked up the candy bar and handed it to Ben, who reached across, collected the money, and gave the candy bar to Torrence.

"You like Three Musketeers?" he asked.

"I sure do," Torrence said.

"Keep it. You're earning it today."

For a second Paula thought the killer was going to weep.

"Gosh. Thanks, mister. That's awful nice of you."

"You're welcome, Earl. Just a couple more tests to go. Tell me, what is the thing you should do when you cut your finger?"

When Torrence didn't say anything, Ben looked up from his clipboard.

Torrence sat in his seat, staring straight ahead. His eyes seemed to jerk back and forth a little.

"What is the thing to do when you cut your finger?" Ben repeated.

Torrence sat, his eyes seemingly focused on the opposite wall. His mouth hung open.

"Amazing," Ben said.

"Is he okay?" the officer asked.

"I think so. Let's wait a moment."

Paula reached out and touched Ben's shoulder. "Maybe we should call a doctor," she said.

"No. I think he's perfectly fine. Give him a moment."

She watched Torrence carefully. A shallow drop of saliva pooled at the corner of his mouth and rolled down his chin in a thin line.

"Earl?" Ben asked quietly.

Torrence stared ahead, nonresponsive. After another ten or fifteen seconds, his eyes seemed to clear and he turned his head a little.

"Are you okay?" Ben asked.

"Fine," he said, wiping his chin. "A little sleepy. Is this going to take a long time? I don't want to miss my story."

"It's called an absence seizure," Ben explained to Paula after the officer escorted Torrence out of the room for a moment for a bathroom break. "Sometimes they're called *petit mal* seizures. Fascinating."

"What causes them?"

"The same kind of brain dysfunction that causes full-blown *grand mal* epilepsy, except in *petit mal* seizures, the problem is localized to the frontal lobes. There's a storm of electrical activity in the brain. When that happens, the person shuts down for a few moments until the circuits can clear. Unlike people with *grand mal* seizures, people with absence seizures mostly sit and stare into space, unresponsive."

"Does it mean anything?"

"I don't know. I'm going to call a friend of mine in Durham, a top-flight neuropsychologist, to see if he can do a separate evaluation."

"Maybe we should clear this through Mr. Kingsley first."

"Why?"

"Because . . . well, it seems as if we should. If Torrence has this epilepsy, would it mean he's incompetent?"

"Not by itself. The real question is whether it could have contributed to the murder. There are all kinds of epilepsy. In a couple of forms, people can actually act out aggressively while in a seizure and recall nothing about it later."

"That wouldn't help us at all. Keep your head in the game. We're trying to execute Torrence, not save him."

"I know exactly what you and Sid are up to. I don't understand why we keep having this discussion. One thing is for certain. If I'm catching this, Eli Crouch's psychologist will, too."

"Maybe not."

"Oh, she will. Count on it."

"How can you be so certain?"

"Because I know her."

Moments later, the jailer brought Torrence back into the testing room. The young man seemed to have recovered completely from his absence seizure.

"Hold your hands out for me, like this," Ben said as he extended his arms and held his hands out, palms down.

Torrence copied him.

"Now, I'd like you to flip your hands up and down, as fast as you can, like this."

Ben flipped his hands palms up, and then back palms down. Torrence did the same, averaging one flip about every two seconds.

"As fast as you can," Ben urged him.

"This is as fast as I can."

Ben glanced at Paula. For the first time, she noted a glimmer of concern cross his brow. He turned back to Torrence.

"That's fine, Earl. Now, I'm going to hold out my index fingers. I'd like you to grasp them and pull."

The corrections officer standing in the corner of the room suddenly stood alertly.

"It's all right," Ben assured him. "This is necessary contact."

He held out his hands with his index fingers extended. Torrence grasped them and pulled gently.

"Don't worry about hurting me," Ben said. "Just pull."

Torrence's hands slipped off Ben's fingers.

"Try again," Ben said.

Torrence grabbed Ben's fingers again, and yanked. His hands slipped off.

"Grab really tightly."

Torrence tried, but his hands slipped away.

"That's as tight as I can grab," he said.

Ben made a hurried note on the clipboard and smiled at Torrence. "That's all right, Earl. Don't worry about it. Let's try this." He held his pen upright. "I'm going to move this pen, and I'd like you to follow it with your eyes without moving your head. Can you do that?"

"Sure."

Ben waved the pen back and forth and watched Torrence's eyes.

At first Torrence's eyes tracked the pen, but when Ben started moving the pen in a circle, Torrence's eyes began to flit and dart as he tried to follow it.

Ben turned to Paula. "Overactive nystagmus. It isn't really diagnostic, but I've noticed that it's a relatively common occurrence in people who have a documented history of ADD."

"Attention-deficit disorder?"

"Yes."

He wrote another note and turned back to Torrence. "All right, Earl. Now I'm going to ask you a few questions and I'd like you to answer them to the best of your ability."

Over the next half-hour Ben walked Torrence through five or six subtests of the larger intelligence test he had come to administer. Torrence complied gamely, but soon after the beginning of each subtest he would begin to falter.

As the test progressed, Paula began to feel sorry for the inmate. Then her mind drifted back to the crime scene photos, multiple angles with garish lighting, showing in all its gruesome vividness the brutality that had been inflicted on Amber Coolidge. Each time the images flashed across her mind, she could feel all sympathy for the monster who sat across from her melt away.

NINETEEN

The testing took a little over four hours to complete, including a couple of breaks. At one point Paula thought she was going to fall asleep, and wondered how Ben managed to remain alert. She had expected the testing might be dramatic or revealing. In the end, she found it merely tedious. Several times she thought she saw a flash of concern cross Ben's face, but then it was gone and he trudged along from subtest to subtest. Whenever Torrence seemed to tire, Ben would suggest a break.

Finally, they were finished. Ben thanked Torrence for his participation and asked the guards to escort him back to his cell.

"If they confirm the *petit mal* seizures, it would be good news for your boy Torrence," Ben said on the drive back to Asheville.

"My boy?"

"You know what I mean. While the evidence is a little inconclusive, there is some strong correlation data linking *petit mal* epilepsy and lowered intellectual functioning."

"Once again, in English."

"People who have these kinds of seizures often have low IQs."

"Well, why didn't you say so?"

"I did."

"You say *often*. How often?"

"Hard to say. There's a lot of variation in the research. The coefficient is significant in almost every case, though."

"What about that grip thing? You looked troubled when you had Junior pull your fingers."

"He's a large man. He should be able to pull my fingers off if he wanted—though I sincerely doubted he'd try. He had the grip of a five-year-old."

"What do you make of that?"

"Does Torrence look soft to you?"

She thought about it. "A little like the Pillsbury Doughboy."

"His eyelids droop. He's jowly. He has a weak grip. It could be related to months of relative inactivity, watching television and waiting for his day in court, or maybe it's something else."

"What are you thinking?"

"I want to know if he has some kind of degenerative neurological process going on."

"Why?"

He looked over at her, momentarily mystified. "Because I don't know."

"That's all?"

"Of course."

"Having a neurological disorder might keep Junior out of the death chamber," she said.

"That's not the point. The presence or absence of a neurological disorder could impact the findings of my evaluation."

"Excuse me, Dr. Long, but that is the point. We aren't assessing Junior Torrence for a long-range treatment plan. We're trying to hold him responsible for killing Amber Coolidge."

She drove on another couple of miles in silence. When she looked over again, Ben's chin had drifted toward his chest, as if he was falling asleep.

"What about the tests you completed?" she said, perhaps a bit more loudly than she intended.

His head jerked upright.

"What?"

"The tests. Any conclusion?"

"Bits of this. Bits of that. He has some short-term memory deficits, some problems with relatively simple calculations, and his vocabulary could stand a little improvement. I really didn't have time to boil down all the numbers. We're still a long way from knowing how he ticks."

"You said something about attention-deficit disorder."

"Just a clue. You saw how his eyes bounced all over the place when he tried to follow the pen. There's no conclusive research evidence, mostly because I never got around to keeping any accurate records, but I noticed over the course of my practice that clients who had been previously diagnosed with ADD tended to have that kind of eye movement. I called it 'overactive nystagmus,' but of course that's not really accurate."

"It isn't?"

"No. Nystagmus is a normal occurrence in everyone. It keeps our rod and cone receptors from focusing for too long on any one object. Our eyes are always flitting hither and yon, if only in tenths of millimeters, and almost imperceptibly. We're not aware of it. What Torrence's eyes did was more in the nature of a tic."

"What would it indicate?"

"Some glitch in his cerebellum, more than likely. Fine motor control is centered there. Can't say for sure how that would be connected with ADD, since the neurological deficits associated with hyperactivity tend to be centered in the prefrontal cortex, which is way over in the next county, in terms of brain geography."

"You have totally lost me. Which, I might add, isn't the first time."

"Sorry. Talking to myself. Wool-gathering. Fact is, I haven't come to any conclusions one way or the other regarding Torrence. I have a lot of ideas. I'll have to test them out one by one. I want to have him evaluated by a friend who specializes in neurological disorders. If he gets a clean bill of health, then we're back on track."

Ben lived an hour from the Henderson County Jail, if one could have driven there directly. However, it was necessary to add in the twisty drive up the mountain to his house. Almost two hours after leaving the evaluation with Torrence, they arrived at Long's home.

"Would you like to come in?" he asked.

"For what?"

"I made an experimental purchase of several bottles of Canadian ice wine the other day. I thought I'd like to try it tonight. Perhaps you would like a taste."

"Ice wine? I've never heard of it."

"I have two of the bottles chilling inside. If you'd care to join me, I'll uncork one and we'll give it a spin."

"Well, maybe just a glass."

Inside the house, he pulled a bottle from the wine cooler. "I've never tried it myself," he said, as he pulled the corkscrew from a kitchen drawer. "It's an interesting process. The wine is made from a very late harvest, after the first freeze. The frozen grapes—only Reisling and Vidal grapes are used—are picked and immediately pressed before they can thaw."

"Couldn't they freeze grapes artificially and press them?"

"That would be cheating. It would also violate regulations put forward by the Vintners' Quality Alliance. No, you must wait for the first frost. It does something to the grapes, you see. Increases the sugar content, or maybe concentrates it. The grapes must be picked before ten in the morning at a temperature no higher than minus eight degrees Celsius."

"What is that, exactly, in our scale?"

"That *is* one of our scales. If you are asking what it is in Fahrenheit, I believe it's around eighteen degrees. It's certainly well below the freezing point. When they press the grapes, all the water is driven out as ice crystals and discarded. This leaves the concentrated juice, with its acids, sugars, and natural nose."

"Nose?"

"The aromatic qualities of the grapes. Here, judge for yourself."

He had uncorked the bottle and poured her a glass. She held it up to the light. It was pale and honey-colored, with an orangey reflection. He watched as she lightly swirled the wine and watched its legs on the side of the glass, then sniffed it.

"Smells wonderful. Fruity," she said. She tipped the glass and took a sip. "Oh, my. Much sweeter than I expected."

Long poured his own glass and worked his way through the tasting ritual. "Delightful. You're right. It's very sweet, but there's an acidic undertone that balances it out. Here."

He had placed a little in her glass for her to taste. Now he poured the glass three-quarters full and did the same with his own. Then he crossed the room to his sofa and sat after turning on one of the end table lamps.

They sat quietly for a few moments, savoring the wine.

"Any progress on the school files?" he asked.

"As we suspected, the school refused to release them directly to Mr. Kingsley. I drafted a request for a subpoena. It should be delivered to a sympathetic judge tomorrow, and we'll have it served before the school office closes."

"A sympathetic judge?"

"Yes. We felt that we would be more successful going to a judge with a public record of supporting the death penalty."

"A manipulation?"

"Social engineering."

"Perhaps Sid was right. You may be learning more from me than you realize. I would suspect—"

The doorbell interrupted him.

"Now, who could that be?" he asked as he placed his wine glass on the coaster. He stood and crossed the room to the front door and opened it.

Paula heard a voice say, "Benjamin, would you like to tell me what you're up to?"

Seconds later, a woman whom Alfred Hitchcock would have referred to as a "frosty blonde" swept into the house. She was fortyish, slightly taller than average, and compactly, athletically built. Her makeup had been deftly applied and her golden hair hung to her shoulders, where it flipped under—a feat Paula had never seemed to master with her own hair. She walked into the living room, then stopped when she saw Paula.

"Oh, you have company," the woman said.

"This is Paula Paige," Ben said, almost an apology. "She's a law clerk in the DA's office."

"Yes, how is Sidney? I haven't seen him in ages."

She didn't wait for an answer. Instead, she turned to Paula and extended a slim, delicately manicured hand.

"Sybil Rock. I'm sure Benjamin has mentioned me."

"No," Paula said as she shook Sybil's hand. "I don't think he has."

"Well," Sybil said, turning her face to Ben without releasing Paula's hand.

"Sybil is a psychologist," Ben said. "She used to work at the DA's office with me. Now, I believe she's more or less freelance."

"We were partners," Sybil said as she relinquished Paula's hand. "For almost—what was it, Benjamin dear? Fourteen years?"

"About that long. Did you drive all the way from Charlotte just to see me?"

"Yes, but I seem to have interrupted something. I should have called ahead."

"No interruption," Ben said. "We were trying some ice wine.

Would you like a taste?"

"*Love* some."

As Ben retrieved a stem from the cabinet and poured a glass of the ice wine, Sybil lowered herself to the sofa and drew one leg up under her, as if she had done so many times.

"How long have you known Benjamin, Paula?"

"A few weeks."

"Really," she said as if she were surprised.

Ben returned from the kitchen and handed Sybil the wine glass, then returned to his place on the other end of the sofa.

"You're in private practice?" Paula asked.

"Yes. All those years spent in the DA's office left me with skills that are very attractive to defense attorneys."

"Sybil is a hired gun," Ben said. "You don't mind me saying that, do you, Sybil?"

"Goodness, no. Best move I ever made."

"Yes," Ben said. "I'd imagine it was. Sybil is currently employed by Junior Torrence's attorney to help find him incompetent to stand trial. She's here to pump me for information."

Paula took a sip from her glass. "You gathered all of that from one sentence?"

"Sybil and I have known each other for a long, long time. I knew what she wanted the minute I opened the door. Her motives are transparent to me."

"And vice versa," Sybil said. "We were a great team, once. Then Benjamin had to break up the act."

"There was more to it than that and you know it," Ben said.

"So. Is Junior competent, or not?" Sybil asked casually.

Paula said, "Ben, I'd ask you not to answer that question."

"Nonsense," Ben said. "Nothing I have to say will deter Sybil for one-tenth of a second."

"Damn it, Ben," Paula protested. "You work for Sidney

Kingsley. I don't think he would like you divulging our findings."

"I work for myself. I'm only billing Sid. I don't see why you're
so upset. Sybil knew I was evaluating Junior for retardation
before she left Charlotte."

"How can you know that?" Paula asked.

"After we ran into Eli Crouch the other day, he undoubtedly
called her—perhaps within seconds of leaving our sight—and
informed her that I'm evaluating Junior Torrence for the DA's
office. She wants to know why."

"Very good," Sybil said. "I'm so pleased to find that you
haven't gone all rusty and dull in the halls of academia. The ice
wine is delicious."

"I'm glad you like it."

"And extremely expensive, as I recall."

"I have very few vices," Ben said. "I think I can be forgiven
for indulging one or two of them."

Paula glanced at her glass. She wondered, briefly, exactly
what the word "expensive" meant in this case.

"Eli is very, very good at what he does," Sybil said. "What he
does, of course, is get juries to bring back acquittals. Junior Torrence is going to be found incompetent to stand trial. Eli almost
never fails."

"That's very possible."

"How did Sidney lure you into this case? I thought you were
irretrievably retired."

"I am. Sidney didn't lure me. I'm doing this for my own
reasons."

"Like when you quit the DA's office without warning?"

"Maybe I should leave," Paula said. "It sounds as if you two
have a lot to discuss and it's apparent that Dr. Long doesn't
want my legal input."

She placed the half-empty glass on a coaster and stood,

smoothing her dress.

"Have I hurt her feelings?" Sybil asked as if Paula weren't in the room.

"No. I think *I* have," Ben said. "I seem to be doing that a lot lately. Ms. Paige, the discussion Sybil and I are having has been ongoing for several years. She's never forgiven me for abandoning her."

"Best thing you ever did for me, actually," Sybil said.

"So you say. Ms. Paige, please don't feel that you have to leave."

Paula stood by the piano. Her face betrayed her irritation. "I don't like being talked about while I'm in the room. In any case, it's getting late, and I have to get down the mountain. Early morning tomorrow."

"Stay a few more minutes," Sybil said from the sofa. "We've barely met and you haven't finished your wine. It's a shame to waste it. I can't wait to hear your impressions of Benjamin. Is he still distant and impenetrable?"

"I think you're playing games," Paula said.

Sybil held her glass up to Ben. "She's sharp. I'll bet Sidney paired her with you."

"You're talking about me as if I'm not here again," Paula said.

"And yet you still don't leave. I haven't driven you off, at least not completely. Curious?"

"A little," Paula said as she stepped back toward her chair. "Besides, as you say, I haven't finished my wine. You and Ben were partners?"

"Professional partners. We worked together for years, doing forensic evaluations on convicted prisoners. Have you ever noticed, dear, how two people who work in such close proximity become almost intimate?"

"Stop it," Ben said.

"I mean, they learn each other inside and out. After five or six years, they finish each other's sentences. I think it's possible for two people who work together closely to become more intimate than those who are married."

"I disagree," Ben said.

"So do I," Paula said.

"Really," Sybil said. She drew it out to three long suggestive syllables. "Then, of course, I heard that Benjamin was evaluating Junior Torrence and I had to find out why. Well, the *why* was obvious, I suppose, but I wanted to know how Sidney had convinced him to take the case."

"He didn't," Ben said. "I made the decision on my own."

"Even more intriguing."

"I had my reasons," Ben said.

"Care to share them?"

"Some other time."

Sybil glanced at Paula. "Oh. Not in front of Paula. I understand."

"I don't think so," Paula said. "In fact, Dr. Long and I have discussed his reasons. I think he just doesn't want to air them here and now. You know. With *you.*"

"Of course. That must be it. I suppose it really isn't important. Junior Torrence is incompetent, and he isn't going to be held responsible for that poor girl's murder. I guess that's the main message I wanted to deliver."

"You mean it's the message Eli Crouch wanted you to deliver," Ben said.

"He and I are of one mind on this. He has become extremely wealthy over the years swaying juries to his way of thinking. This time will be no different."

"Be that as it may, whether Junior Torrence is executed or not is of no real interest to me. You know how I feel about the *Atkins* decision."

"And I know *why* you feel that way. I do love this wine. Is there more?"

"I'll open another bottle." He rose from the sofa and walked to the kitchen.

"I shouldn't drink any more," Paula called to him. "I'm driving."

"And you think I'm not?" Sybil said.

"I didn't say that."

"It was implied. So, tell me what you've discovered about our boy."

"Torrence?"

"No, silly. Benjamin. You two looked so cozy when I arrived. I figured you've gotten to know him, if only a little. What do you think?"

"He's very skilled. Beyond that, I have no real opinions."

"How evasive. Has he taken you out to visit his mother's grave yet?"

"No."

"I'd imagine not. He wouldn't. In fact, he's never been there himself."

Paula looked up from her glass.

"Not once," Sybil continued. "He was still in intensive care when she was buried and he never went to the cemetery. I tried to make him go eight or nine years ago. I thought he was going to go apoplectic on me."

"Why would you try to make him go?"

"Closure, dear. The man is in serious denial."

"Yes. We've talked about it."

"Well, there you are."

Ben returned to the living room with a newly opened bottle of wine. He freshened Sybil's glass, held the bottle up to Paula, and then placed it back on the table when she declined.

"I was trying to pry some information about you from Paula," Sybil said.

"What you need is a nice vacation," Ben said. "You never come off the clock."

"Occupational hazard. You two have been working for . . . how long, did you say?"

"Several weeks," Paula said.

"Does Sidney Kingsley pay you to keep Benjamin company after hours?"

Paula smiled, even as she tried to contain her claws. "Mr. Kingsley doesn't pay me enough to keep him company at all. I'm a law clerk. By definition I am chattel. I go where he directs me and I do what he tells me."

"I suppose Sidney told you to hang out at Benjamin's house and drink wine with him."

"No. That was my decision. If I were a suspicious person, I'd suspect you're jealous."

"Okay," Ben said. "That's enough from both of you. This is still my house. We're going to be civil here." He replenished his glass and sat back. "Allow me to fill in all the blanks. First, Ms. Paige, Sybil and I worked very closely for over a decade, during the worst period of my life. During that time she was my closest confidante and probably my best friend—at least to the extent that I am able to have friends. I'm not certain whether that says more about her or me. She is naturally protective of me, though I have assured her on many occasions that I am perfectly capable of managing my own affairs, such as they are.

"Second, Ms. Paige has been assigned to help me in any way I find necessary to complete my evaluation of Junior Torrence. As it happens, we returned from the first day of my evaluation only an hour ago. I am not yet prepared to discuss the results, and at the exact moment you knocked on the door we were discussing a subpoena to obtain Torrence's confidential school records. We were—therefore—working, no matter what we were drinking at the moment.

"Third, this is a small house, and when I am in the kitchen I can hear every word spoken in the living room. At this moment I am uncertain which of us this should embarrass the most. I suggest we relax and enjoy our wine."

Sybil lifted her glass to take a sip. "So, Benjamin, does this mean that you're coming out of retirement?"

"I don't think so. Taking this case has overtaxed me. I don't think I'd like to do this on a full-time basis again. I'm only performing a favor for a friend."

"Do you really believe Torrence is competent?"

"I think it's too early to decide one way or the other."

"If you determine he is competent, would you give me a heads-up?"

"Excuse me," Paula said. "I don't think it would be appropriate for Dr. Long to provide that information directly. Whether Dr. Long finds Torrence competent or not, I'm sure the evaluation report would be made available to Mr. Crouch during discovery."

"Of course," Sybil said.

Half an hour later, Sybil drained the remains of her third glass of ice wine and uncoiled herself from the sofa.

"I need to head back," she said. "I'm staying in the cabin at Lake James tonight and driving to Charlotte in the morning. It was good seeing you again, Benjamin. It's been way too long."

"Yes. I've missed our talks."

He walked her to the door and opened it for her. She reached out to hug him and kiss him on the cheek. He backed away rigidly. His face looked panicked.

"Well," she said. "Goodnight, then."

She patted his hand and walked out to her car.

Ben closed the door and returned to the couch.

"That was unnecessary, you know," he said to Paula.

"What?"

"Staying here. I wouldn't divulge anything she didn't already know."

"It seems that she knows almost everything."

"Yes. That was my impression."

"I do have to go. I hope I wasn't too unpleasant around your former partner."

"Think nothing of it. Please get back with me as soon as you receive Torrence's school records."

Paula put on her sweater and walked to her car. She drove down the winding gravel drive to the main road down the mountain. At the stop sign she saw Sybil's car parked on the shoulder. Sybil had stepped out of the car and was leaning against the driver's door.

Paula pulled up alongside, and pulled herself from her own car.

"Car problems? Anything I can do?"

"No problems. I was waiting for you to leave. I was hoping to have a word with you in private."

Paula looked one way and then the other, up and down the mountain road. "This seems private enough."

"I wanted to warn you . . . no, wait, I wanted to *advise* you regarding Benjamin."

"Okay."

"For almost fifteen years I was his closest friend. I wasn't kidding about the intimacy thing. I know more about Benjamin than probably anyone else in the world."

"You're in love with him."

"Not the way you mean. His peace of mind is very important to me. Anson Mount cut away a lot more than his spleen. Benjamin is brilliantly deductive and incisive, and the best psychologist I know. When Mount killed Laura, Benjamin lost all faith in humanity. He became the most cynical person I've ever met. He's come a long way in the last twenty years, but he's still exceedingly fragile."

"I'd probably agree with most of that. What does that have to do with me?"

"All I'm saying is, don't fuck with his head. Another disappointment in his life might send him over the edge."

"I think you might have the wrong idea," she said. "I'm working with Dr. Long because Sidney Kingsley assigned me to work with him. Mr. Kingsley told me he wouldn't reassign me, so I'm stuck on this case to the end of the line. I have no romantic interest in Dr. Long at all. I like my men a little better put together."

"That's my point. Benjamin isn't used to the company of women. Emotionally, he's a twelve-year-old boy who presumes every woman who doesn't reject him has the hots for him. It wouldn't hurt to emphasize your lack of interest, early and often."

"I'll take it under advisement," Paula said.

Sybil shook her head. "Only a clerk, and you already talk like a lawyer. See you around, Ms. Paige." She started to get back into her car.

"Wait a minute," Paula said.

Sybil froze halfway into her car.

"Tell me something. Did you sleep with Dr. Long before or after he quit the DA's office?"

Sybil allowed a sly smile. "Aren't you perceptive?" She slammed her car door and walked over to the passenger side of Paula's car. "No reason to stand out here in the cold. I'm freezing my tits off, and they're barely paid for."

She opened the passenger-side door and slipped inside. Paula sat in the driver's seat and turned the heat up on the dash controls.

"Since you're interested, you might like to know that sleeping with Benjamin was one of the biggest mistakes of my life," Sybil said quietly. "It's what made him retire from practice."

"How so?"

"As I said, Benjamin is extremely fragile. Emotional closeness is practically impossible for him, due to his condition."

"The Asperger's disorder."

"Sidney Kingsley prepped you well. Yes. The Asperger's makes him brilliant and analytical, with all the sexual precocity of a table lamp. He's just so damned *hot*, though."

"Are we talking about the same man?"

"You've only known him for a few weeks. I was the closest person in the world to him for over a decade. This was after his mother was murdered. When we first met, he was almost completely withdrawn. I think he was seeking revenge against every predator on earth.

"I was working for the District Attorney's office. We had an opening and he applied. The DA thought he saw fire in Benjamin's eyes, and hired him on the spot. It was only later that we realized what exactly that fire was.

"For the first five years, our relationship was purely professional but very close. Lots of late nights preparing testimony for the courts, lots of dinners discussing testing results. Over the years, his defenses started to crumble. Slowly—and I mean slowly in the sense that glaciers move—he began to trust me.

"A little over four years ago, we attended a conference in Washington. I had a lot to drink. He had a lot to drink. For a moment I forgot who and what he was. His inhibitions were, for a brief moment, broken down. I took advantage of the situation. I suppose I had thought about it for some time. I know I had fantasized about him. It wouldn't be the first time a couple of coworkers escalated their professional relationship into a personal one."

"You seduced him?"

"Don't be silly, dear. I ravaged him. I took him to my room and climbed all over him like I was a mountaineer and he was the Matterhorn. Afterward, we went to sleep. He woke me several hours later by screaming. He had fallen asleep in my arms and when he awoke he couldn't handle the physical or emotional contact. He jumped out of bed, dressed in about thirty seconds, and ran out of the room. After we got back home, he called in sick for the first week. Then he walked into the office and resigned. I tried to talk to him, but he wouldn't say anything except he couldn't work with me anymore."

"That's why he quit," Paula said.

"Yes. So I'll leave you with some friendly advice. If you should have any romantic designs whatsoever on Benjamin, now or in the future, you can forget them. He isn't equipped." She opened the car door and slid back out into the cold night. "Nice talk," she said. "Goodnight, dear."

TWENTY

"Tell me about Sybil Rock," Paula said the next morning as she sipped coffee in Kingsley's office.

"Sybil? How did she come up?" Kingsley asked.

"I was at Dr. Long's house last night, after we finished testing Earl Torrence. She paid him a visit."

"Oh, my."

"What should I know about her?"

"If you've met Sybil, I presume you already know plenty. She's smart, crafty, very often downright devious, and almost as good at what she does as Benjamin."

"Almost?"

"Actually, since Ben may have become a little rusty, she could have a slight edge."

"She's working for Eli Crouch."

"So I'd heard."

"That makes her part of the enemy camp."

"Yes."

"Should we be worried?"

"Constantly."

Paula took a sip of her coffee. "She wanted to know what Dr. Long was doing, working the case. If she'd been a cat, she'd have had her ears laid back and her fur on edge."

"I don't own cats. Never have."

"It's a bad sign. She was threatened, but trying to hide it."

"Threatened is good. It means she doesn't know for certain

whether Junior is retarded. I read over your brief for the subpoena on Torrence's school records. I'm having it prepared by my secretary to present to the judge in an hour or two. We should have the records by this afternoon."

"Thank you. May I ask a question?"

"Of course. That's what students do."

"What if Dr. Long decides Torrence is incompetent to stand trial?"

Kingsley clasped his hands on the desktop in front of him and stared past her at the collection of diplomas and awards that dotted the back wall of his office.

He drummed the desktop with his fingertips.

"Let's burn that bridge when we get to it," he said.

Kingsley stopped by Paula's desk after lunch and dropped a folded piece of paper on top of her growing pile of folders and papers.

"What's this?" she asked as she picked it up.

"The writ. Judge Holden approved it."

"At lunch?"

"I do some of my best work at lunch, Ms. Paige. I presented your brief over the *consommé,* and he approved the subpoena over the *boeuf bourguignon.*"

"And, judging by your breath, you celebrated with martinis."

"Perceptive, and yet somehow impertinent. May I suggest that you pay a visit to Junior Torrence's school and retrieve his confidential folder? I'm sure Ben will find it useful. Now, if you will excuse me—"

"Wait. Please. Could I speak with you for a moment? In your office?"

"Of course."

She followed him to his desk and shut the door as he walked—a little too cautiously—to take his seat. She sat across the desk from him and said, "You told me that I would learn a lot from Ben Long."

"Yes."

"Could you expound on that?"

"Perhaps it would be more useful if you'd tell me what you've learned so far."

"I think it would all fall under the heading of 'social engineering.' "

Kingsley smiled, though he covered his mouth with his hand in a feeble attempt to hide it. "Ben's lying again?"

"Not according to him."

"And this disturbs you?"

"I have some concerns about the professional ethics of it."

"You do realize that, at one time, I was a defense attorney?"

"With Eli Crouch. Yes.

"Our law office defended criminals."

"And some innocent people."

"Once in a long while. I asked all my clients three basic questions before I took them on. Can you guess what one of them was *not?*"

"No."

" 'Are you guilty?' I never asked my clients whether they actually committed the crime. In fact, I cautioned them strongly not to tell me. I asked them to give me reasons to believe they didn't commit the crime. I asked them for possible alibis. I delved into their pasts for every good deed, every positive accomplishment, every moment of glory, so that I could paint a picture for the court that made my clients look good to the jury, no matter what kind of lowlife, conniving, murderous, psychopathic monsters they might have actually been."

"But that's not a lie."

"Isn't it? If I were to be utterly truthful with the jury, wouldn't I have stood before them and declared that my client was, in fact, a slimeball who deserved to be placed *under* the prison? Instead, I glossed over all that depressing stuff and accentuated whatever essential goodness my client may or may not have lacked. And now that I represent the state rather than the accused, you can rest assured that every word I utter in court is the exact opposite. Now I exclude the good, and the defenders exclude the bad, thereby providing a balanced view of the defendant. The rest is just facts. Is this practice professionally unethical?"

"No. It's what we do."

"Yes! It's our job to convince the jury that the evidence against the defendant is overwhelmingly damning. People like Crouch must convince the jury our evidence is tainted, trumped up, or a contemptuous lie. It's his job to demonstrate beyond a reasonable doubt that there is no way his client could possibly have committed the crime, because they were—at that exact moment—doing something else far, far away. So why does he expend so much effort on portraying our defendants as socially acceptable, warm fuzzy puffballs?"

"Because," Paula ventured, trying to follow his train of thought, "it makes them more likable?"

"Exactly. Juries are dumb, Ms. Paige. That's a good thing because most criminals are stupid and criminals deserve to be judged by their peers. Being dumb, juries tend to believe some of the most incredible things. They believe people who dress in suits are smart and sophisticated, so Crouch dresses his clients in suits. They like to believe people are basically good, so he presents his clients' good sides. Most importantly, fifty years of watching courtroom dramas on television has convinced juries that most people placed on trial are actually innocent. It's the *Perry Mason* syndrome. Everyone wants to believe that, at the dramatically appropriate moment, some seemingly guiltless person in the gallery will stand and stop the proceedings, declaring to one and all he can't sit for another moment knowing the accused may be punished for a crime he did not commit. So Crouch massages their misconceptions. He plays to them. He tells them things that reinforce the beliefs they brought into the courtroom. Criminal court is an adversarial process, where the truth is batted back and forth until—in the worst case—it becomes unrecognizable. Ben does exactly the same thing. He has an uncanny ability to stick his finger in the air, see which way his subject's wind is blowing, and go with that flow. It's all social engineering, in the courtroom, in the examination room, when conducting a background interview. It's all part of the interviewing technique. Do you play poker?"

"No."

"Maybe you should take it up. Poker is a great exercise in social engineering. You never tell the other person what you really have and what you really want. You lead them to believe you really have something other than you have and want something other than you want. You bluff, you lie, and you hide your true intentions. If you're really, really good at it, you win."

"But you have to have the cards first."

"Not necessarily. I've seen men win poker hands by making everyone else fold, and all they had was a pair of deuces. If Ben can teach you how to do that, then by God you'll have a future in this business."

"I see," she said as she stood to leave. "I guess I didn't look at it that way."

She walked to the door and started to open it, but stopped and turned back to him. "Sybil is tall," she said. "I'm tall. She's blonde. I'm blonde . . . ish. Are you engaging in a little social engineering of your own, Mr. Kingsley?"

"Maybe a little. Not the way you're thinking, though. You forgot to mention that Sybil is sharp, and you're sharp. Ben needs support to do what he does. He can't operate in isolation.

He has to have someone to bounce ideas off of, or he'll ruminate himself into a floppy mess. That used to be Sybil's role. Now it's yours."

"You knew that Sybil would be involved in Junior Torrence's case."

"Of course I did. In fact, I told Ben she was involved the day I approached him with it."

"So my role, at least part of it, is to . . . what? Distract him from her?"

"Possibly."

"And to keep his eye off the competition?"

"If need be."

"You want me to keep his head in the game."

"Absolutely."

"And when the case is over?"

"There will be other cases. When it comes to rehabilitation, Ben is a long-term project."

TWENTY-ONE

After obtaining Earl Torrence's school records from the local education center, Paula decided to drop them off with Long at his mountain house.

She wasn't certain why it seemed so urgent to do so. It was the beginning of a weekend and there would be plenty of time for him to go over the records the next week. On the other hand, it seemed as if everyone involved in the Torrence case had developed a sense of urgency, as if this case represented some watershed moment in legal history. It didn't, of course, but the mood was infectious. And she wondered whether Sybil Rock might have decided to wander back up from Lake James, bent on sucking more information out of Long.

As she drove, she thought about the evaluation the day before. She had never witnessed an actual psychological assessment, and had been fascinated at first at the variety of tests and measurements that Long wielded as deftly as a neurosurgeon handles a scalpel.

Hours of observing had left her with a lot of time to make her own observations of Torrence. Now she wondered how he could have killed Amber Coolidge. He never became irritated with the testing, though he did demonstrate the occasional glimmer of frustration as tasks became more difficult. More often than not, he would simply quit or claim inability to do what was asked of him.

She tried to imagine Torrence plunging a hunting knife deep

into Amber's ribcage, but the image wouldn't manifest itself. There was more teddy bear than grizzly in Junior Torrence, she decided. It seemed a pity to put a man to death for a crime he barely remembered and probably never intended to commit.

Suddenly, an idea came to her so quickly and with such shocking clarity that she almost drove off the side of the winding mountain road.

Now she had an even more pressing need to see Dr. Long.

"Are you all right?" Long asked as he opened the door and saw her face.

"I need a moment," she said. "We need to talk."

He looked at her for a long beat, as if trying to determine what she needed. Then he stepped aside and gestured for her to come into the house.

"A glass of wine?"

She shook her head, and held up a hand, as if begging for a moment to think. Then she turned to him. "Intent," she said.

"What?"

"One of the central tenets of first-degree murder. *Intent.*"

"Okay."

"Look at the murder again. Junior Torrence went to Amber's apartment because he couldn't sleep. They watched a movie together. She asked him to go home. He went to the bathroom first and then he killed her."

"I'm not following you."

"When did he form the intent to kill Amber? What set him off?"

"Who knows?"

"Exactly! The only good reason Torrence himself has come up with was supplied for him by Detective Donnelly. Until Donnelly spelled out a scenario, Torrence didn't even think he'd killed Amber. Nowhere in his original story is anything even remotely approaching a conflict that could create the intent to kill."

"What are you saying? Are you suggesting Earl Torrence didn't commit the murder?"

"I don't know what I'm suggesting. You've maintained all along that we're missing a huge piece of the story. Perhaps this is it. I think as soon as Donnelly found the knife and bloody shirt, he decided he had his man and accepted whatever evidence he could find to support that belief."

Ben rubbed his hands together, and reviewed everything he could recall about the case. "I think maybe you've decided that Torrence is too likable to have committed the murder."

"What?"

"Let's face it. He's kind of cute and sort of cuddly and very polite. He doesn't look the part of a killer. There's something about him that makes people want to protect him. Right?"

"I suppose."

"Stay with me for a moment. This is important. All the evidence points to Torrence. By his own admission, we know he was in the apartment. He recalls seeing Amber's body on the floor. The knife and the bloody shirt were found in his possession, at his own apartment, meaning he had to take them there, presumably to avoid being caught. There's nothing here that changes the facts."

"What about that knife? Did he take it with him to Amber's apartment?"

"How the devil would I know?"

"Don't you think it's important? You saw the evidence photographs. That was one big-assed mother-honking knife. I have a difficult time believing that it belonged to Amber. That would mean Junior had to have taken it with him."

"I'm sure it's covered somewhere in the investigative reports."

"We can reread the transcripts, but I don't think so. I think the evidence only deals with the possession of the knife after the fact. I don't recall any information indicating the origin of the knife."

"Your point being?"

"If Junior Torrence didn't take the knife to Amber's apartment, then he didn't go there with the intent to kill her. If the knife was already there and he became involved in some kind of argument or conflict with Amber and used the knife to kill her because it was convenient, then this becomes a crime of passion, devoid of premeditation. Without premeditation, this isn't a death penalty case!"

Ben leaned forward and stared at the floor. Then he stood and walked around the room, the way a caged cat might.

"You're out of your depth," he said. "You're a third-year law clerk second-guessing the decision of the District Attorney to charge Earl Torrence with murder. Not just any District Attorney either, but Sidney Kingsley, the best I've ever met. I think you're jumping to conclusions."

"Look at the *facts.*"

"That's exactly what I'm doing. I'm not supposed to decide what his motive was. I only need to determine whether he's fit to stand trial."

"Or maybe you don't want this to turn into something other than a capital case because you want Junior Torrence to fry!"

He turned to her, a mystified gawp covering his usually stoic features.

"Junior Torrence killed Amanda Coolidge the exact same way Anson Mount killed your mother and damned near killed you," she said. "He's represented by the man who kept Anson Mount out of the chair. This isn't about whether Torrence is competent or whether he planned to kill Amber. Maybe you're looking for a way to stick it to Eli Crouch. I think you want to ram this case down his throat to get back at him."

"I've had no thoughts of the kind. That would be unethical."

"It's easy to hide behind ethics. I've seen you in action, remember? I've seen you lie with the skill of a three-card monte dealer. You call it social engineering, but it's just lies. Maybe you've told yourself so many of them that you can't figure out what's real anymore. I'm telling you Junior Torrence might not have planned to kill Amber Coolidge. Will you, for the love of Christ, please consider that possibility?"

Ben turned and walked stiffly out the open sliding door to the deck. He grasped the sill of the deck railing and stared out over the lights of the valley below. Paula could see his chest heaving and bursts of fog exploding from his nostrils as he exhaled. It was as animated as she had seen him, with the possible exception of the fury he had shown after her offhand comment about canonizing Laura.

She waited for several moments and then picked up her jacket to go. As she reached for the front door latch, he walked back into the living room.

"It's too much," he said. "I can't take this anymore. I thought I could handle it, but I can't. I quit."

"Again?"

"I was right the first time. I don't know what I was thinking, accepting this case. It's made my mind a mess. I can't keep up with it all. I have my obligations to the school. I need to focus on that."

"I see," she said, her hand still on the latch. "I guess that's it, then."

She twisted the latch. The door fell open.

"Tell Sid I'm sorry," Ben said without looking at her.

"I'll tell him you gave up."

She didn't wait for his response. She closed the door behind her and walked across the gravel lot to her car.

★ ★ ★ ★ ★

She was halfway down the hill to the highway when she remembered the folder on the back seat.

"Shit!" she said as she pulled the car over to the side of the road.

There was no point in taking it back to Dr. Long. He was quitting the case, right? She could leave it on the back seat and add it to the mountain of files on the Torrence case when she returned to her office. The next psychologist might listen to reason, and there might be something in the school files that he—or she—might find useful.

Dr. Long had asked for these records, though. He had thought there might be something in them that would shed light on Junior Torrence, and maybe even on his motivation for killing Amber Coolidge.

Dr. Long had quit the case. On the other hand, Paula wasn't the person who had hired him. She wasn't able to accept any resignations. Maybe if she gave him the files, he would look them over. Maybe if he looked them over, he would see something that would spur him to return to the case.

She turned around at the first driveway and drove back up the mountain.

When she arrived at his house, most of the lights were off. A faint glow emanated from the rear of the structure, near the area of the living room and rear deck. As she approached the front door, Paula heard music. At first, she thought it was a selection from Ben's seemingly boundless supply of classical recordings, but as she reached the porch she realized he was playing the piano. She knocked tentatively at the door. The music stopped abruptly. Seconds later, the door opened and he peered out.

"I'm sorry," Paula said. "I forgot to give you the copy of Torrence's school records."

She held out the folder, as if in explanation.

"Oh. I see. Yes. Of course. Please come inside."

"No, that's all right. I wanted to make sure you received it."

He opened the screen door. She handed him the folder.

"Well, thank you."

"Excuse me, but were you playing the piano just now?"

"Yes."

"At first I thought it was a CD. I didn't know you could play."

"I learned when I was a child."

"It's very nice."

"Playing the piano?" he asked, looking puzzled.

"Yes. No. *What* you were playing. What was it?"

He looked back toward the living room as if he weren't sure himself and might be hoping the piano could clue him in. "Bartok," he said at last.

She looked at her car. "I suppose I should be going," she said. "I just wanted to make sure you got the folder."

"So you said."

She turned and started to walk toward the car. Then she stopped and looked back at him. He was still standing behind the screen door, in the spill of the yellow porch light, holding the folder. His face looked bewildered.

"Could I ask you something?" she said.

"Of course."

"Would you play something for me sometime? On the piano?"

He looked almost panicked. "No. I don't think so."

She waited for an explanation. When it was apparent that one would not be forthcoming, she said, "I see," even though she really didn't. "I'll be going, then."

"Goodnight."

He closed the door.

Paula walked back to her car, shaking her head.

TWENTY-TWO

When she arrived at the office on Monday morning, Paula found two messages waiting for her. One was from Ben Long, asking her to call. The other was from Sybil Rock. She called Ben first, at his office at the university.

"I don't have much time to talk," he said. "My class is in five minutes. I was wondering whether you could acquire some information for me."

"I thought you were quitting the case."

"I read the records you gave me last night. I have some questions."

She covered the mouthpiece of the telephone and sighed. It was as if their confrontation the night before had never happened.

"Certainly. What do you need?"

"Edward Torrence told us that he had practically raised Junior. I want to know why. I would also like to know what became of their paternal grandparents."

"Why?"

"A hunch. I really don't want to discuss it yet."

"I'll see what I can do."

"Thank you. I really do have to run."

"Wait a moment," she said. "I have a message here from Sybil Rock. She wants me to call her."

"I see."

"What do you think I should do?"

There was a brief silence on the line and then Ben said, "I think you should call her."

He begged off again, and cut the connection.

Paula dialed the number on the message from Sybil.

"I'm returning your call," she said after Sybil picked up the receiver.

"Thanks for getting back to me so quickly. I've received word that you plan to get a court order for a neurological exam on Earl Torrence."

"That's right. Mind telling me who told you?"

"Of course I do. What do you hope to find?"

"While we were interviewing Torrence the other day, he had some kind of seizure. Dr. Long wants to know if it means anything."

"What kind of seizure?"

"Dr. Long called it an absence seizure."

"Really," she said, drawing the word out and managing not to make it sound like a question.

"Is this a surprise to you?"

"We'll call it *news*. You realize, of course, that seizures are of absolutely no consequence when it comes to competency?"

"I have no idea. That's Dr. Long's area of expertise."

"Why don't you call him by his first name?"

"I beg your pardon?"

"You've referred to him as Dr. Long three times in this conversation. I was under the impression that you and Benjamin had developed a somewhat more familiar working relationship."

Paula sniffed.

"Allergies, darling?"

"Bullshit," Paula said, "always makes my nose itch. You're baiting me."

"Only a little. Shall we have an agreement, you and I?"

"Unlikely."

"Just a small conspiracy. How about we both refer to him as Benjamin or Ben in casual conversation?"

"I don't think I like that idea."

"Why not?"

"Because engaging in a little lighthearted conspiratorial banter with you might be construed as inferring an alliance. No matter how you want it to seem, we are adversaries in the Torrence case. I don't think I wish to conspire with you."

"Do you plan to get your court order today?"

"As soon as possible."

"I wanted to give Eli a heads-up. He might want to put in his two cents' worth. Subjecting that poor Torrence boy to endless physical and mental evaluations might be interpreted as cruel and unusual. We are obligated, after all, to act in Earl's best interests."

"Did you pull this kind of nefarious stunt when you were working with Dr. Long?"

"Dear me," Sybil cooed. "Who do you think *taught* me?"

Ben collected his materials and crossed the university parking lot to the hall where he taught Abnormal Psychology. It was almost time to break for Thanksgiving, a time when he traditionally gave the students their last quiz before finals.

He walked into the classroom and placed his briefcase and the sheaf of quizzes on the table at the front of the room, next to his lectern. He looked up at the class and froze when he saw Sarah Ashburton sitting in the front row.

She smiled at him sheepishly. The other students regarded her with caution, as if frightened that she might explode at any moment.

"Ms. Ashburton. I didn't expect you to be back this semester."

"I checked my syllabus," she said. "It said there was a quiz today. And I believe this is overdue."

She pulled a bound manuscript, maybe fifteen pages thick, from her book bag and walked it to the front of the room, where she handed it to him. He looked at the cover page.

"My term paper," she said.

The cover read *Self-Mutilation as a Strategy in Relief of Acute Anxiety.*

"Oh my," Ben said.

"I figured I should write what I know."

"This isn't entirely subjective," he said. "I mean, I hope you included an adequate number of peer-reviewed sources."

"The bibliography runs to two pages."

He flipped through the folder and looked over the bibliography. "Yes, very impressive. There is, of course, the matter of your midterm and the last two quizzes."

"I spoke with the department chair. He assured me that I could make them up before the final, under the circumstances. I've reviewed the chapters I missed while I was away and I'm ready to take the quizzes, including today's."

"Class, please excuse me," Ben said. "Ms. Ashburton, could I see you privately for a moment?"

Without waiting for an answer, he strode to the back of the room and into the near-empty hallway. When he turned to look back, Sarah had followed him out the door.

"Please close the door," he said.

She eased the door shut and turned back to him.

"Are you sure you don't want to take an Incomplete?" he said. "For that matter, it isn't too late in the semester to withdraw from my course and try again. You can get an administrative withdrawal based on hardship, and I'd be happy to inform the dean that you were passing when you . . . uh, left."

"When I slit my wrists, you mean?" she held out her hands,

palms up. "It's all right, Dr. Long. Part of my treatment in the hospital dealt with learning not to keep secrets. I slit my wrists because I couldn't handle my secret cutting anymore. One of the things I've learned is to express my anxieties and insecurities openly."

"I see."

"I would hope so, considering your profession. Please don't make me take an Incomplete or withdraw. I know I can pass your course. I can pass all my courses. I don't want to fall too far behind."

"How about this? Take the quiz today. Then come by my office after class and take the quizzes you missed. If you have a B or better, you'll continue. If your grade is C or worse, you'll withdraw and try again next semester."

"I can pass with a C."

"But it won't do your grade point average any favors, and I seem to recall you were interested in attending graduate school."

She looked down at the worn linoleum floor. "I hadn't thought about it that way."

"Sometimes you have to look at the big picture. Do we have a deal?"

She nodded.

That evening, as the last strains of Rimsky-Korsakov's "Cappricio Español" echoed on Ben's stereo, he penciled a large A on Sarah Ashburton's term paper and slid it on top of the quizzes she had completed in his office that afternoon. *A deal is a deal,* he told himself, but that still didn't make him comfortable with the arrangement.

He wasn't giving her anything. She had earned every grade. Her term paper was top shelf. The quizzes were almost perfect. There was still the matter of the final exam, but he was sure she'd ace it.

Still, it seemed a great deal of pressure for the young woman to place on herself, so soon after leaving the hospital. Stress and fear of failure had led to her self-mutilation. While it was necessary for her to learn new ways to deal with pressure, it wasn't necessary for her to do it all at once.

He decided not to think about it any more that evening. He put the papers away, poured another glass of Mouton Cadet, and placed a relaxing CD of Gregorian chants into the machine. As he started to return to the living room, the folder containing Junior Torrence's confidential school records caught his eye. He'd carefully placed it on the coffee table after reading through it the night before, then had spent most of the night running the information over and over through his mind.

He had found exactly what he had expected. The record actually began in kindergarten, with teachers' remarks indicating that Earl Torrence was a slightly larger-than-normal child who had a tendency to go off-task and had trouble following complex directions. Torrence had been a kindergarten student in the early 1980s, a short time after the *Diagnostic and Statistical Manual of Mental Disorders* of the American Psychiatric Association had coined the term "attention-deficit disorder." Slow to adopt the term, Earl's teachers and counselors had tended to use the older, more accepted phrases, "minimal brain dysfunction" and "soft neurological signs," to explain his behavioral deficits. They meant essentially the same thing. Earl Torrence had behaved in a disorderly fashion, grossly different than the other children in his group, and it was necessary to explain that behavior.

The diagnostic tools available in the Reagan era, Ben recalled, had been crude at best. While there were CAT and PET scans, functional magnetic resonance imaging was way in the future. A CAT scan was unlikely to find much interesting in a child with Torrence's reported problems because they were largely chemical, and axial and emission tomography was intended to uncover structural abnormalities. It was unusual to find brain lesions in kids with minimal brain dysfunction. Diagnosis, even as was the case today, was most typically made by inference and indirect symptom analysis. Even in modern times, MRIs weren't used to diagnose attention-deficit disorder. They were just too damned expensive.

Having been labeled in kindergarten, Earl was a marked kid for the rest of his school career. The final remarks by his kindergarten teacher included a warning of sorts to his first-grade teacher.

Earl Torrence requires strong management to remain on task and to avoid aggressive behaviors in class. Preferential seating and small tasks work best. Complex instructions should be avoided.

As the twig is bent, Ben mused.

The rest of the folder had read like subsequent verses of the same song. By fourth grade, some sharp-eyed school psychologist had changed the diagnostic term to the more correct ADD label, but hadn't bothered to administer an intelligence test to Torrence. A pity.

By the sixth grade, cowed by half a decade of special treatment, Earl had become something of a footnote in each of his classes. Academic success wasn't expected, nor was it encouraged. His primary educational goal was management. Accommodations supplanted lesson plans. It was assumed that he'd float through ten years of school and quit at his earliest legal opportunity, to take a job as a laborer.

There was an interesting note by his seventh-grade counselor. It referred to Earl's "adjustment to his trauma," but was otherwise cryptic. Something terrible had apparently happened to Earl as he entered adolescence. Ben jotted a note on the inside cover of the folder, to remind himself to find out what had taken place, and resumed reading.

By the time he reached Torrence's twelfth-grade notes—the youth had defied all his predictors by completing high school after all, perhaps with his brother Edward's support—it was apparent to Ben that the school, in its well-intended attempt to provide Torrence with every possible accommodation and assistance, had failed him miserably.

More interesting to Ben was what was missing from the file. First, there were no records indicating that Torrence had ever been administered an intelligence test.

Second, there was no mention anywhere of *petit mal* seizures.

It was, of course, possible that Torrence's teachers had missed the seizures, since they consisted primarily of staring into space. If they expected little involvement in classroom activities, then absence seizures would have been considered nothing more than boredom or daydreaming.

On the other hand, Ben knew that there were cases of adult-onset epilepsy. He also knew their probable causes.

That was what had kept him awake for most of the night.

That, and Paula's tirade before storming out of the house. Ben had intended to resign from the case, exactly as he had said he would, but on reflection he had realized that part of his reason for quitting was how close Paula had come to the mark with her accusations.

Most people presumed that his Asperger's disorder prevented him from understanding his own motivations, as if it were some kind of limiting disease or intellectual handicap. In fact, the very nature of the disorder caused him to scrutinize every action he took and mentally rehearse every sentence he uttered. He had spent his entire life examining his behaviors before the fact, and deliberating, analyzing, and ultimately deciding what to do or say before he did so, in order to ensure what he said was as accurate as possible. It was his nature to break things down to their basic elements, and he had been as aware of the risk—that he was pursuing Junior Torrence's examination as some kind of retribution against Eli Crouch—as Paula had been.

What had shocked him was that his motivation might be so transparent to her.

Now, after ruminating over the case for almost twenty-four hours, he realized he had missed something fundamental, something that had been clouded by his prejudices.

He dialed Paula's cell phone number.

Paula stepped out of the shower and heard her cell phone play a Liszt rhapsody in the bedroom. She quickly wrapped a towel around her body and dashed out of the bathroom to grab the phone.

"Hello?"

"Ms. Paige, this is Ben Long."

"Can I call you back?" she asked. "It will only be a few moments."

"I won't take much time. Did you get the order for the neurological evaluation on Torrence?"

Water from Paula's soaked hair dripped across her hand and began to flow onto the telephone. "This really is a bad time. I'll call you back in a few minutes."

Before he could argue, she thumbed the END button.

Ben stared at the receiver for a moment and then placed it back on the cradle.

Not wanting to waste time, he brought the box containing Junior Torrence's records into the living room and began rummaging through it, looking for information that might support his suspicions. It was a dangerous approach, he reminded himself. The idea was to draw conclusions from the data, not find data to support your conclusions. He ran a strong risk of error.

On the other hand, he found it intriguing that nobody had ever noted Torrence's seizures. He recalled that Claudia Flatt had told him that she saw Torrence standing on the sidewalk outside the apartment, staring at the front door. What if she had actually witnessed a *petit mal* seizure? She had interpreted it as an indication that Torrence was dull. Maybe it meant something else altogether.

The telephone rang. Ben picked up the receiver.

"Sorry for hanging up on you," Paula said. "I had just gotten out of the shower."

For a fleeting moment, Ben imagined her running across the house in her birthday suit to grab the phone. He tried to push the image from his mind.

"We got the order for the neurological evaluation," she continued. "But there's something you should know. Sybil Rock knew we were going to request it. Whoever her snitch is, she's getting good information."

"I'm not surprised. Sybil has always been very good at getting information. It probably isn't important. She would have found out about the evaluation sooner or later."

"Who do you want to perform the neurological evaluation?"

"His name is Curtis Sorrell. He's very good. He told me he'd think about it. I'll call him later today and ask if he's decided to accept the referral."

Curtis Sorrell was happy to do the evaluation. Ben phoned Paula and told her how to contact him regarding compensation, then returned to the box of papers from the Torrence case.

His recollection of Claudia Flatt's description of Torrence made him wonder what else he might have allowed to slip by. He poured another glass of wine, and set his laptop up on the coffee table to make notes. Then he began a new exploration of Torrence's records. Around five in the morning, he realized that the gnawing suspicion he had missed something vitally important had been correct. He thought of calling Paula, but remembered the other time he had phoned her in the middle of the night. Instead, he recorded his suspicions on the laptop.

TWENTY-THREE

"You want *what?*" Paula asked when Ben called her the next morning.

"You heard me. I need the medical records for Edward Torrence and his parents."

"You don't want much. You know we'll have to inform Edward that we're seeking his records."

"I also need some genetic tests conducted on Edward, as well as on Earl."

"Why?"

"Adult-onset absence seizures are mostly the result of genetic abnormalities, or sometimes brain injury or cancer. I want to know whether we're dealing with something that runs in the Torrence family."

"What has this to do with competence to stand trial?"

"Maybe nothing. On the other hand, if we can demonstrate that Earl Torrence has a history of seizures dating back to childhood and that they are genetic in origin, then maybe we can make a case with Curtis Sorrell's help for neurological damage arising from seizure activity. It would explain Torrence's intellectual deficits."

"You lost me," she said.

"Do you recall when we met Edward Torrence?"

"Of course."

"Remember his handshake?"

"It wasn't a high point for me."

"His hand was limp. His grip was pathetic."

"So he's lousy at shaking hands. What of it?"

"An otherwise robust man, apparently healthy, with the grip of a five-year-old? Besides the absence seizures, we're also getting a neurological evaluation on Junior Torrence because he shows signs of neuropathic weakness. Maybe there's a familial trait here."

"Does it matter?"

"If it's there and we don't know it, it matters."

"You're talking about some expensive tests to undertake on a hunch."

"Are you going to do this or not?"

She stared at the notes she had jotted on the legal pad in front of her. "Let me talk with Mr. Kingsley," she said. "I'll call you back."

"I don't think Edward will go for it," Kingsley said.

Paula sat across the desk from him and scanned her notes. "Ben seems pretty confident this would be important information."

"Important for whom? Keep in mind that, for Edward, we're the bad guys. We're trying to put his baby brother in the death chamber. Sometimes Ben goes off in a strange direction simply because it interests him. He has a tendency to take his eyes off the ball. Don't get me wrong. More often than not he finds something useful on one of these tangents, but in this case he may have trouble getting cooperation from Edward."

Cautiously, Paula assembled her mental points. "Earl Torrence is no longer Edward's responsibility. Once he was arrested and placed in jail, he became—for all intents and purposes—a ward of the county."

"A ward of which the county intends to dispose at its first opportunity."

"If, in the opinion of the expert witness you've hired to assist you in frying Junior Torrence, you need information that would support Dr. Long's diagnostic impressions, you are obligated to do everything in your power to obtain that information."

"What would you suggest?"

"That someone speak with Edward. If, as he states, he truly wishes Earl to escape the death chamber, he might want to co-operate with Dr. Long's request."

"A compromise."

She nodded. "In the interest of justice."

Kingsley drummed his fingers on the desktop then turned his chair to stare out the office window. Paula waited patiently. After a minute or two, he turned back to face her.

"If you're looking for some obscure neurological disorder of genetic origin, you don't really need Edward's information. A review of Earl's genetic information and his parents' information should be adequate and sufficient to satisfy Ben's curiosity. We can get the parents' information with a court order. Edward wouldn't have any say in that process. We could bypass him completely. Let's do this. You consult with Edward and see if he'd be willing to allow his records to be included in the court order. If not, we'll go for what we can get without his co-operation."

"Why do I think you'd already thought this through before I came into your office?"

Kingsley steepled his fingers and gazed at her through them. "Probably because you are a bright and perceptive person, who one day will become an excellent lawyer. Will there be anything else?"

"I don't think so. The neurologist is supposed to evaluate Earl tomorrow. We should have some results by the end of the week."

"Very well. Carry on, Paula."

She waited until she was back at her desk to pump her fist in celebration. For the first time since taking the clerkship, she felt like a real attorney.

TWENTY-FOUR

Three days later, Paula met Ben for lunch at Mona Lisa. Ben, as she expected, ordered the *salade nicoise*.

"I think I'll have one of those, too," Paula told the waiter.

Ben raised an eyebrow as the waiter retreated to the kitchen.

"What?" she asked.

"No bistro burger? No pound of grilled flesh?"

"Not today."

"Curious."

She unrolled the silverware from the cloth napkin and arranged it in front of her.

"We got the court order," she told him. "Judge signed it this morning. I should have Earl's parents' records assembled by the end of the day tomorrow. Fortunately, the medical practice they used is still in business."

"They died in a car crash."

"I believe so."

"When Junior was in the seventh grade."

"I don't know the exact date."

"I do. I ran across it in Torrence's school records the other night. The seventh grade would have made Earl Torrence—what?—thirteen years old?"

"Sounds about right."

"Edward is seven years older."

She did some rapid mental calculations. "Yes."

"So he was twenty when he took charge of Earl."

215

"Is there a point here?"

"No other siblings."

"I don't see the significance."

"It's a little odd. Nothing really out of the ordinary, of course. People have widely spaced kids all the time. Makes me wonder why Earl's parents waited seven years after Edward to have him."

"Who knows? Maybe he was a *whoops.*"

"Meaning they intended to stop with Edward and Earl happened along by accident?"

"Yes. Despite the best of intentions, birth control fails, or someone miscounts the days in the month, and the next thing you know you're out shopping for bassinettes."

"Or maybe we should consider the most parsimonious explanation, which is that they decided to wait seven years."

"That happens, too."

He assembled his own silverware on the table. "Edward refused to release his own medical records?"

"He claimed they weren't relevant and if we wanted them we'd have to get a court order. Mr. Kingsley was reluctant to file against Edward since we might need him to provide information on the stand that supports our claims, so we have what we have."

"It will have to do. I received a phone call from Curtis Sorrell. He's worried."

"Why?"

"The findings are not encouraging. He wants to do an MRI."

"What's he looking for?"

"Damage. He thinks things are breaking down in Junior's nervous system. They're arranging for him to be taken to Duke University Medical Center for tests."

The waiter returned with their bread. It was dark brown, and rich in molasses. Paula pulled a piece from the basket and began to butter it.

"The state wastes no expense," she said. "After all, it would be a shame for Junior to drop dead before we have a chance to kill him."

Ben had been reaching for a roll. His hand stopped midway to the basket. "Yes. It would be a shame, wouldn't it?"

"What are you thinking?"

"Nothing more than that. It's curious. Another spiky piece of the puzzle that needs to be smoothed out."

"A little bit of brown that needs to be green?"

"Never quote me to myself," he said as he took a roll from the basket. "What are you doing for Thanksgiving?"

Paula realized that she had been so wrapped up in the case that she had forgotten the holidays were impending. "I hadn't thought about it."

"No family to visit?"

"My parents live in Florida now, in a retirement home."

"No brothers or sisters?"

"One brother. He lives in Italy."

"How charming. You should visit him for Thanksgiving."

"It's Italy. They don't celebrate Thanksgiving. He'll be work-ing."

"I see. Well, in that case, how would you feel about having Thanksgiving dinner at my home?"

She placed the roll on her bread plate. "Why?"

"I don't understand the question."

"Why do you want me to have dinner with you?"

"It seems obvious to me. I'll be alone. You'll be alone. Why should we spend the day by ourselves?"

"My first answer would be because you like to be alone. Are you succumbing a little to the herd mentality?"

"Not at all. I'm being practical. Thanksgiving is a holiday built around the concept of plenty. It is a time for making copious amounts of food. It is efficient to have more than one person to eat it. Less wasteful."

"Aren't you forgetting something?"

"What's that?"

"You don't eat turkey."

He took a bite of the roll. "That's true," he said after swallowing. "On the other hand, neither did the Pilgrims at the first Thanksgiving feast."

"Shooting a deer from the back porch, are we?"

"They aren't in season, and besides they are meat. I do plan to bake a delicious sea bass, with oyster dressing and pumpkin raviolis to go with the traditional vegetables."

She eyed him suspiciously. "You were planning to do all this and eat alone?"

"If I were planning to eat alone, why would I have invited you? In point of fact, I only came up with the dinner menu in the last minute or so, after the idea of inviting you crossed my mind. If you'd rather not . . ."

"It sounds very nice. You are a strange man."

"So you've noted."

"On the other hand, what's Thanksgiving without a feast?"

"So I've noted."

"Why do I get the impression that you've spent more than one Thanksgiving by yourself?"

"Because you are a logical person. People like me are very likely to spend most of their time alone. As you already noted, we like it that way. What say you drop by around five that afternoon?"

"Can I bring anything?"

"Not that I can think of."

The waiter returned to the table with their lunches. Long carefully cut a slice of potato and a slice of the seared tuna and placed them in his mouth. He chewed slowly and deliberately.

"Do you think Edward is hiding something?" Paula asked between bites of her salad. "His refusal to relinquish his medical records seemed more than simple reluctance to assist the prosecution of his brother. He sounded almost vehement about protecting the information."

"If I'm right, Edward has a great deal to hide and more than adequate reason to hide it."

"What do you suspect?"

"I am uncomfortable discussing my suspicions, at least until we have more evidence."

"You think Junior might not have killed Amber?"

"I have modified my view of the world to include that as one of a myriad of possible universes."

"You're beginning to doubt the physical evidence."

"The physical evidence? Not at all. The physical evidence is—while circumstantial—sufficiently damning in my opinion to place Junior at the scene of the crime."

"But not as the murderer."

"Ms. Paige, you are talking about the man your office is actively prosecuting for the murder. I would suspect that it is a bit late for second thoughts."

"That doesn't stop you from having them, though."

"I don't know. The problem still doesn't look right. The more information we gather, the more I can't make the pieces fit together. Sometimes that means that I simply need more data. Sometimes it means my primary assumptions are incorrect."

"Such as the assumption that Junior Torrence committed this murder?"

"That would be one worth examining. On the other hand— and I should caution here that we are now entering the realm of pure conjecture—whether Torrence killed her or not, Amber Coolidge is most decidedly dead. If Junior didn't kill her, who did?"

"Edward?"

"He had an alibi. The sports bar."

"Have you ever been to a sports bar, Ben?"

"Why on earth would I go to a sports bar?"

"They're loud, often smoky, and almost uniformly alcohol-drenched. If someone were to disappear for a half hour, chances are he wouldn't be missed."

"All right. Let's give him opportunity. What about motive? Why on earth would he kill his fiancée?"

"The universal question. People kill their fiancées and spouses all the time. Hell, if a woman is murdered, the automatic prime suspect is her husband."

"You are quoting statistics. They do not constitute motive. If we are to argue that Edward killed Amber, we cannot base our suspicions on the assumption that 'everyone is doing it.' "

"He didn't want to get married?"

"Breaking an engagement seems considerably more pragmatic than murder. Killing your fiancée to avoid a trip down the aisle would appear to be a drastic solution to the problem of potential social embarrassment."

"Maybe you were right in the imaginary story you told Junior. Perhaps Amber was cheating on Edward."

"Unlikely. If she were, I would expect her lover would have surfaced by now, if only to inform the police of the potential motive for Edward killing his paramour."

"Unless he has too much to lose by exposing himself. He might be married."

"Or she," Ben said.

"What?"

"If we are to engage in such flights of fancy, why not go all the way? What if Amber had been cuckolding Edward with another woman?"

Paula speared a string bean with her fork. "I think you're allowing your adolescent fantasies to get the best of you."

"Still, if we wish to ignore the mountain of evidence against Junior and instead entertain the notion that Amber was murdered by Edward, we should at the very least figure out his motive. Opportunity? Maybe. Means? We have the knife of unknown origin. That leaves motive. I can think of only one way to determine what it might have been. I think it's time we had another chat with Edward."

TWENTY-FIVE

Edward Torrence was still in his business suit when he answered the door.

"Mr. Torrence," Paula said. "I'm sorry for barging in on you without calling first, but Dr. Long and I were hoping we could ask you a few questions about Earl."

Edward glanced back and forth at Paula and Ben, then pulled the door all the way open. "Sure, of course. Come on in."

They followed him into the living room. He pointed toward the sofa. "Please, have a seat. Can I get you something to drink?"

"No," Ben said. "Thanks anyway."

"All right, then." Edward sat in an oversized chair across from the sofa. "How can I help you?"

"We've been to see Earl," Ben said. "The evaluation, you know."

"Yes. How is it going?"

"I'm finished."

Edward leaned forward and crossed his forearms on his knees. "What did you find?"

"I still have to analyze the data. I hope to have a report ready by the end of the week. As you are probably aware, I have requested another evaluation by a neurologist."

"Yes. I was told about that by Mr. Crouch."

Paula picked up the discussion. "After Dr. Long finished testing Earl, we had a chance to talk with him about the trial. I was wondering if you could help clear up a few questions we had."

Edward shrugged. "Of course. Anything I can do to help."

"Except release your medical records," Ben said.

"What?"

"Dr. Long," Paula cautioned.

"You said you'd do anything you could to help," Ben continued. "But you refused to allow us to access your medical records."

"I didn't see how they were pertinent. I'm sorry, Dr. Long, but I'm not ready to throw my entire life open for scrutiny. I know the DA can subpoena my records, and I'll do what I can to help Junior, but please allow me to retain some small shred of my dignity."

He stood, took off his suit jacket, and laid it across the back of the chair. "I need a beer."

He walked into the kitchen and returned a moment later with an open bottle. After sitting, he took a long drag from it. His hand trembled under the weight of the bottle.

"That reminds me," Ben said. "The police report indicates that, on the night of the murder, you were in a sports bar, drinking with friends."

"I was in a sports bar, but I was alone."

"Alone?"

"Yes. It was the basketball playoffs. I decided to go to a sports bar to watch the semifinals."

"Not to Amber's apartment?"

"Amber wasn't a basketball fan. She wasn't a sports fan in general. It was one of our few incompatibilities. I suggested coming over that evening, but she said she'd rather not spend several hours watching—as she said—'several pituitary mutants bouncing a ball up and down the court.' "

"Sharp words," Paula said.

"Amber could be very direct."

"You mentioned incompatibilities," Ben said. "Besides sports, what was there?"

"Why do you ask?"

"Because I don't know."

"I mean, what's your motive for asking? How is it relevant to Junior's case?"

"You stated that Earl could not have committed the murder because of his handicap. For the moment let's say that I agree with you. Amber is no less dead. Someone had to have killed her. If it wasn't your brother, then we need to begin examining other potential suspects."

Edward's mouth dropped open. "You don't think—"

"I didn't start this line of conjecture, Mr. Torrence. You maintain the man who confessed to the murder is innocent."

"That confession was retracted!"

"It exists, nevertheless. You maintain your brother is innocent, despite the evidence against him and his own confession to Detective Donnelly. According to your report, you were alone in a sports bar, watching basketball, at the time your fiancée was murdered. The police report indicates you were with friends. This is an inconsistency. You stated that Amber did not share your interest in sports and implied there were other incompatibilities. Incompatibility leads to interpersonal stress. Interpersonal stress leads to conflict. Conflict leads to—"

"Stop it! You're blowing things all out of proportion. All couples have some kind of incompatibility."

"No doubt. What were yours and Amber's, besides sports?"

"None of your damned business. I thought you wanted to talk about Junior and you've turned it into some kind of damned inquisition."

"How did you pay for your drinks at the bar that night?" Ben asked, seemingly unperturbed by Torrence's outrage.

"I think you should leave."

"I was just wondering," Ben continued. "Because if you paid

by credit card, there will be a record of the exact time you paid, which should correspond roughly to the time you left. If that time is before eleven o'clock, I would imagine that Detective Donnelly may wish to ask you a few more questions. Don't bother getting up. We'll let ourselves out."

On the road up to Ben's mountain house, Paula asked, "What do you think?"

"It's curious," Ben said. "I never directly implied Edward killed Amber, yet he became defensive when I asked him about their incompatibilities."

"Do you think he could have murdered her?"

"*Could* have? Of course. Statistically speaking, and as you've already pointed out, most murders are committed by partners, whether married or not. The odds tend to run against him."

"And up to this point, the primary evidence that kept suspicion from falling on him was the police report stating that he had been at the bar with friends."

"Correct. It brings into question the thoroughness of Detective Donnelly's investigation."

"And if Detective Donnelly didn't investigate all possible avenues?"

"Then he may have arrested the wrong person. I was very interested in Edward's defense of his brother."

"Wait! Isn't that sort of an important point, that Junior might have been wrongly arrested?"

"I suppose. It's a legal matter. That's rather outside my area of expertise."

"You aren't convinced?"

"We remain at this time in the realm of conjecture we discussed earlier. Remember, you were the one who introduced the element of doubt with your questions regarding whether Earl Torrence acted with intent. Whether he did or didn't is immaterial if, in the end, he killed Amber. There is substantial evidence to suggest he did. In either case, my role in the case would remain the same—to determine whether Torrence is competent to stand trial for the killing."

"Edward's behavior, though—"

"Could be explained by any number of things. He has endured a great deal of stress for a lengthy period of time. That sort of experience tends to make people irritable. His behavior may mean nothing at all."

"But you kept digging at him."

"I wanted to see how irritated he might become."

"Because you suspect him?"

"No. Just curious."

Paula didn't know what to say, so they rode for a mile or two in silence as she ran the conversation over again in her head.

"He regards Earl as a child," she finally said.

"We haven't established retardation. Remember?"

"I didn't mean he regarded Earl as having the mind of a child. He actually thinks of Earl as *his* child."

"How so?"

"Edward raised Earl from early adolescence. He's provided for all of Earl's needs. He even insists on calling Earl *Junior.* He's acting toward Earl the way any concerned parent might."

"I'm not sure I can see that."

"It isn't easy for me, either, but neither of us are parents. I suppose if I had a son and he was accused of a horrible crime, I'd consider rolling the dice rather than guaranteeing he'd go to prison. Especially now, since I've seen what the prisons are like. Who would want their child to go to a place like that?"

"You're suggesting that after Sid refused Eli Crouch's overtures of a plea bargain, Edward convinced Earl to stop pursuing other avenues, knowing it was a gamble, because he cared about him?"

"Exactly. Doesn't make a lot of sense, I suppose, given the potential risk of a death penalty. Sometimes I'd imagine that rationality and a sense of parental obligation don't go hand in hand."

"No," Ben said. "I don't imagine they do."

TWENTY-SIX

At three-seventeen in the morning on the day before Thanksgiving, Ben sat upright in bed.

He had been awakened by a troubling dream. Normally he would have dismissed it as nothing more than a nocturnal phantasm, rolled over, and gone back to sleep.

This time, however, he realized that his mind had been quietly analyzing all the data on the Earl Torrence case, spurred on by his ongoing sense of discomfort with missing pieces. As the dream progressed, he became aware of a startling change of color in his head, and he concluded that—whatever the dream had uncovered—he needed to act on it.

He rose from bed, dashed to the living room, and wrote down as much as he could recall. He made a note to himself to investigate his hunches the next day, between classes.

When he arrived at his office, there was a voice mail on his telephone from Curtis Sorrell.

He was already running late for class, so he saved the voice mail and rushed back out of his office to his Developmental Psychology students.

When he returned at lunchtime, he found a second voicemail from Sorrell.

He dialed the number and Sorrell answered on the second ring.

"Curt, this is Ben Long."

"Hope I didn't alarm you with the voice mails."

"Not really."

"I wanted to make sure you knew I'd finished the evaluation on your boy Torrence, and I've also received the results of the MRI from Duke University."

"What did you find?"

Sorrell told him.

"This is important," Ben said. "I need you to send me the report overnight. Email me a copy as soon as you've written it. I can't stress to you how important this is. It may explain everything."

"I don't see how."

"Let me worry about that. Will you send it?"

"Sure."

"Thanks, Curt. I have to run. Still have a ton of research to do."

He assembled the notes he'd scribbled at the kitchen table in the blue-black hours, and grabbed a legal pad before dashing across the campus to the main library reference room.

A half-hour later, deep in the stacks, he rooted through drawers full of microfilm rolls. It took him a few minutes to find the strip he needed, even less time to thread it into the reader and start scanning the contents. When he found the reference he needed, he made a quick copy and stashed it in the back of his legal pad.

He left the library and rushed to his office, where he opened a word processor in his computer and started assembling all the data he'd acquired. He included the preliminary findings of his evaluation, the information from the reports by Detective Donnelly and Claudia Flatt, and finally incorporated the information from Curtis Sorrell's neurological assessment and MRI studies.

He checked his watch and realized he was almost late for his

Introductory Psychology class. Before leaving, he picked up the telephone and dialed the law firm.

"What's happened?" Paula asked.

"What makes you think something's happened?"

"Your voice. You sound almost animated. You've finished analyzing the evaluation?"

"Not quite. I'll do that tonight. I have found some important information, and I need one more thing from you. Did you receive the medical records for Earl's parents?"

"They arrived this morning."

"Great. Bring them with you when you come for dinner tomorrow. I need you to get a court order for more medical records."

"What now?"

"Something occurred to me after hearing from Curtis Sorrell. We're not going to find what we need from Earl's parents' records."

"Why not?"

"They died too soon."

"What?"

"I can't explain yet. I need records for Earl's grandparents."

"I don't know—"

"Talk to Sidney. Get him to approach some sympathetic judge, preferably one who knows me. We've done this sort of thing before."

"Which grandparents?"

"Both sides."

"This could take a while."

"You'd better hurry then. If you can get the order today, maybe we can have the records by the first of the week."

"His grandparents?" Kingsley asked.

"That's what Dr. Long said," Paula told him. "He said we

wouldn't get the information we need from Torrence's parents' medical records because they died too soon."

"Now what in hell does that mean?"

"I have no idea. But half the things Ben says make no sense when he says them. They always seem to come together later. Can we get the order?"

"I suppose. There are judges over at the courthouse who'll sign anything you put in front of them. How soon does he need it?"

"He said he'd like to have the records by the first of the week."

"Tomorrow's Thanksgiving. The whole world's closed until Monday. Half the judges probably only scheduled morning sessions today. If I'm going to get an order, I need to hustle over to the courthouse soon, before everyone clears out. Can you draft it right away? I'll make a few calls, see who's available."

"Okay. Also, we received the medical records from Torrence's parents today. Dr. Long wants me to bring them when I go to his house for dinner tomorrow."

"Sure. Just make copies and . . ." Kingsley stopped and looked up from the PDA that he had been scanning for phone numbers of receptive judges. "Did you say dinner?"

Paula stopped at the door. "Yes."

"Tomorrow? Thanksgiving?"

"Yes."

"Well, I'll be damned."

She had the door halfway opened. She closed it gently. "You want to explain that?"

"I suppose it's too much to ask, but I don't imagine he's roasting a turkey, is he?"

"No. Sea bass. What are you getting at?"

Kingsley sat at his desk and rocked his chair back and forth. "This is very interesting. How exactly did he invite you?"

"Do we have time for this?"

"Not really. So give. How'd he invite you?"

She crossed the room but didn't sit. Instead, she stood at the edge of his desk. "He asked whether I had plans for Thanksgiving. I didn't. He didn't. We decided to have dinner together."

Kingsley stroked his chin. "Just like that."

"Yes. Are you implying something? Because I can assure you there's nothing going on."

"Oh, I don't doubt *that.*"

She turned and walked back to the door. She laid her hand on the knob but didn't open it. "I'm trying to decide whether I should be insulted."

He placed his hands behind his head and chuckled as he leaned the chair even farther back. "It's not you, Paula. Ben is acting very much against the grain. I think asking you to join him for dinner for Thanksgiving is about the closest he's come to emotional intimacy since Laura died."

"Don't bet on it. He's gotten intimate a time or two."

She immediately regretted saying it.

Kingsley's eyes narrowed, the way a predator's do upon the first sight of prey. "How do you mean?"

"I'd be betraying a confidence."

"Whose confidence? Ben's?"

"He doesn't know I know."

"You're not talking about Sybil, are you? Jesus, Paula, that was about as non-intimate as you can get."

"I'm not interested in discussing it. I'm sorry I said anything. Can I go? I need to draft the order."

Paula returned from lunch to find a note on her desk from Kingsley. It read "Please see me."

He stood by the bookcase next to his picture window. He had pulled a hefty book from the case and had placed it on a lectern kept there. He'd placed a legal pad on top of the book and seemed to be making notes from one of the citations.

"Have a seat," he said. "I'll only be a second."

She sat in one of the plush leather-upholstered chairs on the client side of his desk and waited. He jotted down some more notes, closed the book, and placed it back on the shelf. Then he crossed the room to his desk and picked up a manila envelope. "Judge Pickens signed the order before lunch."

He handed it across the desk. She grasped it, but he didn't let go.

"Is there a problem?" she asked.

He released the envelope, somewhat self-consciously, and sat in his own chair.

"Maybe. I wanted to apologize for the way I acted this morning. Whatever's going on between you and Ben is your own business."

She started to protest, but he held up a hand to silence her.

"I should also say that—knowing Ben—whatever *is* going on is probably completely innocent and, for that matter, completely chaste. Sorry, bad choice of words. How about businesslike?"

"How about nonexistent? Would you like a clue as to how close he feels to me? I caught him playing piano one evening while I was delivering some reports to him. I asked him if he would consider playing something for me sometime. I thought for a few ridiculous moments he'd say yes, but he blew me off. Sometimes he's infuriating. You've got him nailed, Mr. Kingsley. He has all the emotional depth of a flatworm."

Kingsley smiled. "Gets to you, too, doesn't he?"

"Frankly, most of the time he's intolerable."

"Most of the time?"

"He doesn't make himself easy to like."

"No."

"He's the most self-absorbed man I've ever met."

"Yes. But brilliant."

"Brilliance doesn't excuse bad manners."

Kingsley fiddled with a pen on his desk. "No, I suppose not. I'd imagine that's the way it is when you're dealing with someone who has Asperger's, or perhaps he's King of the Geeks. I don't know. He's my friend. We've known each other for longer than I like to think."

"What's your point?"

"Sometimes friends have to overlook their friends' idiosyncrasies and shortcomings. Sometimes it's a good idea to remember that whenever you point your finger at someone, the other three fingers point back at you."

TWENTY-SEVEN

Ben was at the desk in his office, again examining the data from his tests on Earl Torrence, when he heard a knock at the door.

When he opened it, he found Stanley Claussen, the chair of the university social and behavioral sciences department. Claussen, a retired psychiatrist, was a large, florid man with a thick, graying beard that Ben had always presumed to be some kind of compensation for the lack of hair on his head.

"May I sit?" Claussen asked.

"Of course," Ben said, gesturing toward one of the chairs.

Claussen settled into the chair and seemed to think for a moment or two, as if he weren't certain how to start.

"Is there a problem?" Ben asked.

"You have a student. Sarah Ashburton. I was wondering if you could take a moment to describe your relationship with her."

"Why? Is there some question of propriety?"

"Humor me."

Ben understood humoring people. He hated it, but he understood it. It was one more accommodation that the neurotypicals expected.

"She's in my Abnormal section. She came to me a couple of months ago with a personal concern. I referred her to a colleague, and she subsequently attempted to harm herself and was hospitalized."

"I see," Claussen said. "Then she came back to school?"

"Yes. She showed up back in class a week or so ago, after her release from the hospital. She was still within the administrative withdrawal period for her coursework. I suggested she could either take an Incomplete or I'd approve an administrative withdrawal for her and indicate she was passing. She insisted on completing her coursework, so I allowed her to make up her missing tests. She also completed her term paper."

"How did she do? On the tests and the term paper?"

"Quite well. Is there a problem?"

"That is the extent of your relationship with Ms. Ashburton?"

"I visited her when she was in the hospital. Otherwise, yes. What is this about?"

Claussen cleared his throat. "Well, then, this is difficult. It seems that Ms. Ashburton got into an argument with her parents last night. Something about her medications."

"She was on serotonin-selective reuptake inhibitors for relief of anxiety," Ben said.

"Yes. So I understand. Her parents, it seems, have little regard for medications."

"They have religious objections. Sarah doesn't share them."

"That seems to have been the basis for the argument. I'm sure your involvement with her is exactly as you've described it, Ben, but I had to ask. In light of . . . well . . ."

He pulled a folded sheet of paper from his jacket pocket and offered it to Ben, who took it and opened it. It was a copy of a handwritten note.

This isn't fair to anyone. I wish I knew another way, but I can't deal with this anymore. I'm sorry. Please tell Dr. Long that he is in no way to blame for this. He has been completely sweet about me and my problems through all this. I hope that you will forgive me, and that God will forgive me and accept me into His presence.

Ben read the note over twice then handed it back to Claussen.

"She tried to hurt herself again," Ben said.

Claussen said, "The, ah, medication she was taking is remarkable, almost a miracle drug. Good for what ails you, psychiatrically speaking. There's one drawback. It increases physical energy before it reduces depressive and suicidal thoughts. Give it to a suicidal young girl with low energy and poor motivation to follow through on her impulses and, before she stops considering harming herself, she will find the energy to actually make an attempt. That's why the manufacturers have strongly urged doctors to enlist the aid of patients' families to monitor for potential suicide during the first month or so of medication. Sarah's parents, due to their disregard for medications in general and—I'd suspect—their religious repugnance for suicide, probably didn't watch Sarah all that closely. Instead, they imposed their values on her and condemned her for doing the one thing that probably could have prevented her from harming herself."

"Yes," Ben said. "I've seen it before. Is she hospitalized again? Can I visit her?"

"I'm afraid, Ben, that this attempt was somewhat more tragically successful than her first one. By the time the ambulance arrived at her house, she had lost a great deal of blood. They administered a transfusion at the hospital, but she had lost most of her platelets—the clotting factor, you know."

"Yes." Ben knew what was coming but dreaded it.

"She, ah, couldn't clot. The body has remarkable systems, but it tends to react badly when the platelets are depleted. She started bleeding internally. There was really nothing the doctors could do."

"I see."

"You understand why I had to ask about your relationship

with her, don't you? A note like this could raise questions."

"I understand completely. You were perfectly correct to ask."

"I haven't heard about the arrangements. When I do, I'll be certain to let you know. I'm sorry, Ben. It's hard to lose a student this way."

"Yes," Ben said. "Thank you, Dr. Claussen."

Claussen stood, placed a hand on Ben's shoulder, then left the room, closing the door as he walked out.

Ben sat at his desk for a long time, staring at the wall and trying to sort everything in his head.

TWENTY-EIGHT

When Paula arrived at Ben's house on Thanksgiving Day, he answered the door wearing a plaid flannel shirt, jeans, and a ridiculous-looking Pilgrim hat.

"Where on earth did you get that?" she asked as she walked through the door.

"The shirt? J.C. Penney's."

"The hat."

"Been in the family for generations. Can I get you a glass of wine? I have a wonderful pinot grigio that will go perfectly with the sea bass. There's no harm in trying a little taste now, though."

"Well, since you twisted my arm. Where can I put my coat?"

He took it from her and hung it meticulously in the entry hall closet. Then he walked to the kitchen and poured wine from an already opened bottle into a glass. After he handed it to her, she crossed the living room to the sliding glass door and looked over the mountains.

"Such a lovely view," she said. "I can't imagine how you ever dredge up the strength to leave this house and go to work in the morning. If I lived here, I'd lie on the sofa and look out the window all day."

"That's silly," Ben said, sitting in the chair next to the fireplace. "They'd foreclose on you eventually."

"I was speaking figuratively."

"As I surmised. And, as you already know, I am impervious

to figurative speech. Tell me, did you get the court order for the grandparents' medical records?"

She grimaced. "It's Thanksgiving."

"Yes."

"That makes it a holiday. On this planet, people don't work on holidays."

"It was a small question."

"Then I'll give you a small answer. Yes. You should have the records by Monday. Change the subject."

He looked confused. It occurred to Paula that changing the subject could be a considerable task. Multitasking didn't appear to be Ben Long's forte.

"Tell me about dinner," she said, giving him a hint.

"Ah, dinner. Yes. The sea bass was flown in from Ecuador—or perhaps Chile—only yesterday. I know a man who owns a restaurant supply house. He provides fresh fish to most of the top-shelf bistros in the western part of the state. This particular specimen is approximately eight pounds."

"Eight pounds of fish? How many people are coming for dinner?"

He seemed confused again. "Just the two of us."

"Good," she said. "I was worried. The best part of Thanksgiving dinner is the leftovers. I can't wait for lunch tomorrow. Maybe a baked sea-bass sandwich, or maybe some nice sea-bass salad."

"Why do I think you're chiding me?" Ben said as he retreated to the kitchen.

"Oh! I know! Sea-bass tetrazzini!"

She took a sip of the wine and looked out over the landscape again. The sky was a brilliant Carolina Tarheels blue, the air swept clean by a Canadian high-pressure system that had jetted through the state the night before. She was certain that she could see for thirty miles or more, before the smoky mists of the Blue Ridge enveloped the mountains like a sheer curtain.

"Say," she called out. "I don't suppose your family passed down any of those old Puritan bonnets, did they? I'd hate to feel underdressed."

He didn't reply.

She walked into the kitchen.

"Anything I can do to help?" she asked, and then stopped.

Ben stood at the sink, holding a nine-inch carving knife. He had been chopping onions for the oyster stuffing. Now he stood rigid, staring at the keenly honed edge of the blade.

"What is it?" she asked.

He looked at her but didn't answer. His eyes glistened with moisture.

"Dr. Long, you're scaring me."

He looked back down at the knife. "I remember," he said. "Anson Mount stabbed me. I couldn't recall it for a very long time. Not amnesia, exactly. Something about blood loss, anoxic brain trauma, something. I remembered, though. Later."

"What's happened?"

"He stabbed me. It took a long time, but I finally remembered the sensation of the blade slipping inside my skin, scraping against my rib. You'd think it would feel cold, wouldn't you? It burned. Burned like acid."

"Come sit down."

He held the knife up and stared past it to her face. A lone tear escaped the corner of his eye and coursed down his cheek.

"What am I doing?" he said. Then he placed the knife on the counter and walked past her to the sliding door. He yanked it open and leaned against the deck railing. He gulped several great breaths of the frigid mountain air.

She walked up behind him and placed her hands around his shoulders.

Immediately, he threw up his arms and shrieked. She drew

her hands back reflexively. He clasped his head and rocked back and forth, his eyes squeezed tightly shut and his face locked in a tortured grimace.

She wrapped her arms around herself, backed away to a safe distance, and waited for him at the door. After a few moments he lowered his hands and turned toward her.

"I turned her away. She came to me for help, and I sent her to someone else."

"Your student?"

"Sarah. I thought she was better. She came back to class after she got out of the hospital. She was doing well in class. I never thought . . . never *considered* that she might . . ."

Paula stood a foot away from him. Even so, she could almost feel him stiffen, as if repulsed by human contact.

"What happened to Sarah?"

He took another gigantic breath and exhaled it as a sigh. "She killed herself," he said. "With a blade. Slit her wrists. She told me when she was in the hospital that she had learned how to do it the right way. I never imagined that she meant she would get it right the next time."

"Oh, my God," Paula whispered. "I'm so sorry."

"I remember how it felt. It burned. Anson Mount stabbed me first. Then he tried to rob Laura and she tried to fight him off. I lay on the ground, bleeding from four different wounds, and watched as he went after her with the knife. She fell right next to me. I heard the breath go out of her."

"It was terrible," Paula said quietly.

"Amber Coolidge, killed with a knife. Laura. Sarah Ashburton. I was standing in the kitchen, slicing onions, and I watched the blade as it slid through the skin, and I *felt* it again."

"Come inside," she said. "Tell me what to do. I'll prepare the food." She reached out again, gently and carefully placed a single hand on his elbow, pulled against his weight gently. He yielded, stiffly, and followed her back into the living room. She shut the sliding door.

"Excuse me," he said. He pulled away from her, crossed the house to his bedroom door, and closed it behind him.

She waited in the chair next to the fireplace. After about ten minutes, the door opened and he reappeared. His face was flushed, but his eyes were clear.

"I'm sorry. Can't imagine what came over me. Fatigue, maybe. So much work. Thank you for offering to help in the kitchen, but I couldn't allow it. You're a guest. Please, make yourself comfortable. Have another glass of wine. Dinner should be ready in an hour."

"Can I turn on the TV?"

"Whatever for?"

"It's Thanksgiving," she said. "Football."

"Football. Yes. I suppose that's only right. There should be football on Thanksgiving. Yes. By all means. Turn on the television."

He returned to the kitchen. Paula watched as he disappeared around the corner. She realized, as she sipped her wine and watched the Cowboys take on the Vikings, that—for perhaps the first time, and for however brief a moment—she had seen Ben Long behave like a real human being.

Like a *neurotypical.*

She wondered if she would ever see it again.

Twenty-Nine

Sarah Ashburton had lived with her parents in a three-bedroom frame house in Weaverville, a small town to the west of Asheville. The house was quaint, in no way ornate, and was reached by way of a gravel driveway from a quiet neighborhood street. Two small dogs lazed on the front porch.

The skies were leaden overhead. The air was damp and cold. The house sat, austere and forbidding, as Ben reached for the doorbell.

The door opened almost immediately. A doughy woman in her late forties peered at him through the screen door. Her shoulder-length hair fell limply around her plump cheeks. She wore a simple black dress and opaque black stockings. Her eyes were bloodshot.

"Mrs. Ashburton?"

"Yes."

"My name is Ben Long. I'm an assistant professor at the university. Sarah was one of my students."

"The man in the note."

"That's correct. I was informed by my department chair that you weren't planning a funeral for Sarah."

She opened the screen door.

"Would you like to come inside?"

Ben stepped across the threshold.

"My name is Kate," she said, extending her hand.

"I'm sorry to meet you under these circumstances," he said,

but didn't take her hand or meet her eyes.

"Please, have a seat."

The inside of the house was warm and inviting, in sharp contrast to the exterior. There was a scent of allspice in the air. Ben noted the lack of Christmas decorations, even though it was almost the first of December. He couldn't recall whether Christian Scientists celebrated Christmas.

"Sarah's father, Nate, isn't home. He had to go to Black Mountain. He should be back in an hour or so," she said.

Nate and Kate, Ben noted, with no particular humor. One of life's little tricks of fate. She seemed to know what he was thinking.

"We've heard all the jokes. Can I get you anything to drink? Some water? Perhaps some juice?"

"Nothing for me, thank you. As I said, I heard you wouldn't be having a funeral, and I wanted to drop by to . . ."

"Pay your respects?"

"Not exactly," he said. "I thought about it and it seemed I should visit."

"What do you know about our religion, Dr. Long?"

"Practically nothing."

"We don't have preachers or priests or parsons. We don't have a traditional church. Some people, I suppose, find Christian Science to be overly dogmatic, but a great deal of our observance is left up to individual preference. How we deal with death, for instance."

She had remained standing while he sat, and she crossed the living room to the fireplace mantel. She lifted a small wooden box and returned to the sofa, where Ben sat uncomfortably. She placed the box on the coffee table in front of him.

"Sarah," she said, nodding toward the box as she sat next to him. "We had her cremated. It's the preferred method."

"Oh." He stared at the simple basswood box. It didn't seem

real. He found it appallingly difficult to reconcile in his mind that the contents of this undecorated container had sat in his office only days earlier, begging to be allowed to finish his course. The concept was too other-worldly for him to get his head around it.

"What did she mean?" Kate Ashburton asked. "In her note she said you weren't to blame for what she did."

"Yes. The note. I suppose—at least in a way—this somehow comes under the issue of confidentiality. On the other hand, she is gone, and it is a fair question. I talked with Sarah several times over the last month or so. As I told you, she was a student in my class. She came to me several weeks ago, very frightened. She asked me for help with a problem she had. I didn't feel I could help her, so I sent her to another therapist. Shortly after that, she tried to kill herself."

"The first time."

"That's right. I visited her in the hospital. I told her that I felt responsible for what happened. Because I had sent her away."

"It's hard to understand our ways," Kate said. "Why we don't use medicine or therapists or modern medical technology."

"Yes."

"When she came to you to ask for help, she was violating one of our most fundamental beliefs."

"She told me that you didn't believe in psychiatric drugs."

"*Any* drugs. Our beliefs are strong. We are not against medicines. We have nothing against pharmaceuticals, in terms of their existence. We simply don't believe they are necessary."

"But if someone is ill—"

"There is no illness. Sickness is an illusion."

"I don't understand."

She patted his hand. He fought the urge to draw it away.

"I know," she said. "It's difficult. Several moments ago, I

presented Sarah to you."

"The box."

"Sarah. She's there. She was here as a baby and as a child and as a teenager, and now she's here as this box of ashes. And, in all those instances, she was nothing but an illusion. Do you believe that we are nothing except ideas in the mind of God?"

"No," Ben said, perhaps more quickly than he intended.

"Then we are immediately at philosophical odds, Dr. Long. Because we believe illness doesn't exist, any more than *we* exist. Being ideas in the mind of God means illness is nothing more than a failing of faith, a moral lapse perhaps, but certainly not *real*. We believe matter is not real, so maladies of the matter are not real. So, Sarah is *here*. It's just her matter that has changed."

"I'm trying to understand. Dr. Claussen—my department chair at the university—told me that Sarah became upset because you condemned her use of the psychiatric medications the hospital prescribed."

"Condemned? Perhaps your Dr. Claussen misunderstood. We would never condemn Sarah or anything she did. We don't even condemn her for what she did to herself. She—all of us—are completely free to act as we feel is right in these matters. Sarah clearly decided that taking medication was the right thing to do. She ignored our beliefs that medications are nothing but palliatives and that the only true cure comes from The Lord. That was sad, but *condemn?* No. We did urge her to stop using the drugs and allow herself to be visited by a Practitioner, but she refused."

"Her note said she couldn't take it anymore."

"Yes. She wasn't talking about her relationship with her father and me. We tend to think she just wasn't strong enough in her faith to allow The Lord to come inside and heal her." Kate reached across the sofa and placed her hand on his arm. "As for you, Dr. Long, I'm sure what she wrote was absolutely true.

What happened wasn't your fault. Perhaps it was ours, for not instilling our faith strongly enough in Sarah. We have to live with that. Sarah's death isn't the true tragedy here, though we loved her dearly and will miss her tremendously. The real tragedy may be that her father and I are left to spend the rest of our lives doubting whether we did right by Sarah. The only cure is to place ourselves in The Lord's hands and hope that He will see fit to take that pain away."

Ben still couldn't take his gaze from the box.

"Of course," she added, "There's always the possibility that you came here to do more than offer your condolences."

"I want to understand why she did it."

"Killed herself, you mean?"

"That's right."

"It's very painful. We view suicide very solemnly. It's a denial of everything we believe. If matter is an illusion, and illness is an illusion, then the act of self-destruction is a denial and rejection of the God that conceives us. It's a denial of faith. Perhaps that's what Sarah meant when she said she couldn't take it anymore. Maybe she couldn't stand to be so far from God."

"She seemed to be doing better."

"By using drugs," Kate argued. "By denying that the true power to heal was God's alone. She gave up on God and turned instead to the medicines. I can't claim to understand what went through my daughter's head, Dr. Long. It seems to me, though, that if she thought the drugs made her feel better, then it could have only strengthened her denial of her faith. That's a terrible loss."

"You're saying because she felt better she felt worse?"

"Doesn't make a lot of sense, does it?"

"No. I'm afraid not."

"I wouldn't expect it to, for someone not brought up in the faith."

Ben sat quietly for a moment. Finally, he stood slowly. "I'm very sorry for your loss," he said, somewhat perfunctorily. "I liked Sarah. She was an excellent student and she had a quick mind. I will miss her."

"Thank you," Kate said.

"I also suspect you spend a great deal of your life dealing with people who don't understand you."

"Oh, yes. We're quite used to that."

"Me, too. Perhaps Sarah understood that. Perhaps that was what led her to come to me for help."

Kate led him to the door, thanked him again for coming, and closed the door behind him.

Ben stood on the porch, looking out into the dreary, misting rain, and the muted light that turned everything in his sight gray.

As he stepped from the porch, he heard a tortured sob from inside the house.

THIRTY

When Ben returned to the school, he found a package waiting for him at the main desk. It had been sent by courier from Sid Kingsley's office. Ben recognized Paula's handwriting on the label.

He took the package to his office and opened it quickly. It took him a little under an hour to digest the contents of the medical records and to make a page and a half of notes on his legal pad.

Then he picked up the telephone and called Paula.

"You received the package," she said.

"Yes. Very interesting materials. I think we're ready."

"You can write your report now?"

"Yes. I think that it would be a good idea to schedule the competency hearing. The sooner the better. You can be assured that Sybil is deep into her own assessment of Torrence. We shouldn't allow her to get too prepared. She can be a considerable adversary in court."

Five days later, Ben walked into Sidney Kingsley's office with a folder of papers under his arm. Kingsley was waiting for him.

"Are we ready, Ben?" he asked.

"Ready? Of course. I wouldn't have asked for the hearing otherwise. Will Ms. Paige be joining us?"

"Would you like her here?"

Ben stared at him for a moment, as if to question whether his previous answer hadn't made it clear that he would only have asked if he had wanted her present.

"Of course," Kingsley said. "I'll bring her in."

He stepped outside the office and returned moments later with Paula. By then, Ben had sat in one of the leather-covered, button-and-tuck chairs on the visitors' side of Kingsley's desk. Paula joined him in the other chair. Kingsley returned to his seat.

"We may have a problem," he announced. "They've assigned Judge Crumpler to the Torrence case."

"I don't understand," Paula said. "Why would that be a problem?"

"Crumpler doesn't like me," Ben said.

Kingsley said, "I wouldn't go that far."

"He doesn't like me," Ben repeated. "I must admit that I'm not very fond of him either."

"More than that," Kingsley elaborated, "Judge Crumpler is a holdover from the sixties. He's not a law-and-order type. He would have found mitigating circumstances in the Lincoln assassination."

"There *were* mitigating circumstances in the Lincoln assassination," Ben countered.

"Ben . . ." Kingsley started, and then caught himself. "In any case, Crumpler's record for finding criminal defendants incompetent to stand trial is approaching legend. I would rather have drawn any other Superior Court judge."

"To paraphrase a national figure," Ben said. "You go into the court with the judge you have, not the judge you want. We will simply have to make do."

"That we will," Kingsley said. "That we will."

An hour later, the three walked into the courtroom. Contrary to the ornate chambers common on television, this courtroom was austere. The traditional judge's bench and witness stand had been erected at the front, but otherwise the room was somewhat ordinary. The walls were painted in neutral beige, and the two tables facing the bench were blonde maple. The gallery was only two rows deep. The seats in the gallery were plain wooden auditorium chairs with fold-down seats. Absent were rich walnut panels or high palladian windows or even a bailiff. The room had been designed for administrative hearings only.

When Kingsley, Ben, and Paula entered the courtroom, they found Sybil Rock already seated at one of the tables facing the bench, with Eli Crouch. Sybil and Crouch turned briefly at the sound of the doors opening. Crouch nodded in Kingsley's direction and smiled at Ben. Then, without a word, Crouch and Sybil turned back to the papers in front of them.

The gallery was almost deserted, save for Detective Donnelly, Edward Torrence, and a tall, broad, black man whom Paula had never met, but whose name she recognized.

A court reporter arrived next and sat to the right of the judge's bench. She extracted a cassette tape from the drawer, took it from its cellophane wrap, and inserted it into a recording machine in front of her. Then she disappeared into the chambers behind the bench, presumably to inform Judge Crumpler that everything was ready for the hearing.

Paula turned briefly to glance at Edward Torrence. He looked a little bewildered. His cheeks were flushed and the redness flooded down to the sides of his neck.

Kingsley, Paula, and Ben sat at the second table between the gallery and bench. Paula looked over at Ben, who seemed placid, almost tranquilized.

"You aren't nervous?" she asked.

"No. I've done this before. Besides, this should be fun."

"Fun?"

"Yes."

"What are you up to?" she whispered. "What's this all about?"

"The unresolved seventh," he replied.

She started to ask what he meant, then noticed he was smiling slyly. It wasn't a look she had seen on his face before. It was a bit unnerving.

At that moment, the door behind the bench opened and the court reporter returned to her desk. Immediately after, Judge Crumpler entered from his chambers. Everyone stood until he was seated.

He was a tall, lean man with a high forehead and unruly silver hair that fell in small ringlets over his ears. He wore thick glasses over a sharp, aquiline nose and thin lips. His eyes were watery blue and piercing.

He announced the case number then added, "Earl Torrence, Junior."

Sidney Kingsley spoke first. "If it please the court to recap the status of this case: Earl Torrence was charged with the murder of Amber Coolidge in her apartment. Detective Donnelly extracted a confession from him, which Torrence later recanted. Mr. Torrence requested the opportunity to enter into a plea agreement, which the State refused, under the circumstances of Mr. Torrence's recanting of his confession. Subsequently, his attorney, Mr. Crouch, asserted that the defendant might not be competent to stand trial.

"A month ago, I asked Dr. Benjamin Long to complete a psychological evaluation on Earl Torrence, to determine whether the defendant is mentally handicapped or otherwise unfit to face charges or assist in his defense. I've asked Dr. Long to present his findings here today, so that we can discuss our procedural options. Mr. Crouch has enlisted the services of Sybil Rock, another psychologist, who has conducted her own evaluation of Mr. Torrence. We are here today to determine whether Mr. Torrence is competent to proceed to trial."

"I was under the impression that Dr. Long had retired from active practice," Crumpler said.

"He had," Kingsley replied. "I was able to convince him to return for this one case."

"I see. Well, then, since they filed the motion, I'll hear first from the defense."

"Defense calls Sybil Rock to the stand," Crouch said.

"I administered the Wechsler Adult Intelligence Scale, the Vineland Adaptive Behavior Scale, and conducted a review of Mr. Torrence's academic and behavioral history," Sybil said.

"And what did you find?" Eli Crouch asked.

"Mr. Torrence scored an IQ of sixty-four on the Wechsler, and his responses on the Vineland indicated significant deficits in four of eight critical areas identified by the American Psychiatric Association as prerequisites for a diagnosis of mental retardation."

"And your own diagnostic impression?"

"I believe that Mr. Torrence qualifies under the criteria set forward by the APA for mental retardation."

"What about his ability to assist in his defense?"

Sybil made a show of consulting her notes. "Mr. Torrence has very limited memory of the events that took place on the night of the murder. In addition, while he appears to understand being incarcerated because he is accused of killing Amber Coolidge, he does not appear to understand the processes that will be used in the court. As he cannot recall the specifics of the killing, it is my belief that he will have a difficult time assisting in his own defense. Further, his apparent mental retardation provides a reasonable probability that he would not relate the crime and its potential punishment, due to the substantial lapse in time between the two. In my opinion, under the M'Naghten standards, Mr. Torrence is not competent to stand trial at this time."

"Thank you, Dr. Rock," Eli Crouch said, and settled back in his chair.

Judge Crumpler swiveled his chair to face Kingsley. "Any questions?"

"None at this time," Kingsley said, barely looking up from his notes. "Reserve the option of cross-examining Dr. Rock at a later time."

"Noted. You may step down, Dr. Rock. Mr. Crouch, do you intend to call any further witnesses?"

"No, your Honor."

"Very well. Mr. Kingsley?"

Kingsley arranged the papers in front of him and glanced over at Ben. "State calls Dr. Benjamin Long."

Moments later, Ben settled into the witness box. After being sworn, he pulled a sheaf of papers from a folder and turned to Judge Crumpler.

"I have brought copies of my *curriculum vitae,* should the court wish to examine them."

"What on earth for?" Crumpler asked.

"I believe that was the practice when I last appeared in court four years ago. To establish my credentials as an expert."

"I see," Crumpler said. "In this case, Dr. Long, I would say that your *vitae* were vetted quite some time ago. I think we can forego that particular formality."

Kingsley checked his notes again and then launched into his questions. "Dr. Long, could you define mental retardation for the benefit of the Court?"

Ben addressed Judge Crumpler much the way he would have started one of his college classes.

"The *Diagnostic and Statistical Manual of Mental Disorders* of the American Psychiatric Association contains no fewer than three conditions that must be met in order to confirm the diagnosis of mental retardation. First, the person must score below seventy on a standardized test of intelligence. Second, the person must demonstrate significant deficits in at least two out of seven specific adaptive skill areas, such as communication, safety, health, self-care, or work. Finally, the condition must have begun before the age of eighteen."

"What if the condition began after the age of eighteen? Say, as a result of a stroke or a head injury—something causing damage to the brain?"

"If a person sustains a traumatic head injury after age eighteen, and that injury damages the right frontal lobes, resulting in an inability to engage in abstract reasoning, and that inability leads to a score below seventy on a standardized intelligence test, that person is not retarded. Unless, of course, it can be demonstrated clearly that he also would have tested below seventy before the age of eighteen, and before he was injured.

"Even when it appears that the retardation existed prior to age eighteen, it may be difficult to prove. There is a statistical construct intended to explain naturally occurring variations in individual scores that can be produced by factors like fatigue, irritation, emotional distress, and the like. Any one of us, if given a standard IQ test ten times, would be likely to produce ten different scores. However, ninety-five times out of a hundred, those scores would fall in a fairly discrete range, usually somewhere around eight points in either direction of an average of all the scores."

"But we don't give people IQ tests ten times," Kingsley clarified.

"Quite true. And that's why we use this standard error of measurement. Using highly refined statistics, we predict the range of scores an individual might produce if he were administered the same test a number of times."

"Dr. Long, did you conduct a standardized test of Earl Torrence?"

"I did. I conducted the same tests that Dr. Rock used, in addition to one or two others. I also requested and obtained an evaluation of Mr. Torrence by a neuropsychologist and neurologist from Chapel Hill."

"And, in your opinion," Kingsley said, his voice suddenly stressed—since he knew what was coming, "Is Earl Torrence mentally retarded or is he not?"

"Earl Torrence *is* retarded," Long said. "And he *isn't.*"

The room exploded with protests. Judge Crumpler turned red in the face and threatened to hold Kingsley, Ben, and everyone else in the room in contempt. Eli Crouch took to his feet and demanded that Ben's statement be stricken. Sybil grabbed his arm and attempted to calm Crouch down. Edward Torrence stood and demanded to know from Kingsley exactly what kind of psychologist he had employed. The poor court reporter attempted vainly to capture the comments as they flew from one end of the table to the other, and finally gave up, crossed her arms, and waited for the conflict to subside.

Through it all, the tall, broad black man smiled and watched the conflagration. He seemed to be enjoying himself.

For that matter, Paula noted, Ben seemed unusually peaceful, sitting in the witness stand as if waiting for a chance to clarify.

Soon everyone seemed to run out of gas, and the room quieted by degrees. Ben glanced down at his papers and around the room.

"May I expand on my diagnosis?" he asked.

"No!" Judge Crumpler commanded from the bench. "I'm

calling a fifteen-minute recess. I want to see both counsels and our *experts* in my chambers."

Judge Crumpler lowered himself into the chair behind the desk in his chambers and stared stonily across it at Kingsley, Crouch, Ben, Sybil, and the large black man whom Ben had asked to attend the meeting.

"Four years," the judge said. "For four peaceful, blissful years, I have managed to keep my court running smoothly. In my opinion, this is attributable largely to Dr. Long's retirement. Now, in a matter of moments, you have managed, Dr. Long, to toss my court into chaos. What do you have to say for yourself?"

"This is a Schrödinger's Cat case."

"A *what* case?"

"In the early twentieth century, physicists were confounded by separate experiments that appeared to show that sometimes light acted like a wave and sometimes it acted like particles. Erwin Schrödinger, one of the early quantum theorists, offered an allegory to explain this conflict. It went something like this: We place a living cat into a box, along with a container of cyanide gas. There is a very small amount of a highly unstable radioactive substance in the box. If a single atom of this substance decays, a relay mechanism will break the container of gas. We cannot know whether or not an atom of the substance has decayed, since it is extremely unstable and can decay in a second, or in a thousand years, so we also cannot know whether the gas has been released. For that reason, we don't know whether the cat is dead or alive. The only way to know is to look. According to Schrödinger, until you look, the cat is dead *and* alive."

"You wouldn't happen to have one of those boxes handy, would you?"

"What does this have to do with Earl Torrence?" Crouch asked.

"Simply this," Ben continued. "It appears that whether your client is retarded depends on when and how you test him."

"No, it doesn't," Crumpler said. "I see where you're going with this, Dr. Long, and it won't work in my court. You want to use this standard error of measurement mumbo-jumbo to confound the court and turn Torrence into some kind of test case challenging the state's definition of retardation. You want to blur the lines separating retarded from not retarded."

"Not exactly. Strictly speaking, that line is already blurry enough. Please, if you'd allow me to continue."

He waited. In the absence of a challenge, he returned to his presentation. "I met with Earl Torrence on several occasions at the Henderson County Jail. I administered a standard mental status exam, during which I noted several symptoms that—taken by themselves—were not terribly suspicious. As a symptom cluster, however, they raised some serious questions.

"Based on these symptoms, I requested copies of Earl's school records. As I suspected, he was labeled as early as kindergarten with having a condition called 'minimal brain dysfunction.' We know this condition today as attention-deficit disorder.

"However, he was also diagnosed at one point in his school years with a receptive language disorder. In simplest terms, he doesn't completely understand what is said to him. The language centers of the brain—for whatever reason—don't work the same way in Earl's head as they do in ours.

"Then, in the middle of administering Earl Torrence's IQ test, I observed him to have a *petit mal* seizure. I completed the test and requested a neuropsychological examination by Curtis Sorrell, a specialist in the field from the University of North Carolina at Chapel Hill. Dr. Sorrell?"

The black gentleman who had sat quietly to that point, and had seemed so amused at the outburst in the courtroom moments earlier, opened a folder. He scanned the faces around the room as he removed a sheaf of papers.

"As Dr. Long indicated, my name is Curtis Sorrell. I am a neuropsychologist on the faculty at UNC–Chapel Hill. I also have an M.D. with a residency in neurology from Duke University. I will be happy to provide my *vitae* for review if it becomes necessary."

"I object!" Crouch interjected. "This witness hasn't been sworn in. His testimony can't—"

"Shush, Eli," Crumpler said. "This is an informal meeting in my chambers. I want to hear what this man has to say. If it seems important, we'll let him tell us all of it again under oath in the courtroom. Go on, Dr. Sorrell."

"Dr. Long asked me to conduct an evaluation of Earl Torrence, after observing what he described as a *petit mal* seizure in the course of testing Mr. Torrence. I met with Mr. Torrence and conducted a Halstead-Reitan test battery. This is a wide-spectrum diagnostic tool intended to narrow down specific neurological disorders, with the goal of finding the exact cause or location of brain disorders.

"I determined that Earl Torrence demonstrated symptoms of a degenerative central nervous system disorder, and I ordered a series of tests at Duke University Hospital."

"Wait, wait," Crouch said. "Could you define 'degenerative central nervous system disorder' for us? I'm just an old country boy and sometimes I can't follow these big medical words."

"Of course," Sorrell said. "The central nervous system, simply put, is the brain and spinal cord. It was my concern that Earl Torrence's brain and spinal cord are deteriorating."

"There are a great many conditions that can cause this deterioration," Sorrell continued. "In order to pin down a specific diagnosis, I ordered a series of tests, including a magnetic resonance imaging, a CT scan, and certain genetic panels.

"As Dr. Long indicated, the tests conducted indicated that Mr. Torrence has a receptive language disorder. Receptive language—that is, hearing and such—is centered in the temporal lobe of the brain, specifically the left side of the brain, roughly between the temple and the area behind the ear. The MRI showed severe atrophy in the left temporal lobe. This would explain his language problems. People with damage to the left temporal lobe also tend to exhibit a poor memory for verbal material. This would almost certainly affect Torrence's performance on the verbal portion of the intelligence test.

"Further, we found genetic evidence of a condition called hereditary ataxia."

"What was that?" Crouch asked Sybil. "What kind of tax did he say?"

"Ataxia," Sybil repeated. "Not *tax*."

"What in the hell is that?"

"It's a description of a set of symptoms," Sorrell said. "The word itself is from the Greek, for 'without order or coordination.' Ataxia can take many forms, from simple deficits in fine motor control, such as the ability to thread a needle, or all the way to paralysis, as in the case of Lou Gehrig's disease."

"What does that have to do with competence to stand trial?" Judge Crumpler asked.

"There are forms of hereditary ataxia that affect the way the brain operates on tasks measured with intelligence tests. In Mr. Torrence's case, genetic testing indicated a specific form of ataxia, called spino-cerebellar ataxia."

"What does that mean?"

"Spino refers to the spinal cord, cerebellar refers to a large portion of the brain associated with motor control and coordination. Mr. Torrence's condition indicates damage to both the brain and the spinal cord. This damage is progressive, which means it will become worse over time."

"How bad?" Kingsley asked.

"The type of spino-cerebellar ataxia indicated by Mr. Torrence's genetic tests is ultimately fatal. Whether imprisoned or not, Mr. Torrence is living under a death sentence. A review of his school records shows that his earliest symptoms probably began to manifest around the first grade, perhaps a little earlier. He's now just shy of his twenty-seventh birthday. At the current rate of deterioration, I'd estimate there is little chance he will live to forty."

"I took the liberty of obtaining a court order for medical records of Earl Torrence's parents and grandparents," Ben said. "Earl's parents died in an automobile accident when he was fourteen. They were in their late thirties. There is no way to assess whether they had the type of ataxia indicated by Earl's genetic tests, but we know from research that they had to each carry the gene. This specific type of ataxia only manifests itself in children of parents who both carry the gene. If only one parent carries the gene, the children will only become carriers. I did check records from Earl's grandparents, and found that Earl's maternal grandfather died of 'a wasting disease.' At that time, we didn't have much in the way of genetic testing, so the doctor didn't have a name for the disorder."

"What are you saying?" Crouch interrupted. "Are you implying that Earl Torrence wasn't originally mentally retarded, but is retarded now because of this ataxia thing?"

"Not exactly. It's a little more complicated than that. As I said, Torrence had a seizure in the middle of his intelligence test. This particular type of seizure is called *petit mal*, or sometimes an 'absence seizure.' The seizure I noted lasted almost half a minute. Afterward, Torrence was tired. This is uncommon in *petit mal* seizures, so I contacted Dr. Sorrell."

"While Mr. Torrence was at Duke University Hospital," Sorrell said, "we hooked him up to an EEG machine to monitor his brain activity. Over the course of almost twenty-four hours, Torrence had a total of seventy-three seizures, measured by abnormal spike-and-slow-wave readings on the EEG. Some of these seizures lasted no more than a couple of seconds. The longest was almost fifteen minutes. This is a very unusual finding. We can only guess, but it is very likely he has always had this disorder and his hereditary ataxia has made it worse."

"And?" Crumpler asked.

"If Mr. Torrence experienced multiple but very brief seizures during the administration of the intelligence test, it could increase the time needed to complete the tasks involved, thereby lowering his eventual scores."

Sorrell placed his papers on the table and invited everyone to examine them, and then took his seat next to Edward Torrence.

"As to the results of my evaluation of Earl Torrence," Ben said, "I performed several tests with him at the Henderson County Jail. I should note that Sybil—that is, Dr. Rock—administered most of these same tests.

"Torrence's IQ is exactly seventy, but in psychology there is no such thing as an exact score. If Earl were to be administered this same test a hundred times, he would be as likely on ninety-five of those tests to score below seventy as he would to score above seventy. That means the two test scores could be considered consistent, and therefore both were accurate. In other words, whether Earl Torrence is retarded, by the state's definition, depends entirely on when you test him. Schrödinger's Cat."

"I wish I'd never heard of that damned cat," Judge Crumpler said.

"Interestingly, by the end of his career, Schrödinger said the

exact same thing," Ben said. "However, in the case of Earl Torrence, there are other factors, and if we are to make a decision
on whether Torrence lives or dies based solely on whether he is
retarded, then he teeters precariously on the fence even after all
our evaluations. In other words, Earl Torrence *is* retarded and
he *isn't,* depending on when you test him."

"In that case, the court would have to find Earl incompetent,"
Crouch said. "The defendant must be able to participate in his
own defense. Sybil's evaluation makes it very plain that he can't.
All Dr. Long's evaluation does is vacillate. He can't come right
out and say that Torrence is competent, so the court must find
him unable to stand trial."

"Hold on, Eli," Crumpler said. "I'm the one who decides
who stands trial and who doesn't. As much as it distresses me
to admit it, Dr. Long has raised some intriguing legal questions,
and I'm going to need a little time to sort all of this information
out. I want each of you to submit a copy of your respective
evaluations to my clerk. I'll review them and make a ruling . . .
hell, I'll be damned if I know when. In the interim, we'll
consider this process in recess."

Detective Donnelly was still sitting in the courtroom gallery
when the group shuffled back in from chambers, nobody looking terribly satisfied. Ben, in particular, looked troubled.

"So, what happened?" Donnelly asked, to anyone who might
answer.

"Recess," Crouch said as he began to stuff papers in his
briefcase. "The judge has some decisions to make. I don't expect
we'll hear any more today."

Paula noted the concern on Ben's face. "What is it?"

"Another piece just fell into place."

"With your evaluation?"

"No. Something else. Do you have an hour or so? I'd like to

gather a little more information and pay another visit to Amber's apartment."

"Of course."

Ben turned to Donnelly. "I was wondering whether you might accompany us on a little exploratory mission later today. I think you might find it enlightening."

"Hell, I got nothin' better to do. We can take my car."

"That would be fine. Could you pick Ms. Paige and me up at the District Attorney's office, say, around three o'clock?"

THIRTY-ONE

At three o'clock that afternoon, Detective Donnelly led Paula and Ben to the back exit of the courthouse, where the police and sheriff's deputies parked their unmarked cars. After seating Ben in the front seat, Donnelly started the engine and said, "You want to tell me what we're chasing?"

"Inconsistencies. In the course of my interviews with various people involved in this case, I found some problems with the facts. I'd like you to drive us to Amber's apartment building."

"Can't say I like the sound of this, Dr. Long."

"Yes," Paula said from the back seat. "What do you mean?"

"I'd like to review some key points. There are questions I can't answer, at least completely, and they may have great bearing on what happens to Junior Torrence."

Ben pulled another folder from his briefcase and placed it in front of him, leveraged against the dash. "During the hearing this morning I realized that I had missed something fundamental in the case. I believe I had the beginning of this revelation several days ago, but I pursued it in the wrong direction. Even so, the information I found in that process did contribute to my discovery today."

"Well, that's all clear as mud," Donnelly said.

"After the hearing this morning, I reviewed the original investigation files and found some problems. According to the files, the 911 call from Claudia Flatt came in at eleven-twenty-five."

"That's right," Donnelly said. "Best as I can remember."

"And she called the police as soon as she heard the scream upstairs. That would mean Amber was murdered around eleven-twenty-five, right?"

"Stands to reason."

"In your interview with Earl Torrence, he told you that he had come to visit Amber because he was lonely and couldn't sleep. She invited him inside and they watched a movie on television."

"Right again."

"Earl said that the movie was about a man who was trapped in a tall building by terrorists."

"Also correct."

Ben pulled a photocopy from the microfilm he had found at the university library several days earlier and placed it on top of the opened file. "This is a photocopy from the local newspaper, published the date of Amber's murder. I obtained it the other day to establish the time the movie ended, in hopes of determining the time frame of the murder. Specifically, it is the television listing for that date. The only movie that fits Earl's description is *Die Hard.*"

He passed the sheet over to Donnelly, who glanced at it between peeks at the road.

"According to the television schedule," Long said, "*Die Hard* ended at eleven o'clock. According to your interview with Earl Torrence, Amber told him as soon as the movie ended he had to go home. Earl said that the next thing he could recall, he was standing over Amber's body."

"Wait. I see what you mean. If the movie ended at eleven and she told him to leave right away, what happened to the twenty-five minutes?"

"Exactly. In my interview with Earl, he provided me with a little more information. He also told me Amber said he had to go home, but he also said he needed to use her bathroom first. This is documented in your interrogation report. He told me he had to sit down, and clarified this to mean he had to defecate. He indicated that this would have only taken a few minutes. However, he said that the next thing he remembered was standing over Amber's body, and his pants were down."

"Pants were down? Torrence never said anything to me about his pants being down."

"Yes. Here's my problem, Detective. The movie's over at eleven. Amber tells Earl it's time for him to go home. He asks to use the bathroom. Let's give him a couple of minutes for that. Now it's eleven-oh-two. He goes to the bathroom, spends maybe five minutes there. In fact, I'll be liberal and give him ten minutes. That makes it eleven-twelve."

"What happened to the other thirteen minutes?" Donnelly mused aloud.

"Exactly. What happened to the other thirteen minutes? Then there's the matter of the knife."

"The knife?"

"Yes. Could you describe the knife used to kill Amber?"

"Sure. It was a hunting knife, a cheap discount store brand with a seven-inch blade."

"Where did it come from?"

"Like I said, a discount store."

"No," Ben said. "I mean, where did it come from that night?"

"What?"

"Did Amber own the knife?"

"It was a hunting knife," Donnelly said. "I can't imagine what a young lady like Amber Coolidge would need with a hunting knife."

"My thoughts precisely. Ms. Paige brought this issue up several days ago, but I was too busy determining Torrence's competence to completely recognize its significance. If Amber didn't own the knife, that means it had to have been brought to the apartment by someone else. Would you agree?"

"I suppose."

"And the only other person we know to have been in the apartment is Earl Torrence."

"Right."

"Then doesn't it stand to reason that Torrence must have brought the knife to Amber's apartment?"

"If he was the only other person there."

"Yes. *If* he was the only other person there, he had to have brought the knife. My question is why?"

"I don't follow," Donnelly said.

"Why did Earl bring the knife? A knife with a seven-inch blade would be almost a foot in overall length, wouldn't it?"

"Including the handle, yes."

"Why would Earl bring something that large to Amber's apartment unless he intended to harm her with it?"

"Well," Donnelly said. "Torrence did say he thought about having sex with Amber. He was slow. Maybe he intended to force her to have sex with him."

"Perhaps. On the other hand, if you'll recall our conversation a couple of weeks ago, it's very likely Earl may have said he had thought about having sex with Amber only after you convinced him that it could have happened."

"I remember. Seems kind of unlikely, though."

"It was my concern after reading the transcript of your interview with Earl that you might have—however inadvertently—implanted a false memory in Earl's mind. As I've already established, Earl's intelligence at best falls into the borderline range, and at worst makes him mentally handicapped. Memory is very tricky. We never remember things exactly the way they happened. Too many details. Gaps in our memory are dealt with in a very elegant manner. We make up stuff to fill in the holes. Some people, especially people who have lower cognitive skills, are susceptible to accepting false memories.

"Because I was afraid that you might have inadvertently extracted an inaccurate confession from Earl, I tested my hypothesis during an interview at the jail. Ms. Paige was present. I was able, with almost no effort at all, to convince Earl that he had killed Amber in order to protect Edward from embarrassment because he, Earl, had caught Amber with another man."

"But the only person there on the night of the murder was Torrence himself!"

"That remains to be seen. I created an implanted memory, fabricated entirely from my imagination. Very likely no more the truth than Earl's statement to you that he killed Amber because she wouldn't have sex with him."

"You're losing me, Dr. Long. This all sounds like random speculation."

"Speculation, yes," Ben argued, "But hardly random. This leads us back to the knife. If, as I suggested, Earl had no intention of attacking Amber, why would he have brought a foot-long knife? Further, even if he did bring the knife, where did he keep it? It was too long to hide in his pants pockets. You never found a scabbard anywhere, did you?"

"No."

"So how did Earl get from his apartment, six blocks away, to Amber's apartment, carrying a twelve-inch hunting knife, without drawing any attention or alarm? Further, as I've already stated, if he had no intention of threatening her, why would he have brought it in the first place? Why didn't she become alarmed the entire time they were watching the movie, if he had this knife in his possession? I can't resolve that conflict, so I have to conclude that Earl *didn't* bring the knife."

"But I found it in his apartment, under his bed," Donnelly said.

"Sure," Ben replied. "After the murder. The fact that he took it home with him doesn't mean he owned it before the murder."

Donnelly gripped the steering wheel. "So we're back to the knife belonging to Amber?"

Ben pulled another sheet from the folder in front of him. "According to the investigation report, the police responded to Claudia Flatt's call and were admitted to Amber Coolidge's apartment by the maintenance man, Sachs. Now, Detective Donnelly, I know you weren't at the scene at that point, but could you tell me whether the front door to Amber's apartment was locked?"

"Yes. The door locks automatically when closed. We'd have used Mr. Sachs in any case, whether it had been locked or unlocked. Procedure. For all we knew, this was a case of a domestic disturbance and a nosey neighbor. It's always better in those cases for the uniformed officers to be admitted by someone in authority."

"I see. And, according to the forensic reports, four sets of fingerprints were found in the apartment."

"That's right. Amber, of course; Edward Torrence; his brother Earl; and Mr. Sachs."

"And how did Mr. Sachs explain his fingerprints being in Amber's apartment?"

"Beg pardon?"

"Well," Ben said, "Amber's prints are understandable. She lived there, after all. Edward and Earl visited frequently, which they admitted. How did Mr. Sachs explain the presence of his fingerprints in the apartment?"

"He didn't. Come to think of it, we never interviewed Mr. Sachs."

"Why was that?"

"Sachs was the maintenance man, for Pete's sake. He'd probably been in the apartment a hundred times, fixing one thing or another. These are old apartments, Dr. Long. They need a ton of upkeep."

"A hundred times," Long said, solemnly. "We'll come back to that. Now, when the police arrived and had Mr. Sachs let them into the apartment, you say the front door was locked."

"Right."

"What about the side door?"

"Side door?"

"Amber's apartment was on the second floor. The first floor apartments have a front and a back door. Those on the second floor are entered from a door in the stairwell, but also have a second door just beyond the bar, in the kitchen. I found it when Ms. Paige and I visited the apartment a few days ago. I thought it was a pantry, but it was locked. When I checked back yesterday, I was told it leads to a set of stairs that exit to the side of the building. It's a fire precaution. Do you know whether the side door was locked or unlocked?"

"I can't recall," Donnelly said, looking perplexed.

"It was locked. There was a very obscure note deep in the forensic report. Almost an afterthought, it seems. It reads 'Officers checked the second exit door, and found it locked.' "

"Okay. So it was locked."

"Yes. Tell me, Detective, was there any specific reason you didn't interview Mr. Sachs, the maintenance man, besides your presumption that he must have been in the apartment a hundred times?"

"Yes," Donnelly said. "We had already found the murderer. I found the knife and bloody shirt in Earl Torrence's apartment and extracted a confession from him. We didn't get all the fingerprint results back until after the confession. There was no reason to interview Mr. Sachs."

"And that's your job, right? As you told me when I interviewed you a few weeks ago? If I recall correctly, in describing your work you claimed that 'people wind up dead and someone has to clean up the mess.' Is that accurate?"

"Sounds like something I'd say."

"And once you've found your killer, the mess is cleaned up, right?"

"Pretty much."

"No reason to pursue the matter any further?"

"Not if I have a confession. In this case, though, I had more. I had the murder weapon in Torrence's possession, along with a shirt covered in Amber's blood. Seemed pretty airtight to me."

"I can see what you mean," Ben said. "Of course, if you had taken a little harder look at Mr. Sachs, would you have been suspicious to discover that he had only started working at that apartment building a few weeks earlier?"

"What?"

"When Ms. Paige and I visited Amber's apartment, Mr. Sachs let us in and showed it to us. He told us that, at the time of the murder, he had only been working for the company that owns Amber's apartment building for a couple of weeks."

Donnelly looked dejected, as if his entire world had collapsed. "Shit fire," he said. "I didn't know that."

"What I can't understand is why Mr. Sachs's fingerprints would be all over Amber's apartment if he had only been employed as a maintenance man for a couple of weeks. Surely there weren't enough things to fix during that short a time, wouldn't you think?"

"Yeah. That does sound strange."

"May I ask your opinion?" Ben said, almost as if asking for a personal favor. "I'd like to present an alternate explanation for Amber's murder."

"Hell, at this point I'd pay cash money for one that makes sense."

"Here's my story. We know several things. First, we know that

273

Earl Torrence was subject to *petit mal* seizures. We know he has—at best—borderline intelligence. We know he visited Amber on the night she was murdered and the movie they watched ended at eleven o'clock. We know she was murdered approximately twenty-five minutes later. We know the knife and the bloody shirt were found in Earl's apartment. We also know he confessed to murdering Amber, but the veracity of that confession is subject to some doubt. Any arguments with those statements?"

"No," Donnelly said.

"So here's what I think might have happened. After the movie, Amber told Earl to go home. He asked to use the bathroom. It was—maybe—eleven-oh-two. Earl went into the bathroom, and during his business there, he had a seizure. Dr. Sorrell documented that Earl had one seizure at Duke University Hospital that lasted fifteen minutes.

"While Earl was in the bathroom, staring into space, probably somewhere around eleven-twenty, Sachs entered the apartment through the side door near the kitchen, after walking up the inside steps from the side yard. As the maintenance man for the apartment building, he would have keys to the door. In fact, since his fingerprints were found in the apartment, he had already been there at least once, perhaps multiple times, maybe to familiarize himself with the layout, or perhaps to engage in some sort of fetish involving Amber's personal items. He opened the door and found Amber in the living room. He brought his hunting knife from his own apartment because he had become infatuated with Amber and threatened to kill her if she didn't submit to his demands.

"Amber screamed for Earl—the scream that Claudia Flatt heard downstairs—and Sachs stabbed her reflexively with the knife. She fell to the floor—the thud Ms. Flatt reported—and Sachs stood over her, trying to decide what to do next.

"At that point, Earl came out of his seizure. I observed him do this and he was slightly disoriented and fatigued. He pulled his pants up and started to open the bathroom door. Sachs heard him, panicked, and dashed for the side door, leaving his knife in Amber's body. Like the front door, the side door locked automatically.

"Earl walked into the living room and found Amber lying on the floor. He had forgotten to fasten his pants and they fell down around his ankles. This is his first conscious memory after he went into the bathroom, so it makes sense.

"He tried to help Amber, perhaps removing the knife from her body, but only succeeded in getting blood on his shirt. He couldn't recall what happened after he went into the bathroom and he panicked. Maybe he thought he had killed her. He had watched enough television to know about fingerprints, so he picked up the knife and stuffed it in his shirt, then ran out the front door and dashed down the stairs. That was the clumping sound Ms. Flatt heard outside her door.

"The rest of the story we know. You found incriminating evidence in Earl's apartment, extracted a confession from him that Earl probably believed to be true because of the way his mind filled in his memory gaps, and for you the case was closed. You'd found the murderer. There was no reason to follow up on Sachs."

The color had risen in Donnelly's emaciated neck and face. He swallowed quickly a couple of times.

"Now, Detective Donnelly, I have one more question. Please understand, we aren't trying to accuse you of anything. You acted the way any good police officer would. My question is this: Is there any possibility that the story I've just told could have happened exactly as I told it? Is it possible that the knife belonged to Sachs, and that Sachs killed Amber, and that you didn't bother to follow up on that possibility because you had already extracted a confession from Earl Torrence?"

Donnelly had pulled up to a red light. He rubbed his face with both hands. His eyes filled with tears. Then, slowly, he nodded. "Yeah. It could have happened that way. Dear God, man. Did I arrest the wrong boy for this murder?"

"A correctable error," Ben said. "It isn't too late to set things straight."

"Sachs doesn't live at Amber's building."

"No. There isn't enough space for a live-in maintenance man. He lives about four blocks away. That way he can be called relatively quickly when something needs to be repaired."

"Hope he hasn't gone rabbit on us."

"He hadn't as of this morning," Ben said. "That's when I spoke with him."

Donnelly almost drove the car up onto a sidewalk. "You *talked* with him?"

"Yes. I needed to ascertain that he was still at his address. I told him he had been extremely helpful when he showed Ms. Paige and me the apartment where Amber was murdered. I asked him whether he would be so kind as to meet us there again. Mr. Sachs seemed very eager to help out. I told him we'd drop by today—Ms. Paige and I—to gather a little more information."

"And he agreed?"

"He seemed pleased to be of service. I, of course, expected him to be. In my experience, real suspects are almost always very willing to help the police. They believe it takes some of the suspicion off of them."

"You socially engineered him," Paula said from the back seat.

"Yes," Ben said. "And I intend to do it again."

THIRTY-TWO

Donnelly pulled to the curb a block from Amber's apartment building and stepped from the car. Ben walked around to the front and sidestepped the detective to slip behind the wheel.

"Remember what I said," Ben told the detective. "If Sachs knows you're around, he won't tell us anything. I need to ensnare him in his own words. Once he admits anything useful, you can show yourself."

"It could be viewed as entrapment. I'm not sure I'm comfortable with this arrangement."

"I will defer to your expertise in that area," Ben said. "If you believe at any point that I am entrapping Sachs, feel free to intervene. Here." He handed Donnelly a key on a metal ring. "This is the key to the outer entrance of the stairway leading to Amber's side door. I obtained it several hours ago from the real estate office, along with permission to enter the premises."

Donnelly shook his head. "All right, Dr. Long. I'll play along with you, but only because your explanation of this murder is plausible enough to bear investigating."

"That is all I ask," Ben said, and drove away from the curb.

"I hope you know what you're doing," Paula said as Donnelly's scarecrow figure diminished.

"I've thought it through very carefully. If all goes according to plan, Sachs will tell us everything we want to know."

"And if it doesn't go according to plan?"

"That's why I invited Detective Donnelly to join us."

Sachs sat on the front steps of the building as Ben and Paula pulled into the gravel drive. He stood, wiped his palms together, and walked up to them as they got out of the car.

"Thank you for agreeing to let us see the apartment again," Ben said. "You've been very helpful in this case."

"Always like to help the law," Sachs said, then tipped the brim of his cap to Paula. "Afternoon, ma'am." He then led them into the central doorway and up the stairway to Amber's apartment.

Ben could imagine Ms. Flatt, her ear pressed to her apartment door, listening intently as they walked upstairs.

Sachs opened the door and held it for them. They walked in and he followed. He allowed the door to close behind him. "Now, what was it y'all wanted to see?"

"We didn't get a good look at the bathroom last time," Ben said. "Nor did I get a chance to do a good examination of the kitchen."

"But she was killed right here," Sachs said, pointing to a spot several feet in front of the hearth.

"Yes," Ben said. "Ms. Paige, would you please go to the bathroom and close the door? I'd like to try something."

Paula looked worried, but she walked into the bedroom and from there to the tiny adjoining bath. After a couple of seconds, Ben heard the bathroom door close.

"Can you hear me?" he called out.

"Yes, but it's muffled."

"Stay there for a moment. I want to check something else."

He turned to Sachs and lowered his voice. "I'm sorry, Mr. Sachs, but I wanted to get her away for a moment while I asked you a few questions."

"Why?"

"She works for the District Attorney's office. The DA hired me to evaluate the man who killed Amber. I can't get rid of her. She's always looking over my shoulder, almost like she's spying on me."

"Man, I know what that's like."

"I don't doubt it. The fact is, I can't seem to turn around without finding her standing there. It certainly makes it hard to concentrate."

"I'll bet," Sachs said with a conspiratorial grin.

"Now, here's my problem, and this is why I wanted to get you alone for a moment. I have reached the conclusion that Earl Torrence didn't kill Amber Coolidge on this spot."

Sachs blinked a couple of times. "He didn't?"

"I don't think so. The DA's office is bound and determined to send Earl Torrence to the death chamber. I can't convince them otherwise. That's why I sent Ms. Paige to the other room. I needed a few moments alone with you to ask some questions they don't want asked. Not only that, but I think I know who actually did commit the murder."

For a second, Ben thought he saw a dark wave roll across Sachs's face.

"Who?"

Ben poked him in the chest with an index finger. "You."

Sachs backed up as if Ben had thrust a copperhead at him. "What?"

Ben smiled and clapped his hands. "Relax, Mr. Sachs. I'm just having some fun with you."

"Don't seem like much fun from my end."

"You should have seen yourself jump. Priceless. No, no, you shouldn't worry yourself. My actual suspect is someone else entirely. Can you keep a secret?"

"I reckon I can."

"I think there is a very strong likelihood Edward Torrence is

279

letting his brother take the fall for killing Amber."

"The boyfriend?"

"Fiancé," Ben corrected. "They were going to be married. On the night of the murder, Edward was supposed to have been in a sports bar. When I questioned him, however, his alibi started to fall apart. I've asked for a subpoena of his credit card records. If I'm right, he left the bar ten or fifteen minutes before Amber was murdered."

The dark cloud over Sachs's face had disappeared. Now he seemed fascinated with Ben's explanation. "You don't say."

"I do say. Hold on a minute."

Ben walked to the threshold of the kitchen and faced back into the living room. "Can you hear me now, Ms. Paige?" he called out.

"Yes," she replied from the bathroom.

"Okay. You stay there. I want to try something else."

He gestured for Sachs to join him in the kitchen. Sachs walked around the bar.

"This is how I think it happened," Ben said quietly. "Edward left the sports bar around eleven o'clock and decided to drop by to see Amber. We already know his brother Earl was here, in the bathroom, exactly where Ms. Paige is now. Edward had been drinking. You know why he was drinking, Mr. Sachs?"

"No."

"What would you say if I told you it was because he and Amber had a fight?"

"They had?"

"Doesn't it sound preposterous?"

"What did they fight about?"

"It might have been Earl."

"Go on."

"I can imagine a situation in which Amber was tired of having Earl around all the time. He was like a huge, overbearing two-year-old. Why, he could barely zip up his own pants after going to the bathroom. Can you imagine what that was like for her? How embarrassing?"

"I sure can."

"So perhaps Edward came up here, and Earl was here—in the bathroom—and Amber started complaining again. Edward, who as I said had been drinking, may have finally lost his temper and stabbed her to death."

Sachs rubbed his craggy face with one gnarled hand. "Just like that?"

"It's what I think happened," Ben said. "I have one problem and that's why I wanted to talk with you today. You're the maintenance man for this apartment. Maybe you can help solve this problem for me."

"I'll help if I can."

"Great. Here's the problem. The nosey neighbor downstairs told the police she only heard one set of footsteps come down the central stairwell that night."

"I'm with you so far."

Ben walked around the bar and called out again.

"Can you hear me now, Ms. Paige?"

"Yes," she said from the bathroom.

"Very good."

He lowered his voice again. "One set of footsteps but two men in the apartment. We know the footsteps Ms. Flatt heard were made by Earl Torrence as he ran away with the knife used to kill Amber. Edward wasn't in the apartment when the police arrived a few moments later. According to Ms. Flatt, footsteps on the central stairs echo very loudly. It would have been almost impossible for Edward to leave without Ms. Flatt hearing him. Do you agree?"

"By the central stairs," Sachs said.

"Exactly. By the central stairs. That means he had to leave by another route, one where he wouldn't have made any noise."

Ben laid the palm of his hand on the door to the side stairs. "This route," he said. "I think, if my suspicions are borne out, Edward took the side stairs. Now, here's where you can help. You work in this building every day. Do you think it would be possible for someone to get out by the side stairs without making any noise?"

"Well, sure. The central stairs aren't carpeted, and the plaster walls make all kinds of racket when you walk on them. The side stairs, though, they have some upholstery on them—you know, to hold down the chance of slipping when it's raining. Also, the side stairs run down the inside of the building behind Ms. Flatt's apartment. There aren't any doors back there, and the walls are insulated right good. Here, I'll show you." He reached for the doorknob.

"Stop!" Ben said. "Don't touch it."

"Why?"

"Fingerprints. If Edward did escape by the side stairs, his fingerprints might still be there. We have to preserve the evidence."

"Oh, yeah. I get it. Like on TV."

"Right. I'm going to call the police and ask them to come out and dust for prints. If I'm correct, they'll find Edward's prints all over the place and we'll have all the proof we need to put him away."

Ben straightened and forced a smile for the maintenance man. "I want to thank you, Mr. Sachs. You may have helped put away a dangerous killer."

Ben thought he could see the wheels turning in Sachs's head.

"Ms. Paige, I think that's all," Ben said.

Paula walked into the living room. "That's it? All you wanted to do was find out if I could hear you in the bathroom?"

"It's an important factor in my theory," Ben said. "I think we can go now. We need to contact Detective Donnelly and ask him to pay this apartment another visit. With any luck he can be here in a half hour."

He opened the door and walked into the central stairwell. Paula turned to Sachs. "Coming?"

"Sure," Sachs said. He followed them onto the stairs. They all walked down to the street level.

"We're parked around the corner," Ben said. "You have a nice day, Mr. Sachs. Thanks again for your help."

He took Paula's arm and steered her toward the corner. Sachs seemed to loiter in front of the apartment.

"You want to explain what this is all about?" Paula asked.

"Yes, but not yet. We're going to turn the corner and then cross to the apartment through the back alley."

Moments later, they returned to the back side of the building, which was comprised mostly of a gravel parking lot for the residents' cars and a low picket-fenced area for garbage cans.

"Sachs's car is still parked out front," he said, pointing to the rear end of the car, which was visible from the side of the building. "If I'm right, he's doing exactly what I hoped he would do."

At that moment, the side door to the apartment flew open and Sachs was thrust out onto the landing, followed closely by Donnelly. Sachs's hands were cuffed behind him.

THIRTY-THREE

"What in hell is all this about?" Sachs demanded.

Donnelly ignored him.

"Son of a bitch went straight for the side stairs," Donnelly said. "Had a rag in his hands when he opened the door from the kitchen."

"Don't mean nothin'!" Sachs protested.

"On the contrary," Ben argued. "It means almost everything."

He pulled a pocket dictating machine from his jacket. "I have our entire conversation on tape. It proves that you knew the possibility the police would find evidence in the side stairway. No sooner were Ms. Paige and I out of your sight than you hurried back up to Amber's apartment, took a rag, and went directly to the side stairway with the intent of eliminating any possible fingerprints."

"So?"

"You have no reason to protect Edward Torrence, which leads me to the conclusion that the fingerprints you intended to wipe away were, in fact, your own."

"You ain't got no proof!"

"Here's what we know," Ben said, clearly savoring the moment. "The police found dozens of your fingerprints all over Amber's apartment, but you had only been working here for a month when she died. That meant you had been in her apartment multiple times. Maintenance men are invisible. Nobody questions their comings and goings. You had a master key, so all you had to do was wait for Amber to leave for work and you had free reign of her apartment, perhaps for hours on end.

"That's what I know. Now here is what I *think*. I believe you became infatuated with Amber. After a while, perhaps you even became obsessed with her. You decided to pay her a visit on the night she died. You used your master key and entered her apartment by way of the side stairs. She tried to fight you off when you attacked her. She screamed. You panicked, and killed her with the knife you had brought to intimidate her. After the killing, you tried to clean the knife with a rag very much like the one you just tried to use on the stairway. What you didn't know was that Earl Torrence was in the apartment. When he appeared in the bedroom, you were startled. You ran to the side stairway, forgetting the knife, and escaped into the night.

"Earl, having just come out of a seizure, was confused. He didn't realize you were there. Thinking he had killed Amber, he took the knife and ran down the central stairway."

"You think you're so damn smart!" Sachs yelled. "Ain't no way you can trick me into confessin' I killed her."

"I don't need to," Ben said. "You can't attack someone the way you did Amber without getting blood on you—a lot of blood. Detective Donnelly will search your apartment. If he finds one drop of Amber's blood there on any of your possessions, it will be enough to incriminate you."

"I ain't sayin' nothin'!"

"That's fine. You have the right to remain silent," Donnelly said to him.

The next day, at a hearing in Judge Crumpler's courtroom, Earl Torrence was exonerated of all charges.

"I was prepared," Crumpler announced when everyone had assembled, "after careful examination of the reports presented by Dr. Long and Dr. Rock yesterday, to declare Mr. Torrence competent to stand trial, despite his clearly evident disability. While he obviously does present with a neurological disorder, which in the fullness of time will result in his demise, I am not satisfied that this neurological disorder meets the criteria to make him ineligible for prosecution.

"In addition, the report by Dr. Long presented reasonable doubt regarding whether Mr. Torrence might be considered mentally retarded. Again, the result would have led to trial.

"I commend Dr. Long and Ms. Paige, a law clerk in the District Attorney's office, for their follow-up work, which resolved completely the issue of Mr. Torrence's guilt or innocence. For that reason, I am ordering that Mr. Torrence be released from custody, and that all charges against him be expunged from his record. Court adjourned."

Eli Crouch stood with the others as Judge Crumpler left the courtroom. Then he turned and crossed to the jury box, where Long, Paula, and Sybil now stood.

"Good work, Dr. Long," he said as he took Long's hand. "I can't thank you enough for clearing my client."

Long stared at the floor as they shook.

Crouch walked over to Kingsley. Sybil lingered behind. She carefully placed a well-manicured hand on Long's shoulder. He turned to her as she reached up to straighten his tie. He stiffened but didn't flinch. However, he didn't allow his eyes to meet hers.

"It's good to see you back in the saddle," she said. "You haven't lost a thing in the last several years. You're as sharp as ever."

"Thank you, Sybil. It couldn't work any other way. As long as I looked at the case with the premise that Earl Torrence committed the murder, none of the pieces fit together correctly. I couldn't rid my mind of the unresolved seventh."

"Oh, hell," Sybil said, dropping her hands. "Not that damned unresolved seventh business again."

She leaned over and kissed him on the cheek. This time he did flinch, and his face turned red. Sybil patted his cheek, then walked over to join Crouch.

Detective Donnelly leaned over the knee wall separating the jury box from the main court floor.

"I'm sorry. I was just doing my job. As a cop I'm cynical enough to believe that there's a little evil in all men, but I hate to think we might have sent an innocent man to the death chamber. Thanks for keeping my conscience clean."

He pumped Long's hand, then shook Paula's hand as well before leaving the courtroom.

Sorrell also stood and shook Ben's hand.

"I'd heard stories, but you're amazing. Keep me posted, okay?"

After he left, Long turned to Edward Torrence. The young man sat in his chair at the defense table, wringing his hands and staring at the floor. Tears gathered at the corners of his eyes.

Ben walked around the conference table and sat next to him.

"One more question," he said. "One thing I still don't understand. Why did you tell Eli Crouch to plead Earl not guilty in court? Is it because you have the same hereditary ataxia?"

Torrence looked up. "You know?"

"You have a limp handshake. When you were holding the beer bottle at your house the other night, your hand trembled. Your left eyelid droops a bit. Your muscle tone could be better. Shall I go on?"

"No. I found out almost ten years ago. It can strike at any age, you know. Dr. Sorrell was right. Both our parents probably carried the gene and it was passed on to both me and Junior. I suppose it just started to manifest itself a lot earlier with him."

"And the not guilty plea?"

"The ataxia is progressing much more quickly with me.

Maybe it's because it started later. I don't know. I didn't want to think Junior killed Amber, but the evidence was so overwhelming and then there was that damned confession. I was afraid that he might have done it after all."

"So you asked Crouch to plead him not guilty, knowing he'd be convicted?"

"Not exactly," Kingsley said as he sat across the table from them. "May I tell it, Edward?"

Edward peered at him through bleary eyes and nodded.

"Edward came to me after Earl was charged. He had hired Crouch to defend Earl, but he and I have known each other for a number of years. He told me he had hereditary ataxia and didn't expect to live more than another ten years. He told me that Earl had the disorder and would also die, and that they would both become incapacitated as part of that process.

"He had read a little in the state statutes and had discovered there was a reasonable chance, given Earl's history of mental and neurological problems and his confession, that his case might be pled down to voluntary manslaughter. If that happened, Earl might be released in ten years. Maybe sooner.

"I told him if he could get Eli to plead not guilty and Earl was convicted, the minimum charge would be second-degree murder, which would mean life in prison; or first degree, meaning life without parole or the death penalty.

"Edward wasn't worried about the death penalty. He knew that, on average, it could take twenty years to move through all the appeals to the execution and there was no way Earl would live that long.

"On the other hand, if Earl got out in ten years, Edward was afraid his own ataxia might have progressed to the point where he could no longer care for Earl, or he might even be dead, in which case Earl would have nobody to care for him at all. Worse, Earl would have no health insurance of any kind.

"Edward reasoned that—in prison—Earl would receive the very best of care as his disease progressed."

"I told Mr. Crouch I wanted to go to trial," Edward said. "He disagreed, said that—in light of the confession and all—he thought he could talk Kingsley into a plea bargain. Sidney, of course, turned him down."

"Remarkably logical," Ben said. "Even intertwined as it is with familial emotion, it was a strategy of which Solomon might have been proud."

"In prison, Junior would have had everything he needs," Edward continued. "His cell would be clean and warm, he'd get three meals a day, and he could watch television until the cows came home. That's all he really wants out of life. Then, when he'd inevitably get really sick in five or ten years, he'd have had the best medical care available, free of charge."

"Yes," Kingsley said. "And, after all, we all believed Earl actually *had* killed Amber, hard as that was to stomach. By turning Crouch down, I inadvertently opened a can of worms. Because he couldn't get a plea bargain, Eli decided to save Junior's life by having him ruled incompetent. He hired Sybil to do an evaluation on him. She must have encountered the same ataxia-related seizures you did, but didn't recognize them, so her test results indicated that he was retarded. That's when I decided to pull you in on the case. I figured you'd recognize the symptoms and compensate for them in your findings. Like the judge said, ataxia doesn't render a person incompetent."

"And now you tell me Junior didn't kill Amber after all," Edward said, tears brimming. "He's innocent. It seems I did the right thing, asking Mr. Crouch to enter the not guilty plea, but for the wrong reason. What happens now? How can I provide for Junior when he gets really sick, if I'm not around anymore myself?"

Kingsley leaned across the table and patted Edward's hands.

"Don't worry about that. I'll work with you to find a way to ensure that he gets the best available care."

Satisfied with the explanation, Long stood.

"Thank you, Ben," Kingsley said.

"You're welcome," Ben said, his voice nearly devoid of emotion. "I must say that Ms. Paige played a huge role in the case. She deserves to be commended."

"Of course." Kingsley looked over at her. "Thank you, Ms. Paige. You can count on an excellent recommendation from the DA's office. I am in your debt."

"Several days ago," Ben said, "I accused you of not accepting Crouch's offer of a plea bargain out of selfish political desires. I have thought this over and I think I may be expected to apologize to you."

"No apologies necessary. Never between friends."

Ben walked through the conference room doors and started toward the front entrance of the office. Paula stopped him halfway there with a tug on his sleeve.

"I wanted to thank you too," she said. "Mr. Kingsley was right. I did learn a lot working with you."

Ben nodded absently. "You're welcome. Now, if you'll excuse me, I have an errand to complete."

The misty rain had disappeared, but the dreary frame house in Weaverville still looked foreboding. The dogs still lazed on the porch. The gravel of the driveway still crunched under Ben's feet as he walked toward the front door.

He rang the doorbell and waited as he heard footsteps inside the house. After a moment, the front door swung open and Kate Ashburton peered out at him through the screen.

"Dr. Long," she said.

"May I come in?"

"Of course."

She held the screen door open for him. He walked into the discordantly warm living room and sat on the sofa. She followed and sat in a chair on the other side of the coffee table.

"Is there something I can do for you?" she asked.

"No. Quite the contrary. I believe what's happened has been tragic for you. I understand, you see, because I lost my mother some years ago. It's hard, and I know you've been trying to find some meaning in Sarah's death."

"Yes," she said. "It doesn't seem to make sense."

"I don't know if this will help, but it's very possible Sarah's problems may have resulted in some good after all. I think it's very likely she kept an innocent man from being convicted for a crime he didn't commit."

"I don't understand."

"It's kind of a long story," Ben said. "You see, a couple of months ago Sarah came to my office and asked me for help with a problem . . ."

THIRTY-FOUR

On Christmas Day, the mountain range outside Ben Long's house looked as if someone had draped a huge India cotton sheet over it. During the night, eight inches of snow had fallen over the Blue Ridge and now the landscape stood starkly silent and still.

Ben Long lounged on his sofa, wrapped in a patchwork quilt he had purchased the year before in a craft gallery in Hendersonville. Next to him sat a half-empty box of tissues. He had built a healthy fire in the hearth.

He had gotten a cold two days before Christmas Eve. It had started as an annoying tickle at the back of his throat and a wet earthy sensation in his sinuses. Now his head was full, his body ached, and his voice had dropped to a raspy croak.

He considered this the most miserable Christmas he had ever known.

Tchaikovsky's Fifth Symphony played on the CD. Long had considered choosing the First—appropriately called "Winter Dreams"—but thought "The Pathetique" better matched the way he felt.

He had risen early, after the nighttime cold medicine he had imbibed had worn off. The residual after-effects included an irritating buzzing/ringing noise in his ears.

Just as the Tchaikovsky switched gears and rolled over to the last movement, Ben was roused from a drowsy, semi-comatose state by the doorbell. Keeping the quilt wrapped around him, he walked across the house to the front door and opened it.

"Do you have any idea how bad the roads are coming up this mountain?" Paula Paige said as she stamped snow off her boots and walked into the living room. "It took me half an hour to get here from the village. Close the door, Ben. You'll catch your death."

"Too late."

"Yes. I heard. I'm so sorry. I was at a luncheon at Sidney Kingsley's house yesterday and he told me you were sick."

"He knew you'd come up."

"Are you accusing Sidney of social engineering?"

"He had a good teacher."

"Is it awful? The cold?"

"It's no fun. What are you doing here?"

"Christmas visit. Beats sitting around the house alone. Get right back on that couch. Pretend I'm not even here."

Ben started to ask another question, but suddenly seemed to lack the energy. He was tired of asking questions. Instead, he simply dropped back onto the sofa and wrapped the quilt around himself even tighter. Paula, who had brought a bulging plastic grocery bag, did something noisy in the kitchen.

After a few moments, she came back into the living room with two steaming mugs. "Vegetable broth, no meat," she said, holding one of them up. Then she hefted the other. "Hot mulled wine. One or the other should make you feel better. I'm betting on the wine."

She set the mugs on the tiled coffee table in front of the couch and turned to look out the sliding doors to the deck. "Isn't it just gorgeous? Nothing but white for miles and miles."

"It's Hell's window dressing," he croaked as he sipped from the broth mug. "Whatever possessed you to drive up the mountain in all this mess?"

She sat in the oversized chair across from the sofa. "Working the Torrence case, I came to think of you as a friend, albeit, a strange, socially retarded friend. Friends take care of friends when they're sick."

"Ah. An errand of mercy." He sampled the broth again. "I wonder what this tastes like."

"It's perfectly awful. It would be infinitely better if it had some chicken in it."

"Or some salt mackerel. Salt mackerel makes an acceptable alternative to chicken in soups."

"I'm sure it does. Speaking of which . . ."

She reached into the bag she had brought with her and pulled out a wrapped parcel. She crossed the living room and handed it to him.

"What's this?" he asked as he eyed the bundle.

"Something from Santa Claus."

He held it gingerly, as if it might explode, then pulled at the paper. Soon he had it unwrapped.

"A book."

"A cookbook," she corrected.

"*The Gourmet's Guide to Preparing Sea Creatures*," he read from the cover.

"I saw it in a shop in Asheville and thought of you. There may be one or two recipes in there you've never heard of."

"I dare say."

He opened the book and riffled the pages, stopped somewhere in the middle, and read a paragraph. Then he closed the book and placed it on the coffee table.

"I didn't get you anything," he said.

"That's all right. You didn't know I was coming. Don't worry about it."

Ben looked out the window at the snow-covered peaks. Off in the distance, he could see some kind of raptor circling slowly, desperately searching for any sign of food on the forest floor below.

Slowly, he rose up from the sofa and walked over to the piano. With the quilt still wrapped around his shoulders, he sat at the bench and started to play Debussy's "Claire de Lune."

He wasn't used to playing for another person and the notes were tentative at first, but as he progressed it became easier and the notes flowed effortlessly underneath his fingers.

Eventually, the very last note—an unresolved seventh—resonated through the house. He pulled the quilt around his shivering shoulders and slowly walked back to the sofa. He settled into the cushions, picked up the mug, and sipped at the mulled wine.

"Thank you. It was a wonderful present," Paula said.

"And cheap," he said, sipping the wine.

"You really are a Martian, aren't you?"

"Don't be silly." He snuffled back some congestion. "There are no Martians. The atmosphere on Mars is incompatible with life. The wine I can taste, though mostly I tasted cloves. I must warn you, when I finish it I will likely go to sleep."

"Probably a good thing. I'll just watch the snow and read a book until you wake up."

"No need. You don't have to stay."

"All the more reason. If I had to, I probably wouldn't. Drink up."

He slowly finished the wine while she examined his bookcase. When the mug was empty, he wrapped himself even tighter in the quilt and propped up the pillows before sinking into them.

"Thank you for coming. You have made a miserable holiday tolerable."

"It was my pleasure."

"I think I'm going to sleep now," he said, his voice barely a whisper. "Merry Christmas, Ms. Paige."

She selected a book and settled back into her chair. "Merry Christmas, Ben," she said.

AUTHOR'S NOTE

One of the benefits of writing fiction is that you get to take some liberties with facts. In the case of *The Unresolved Seventh,* I had my protagonist, Ben Long, note that North Carolina has a faulty interpretation of the real Supreme Court case of *Atkins v. Virginia.* Long notes at one point that the state uses only the IQ score of a defendant to determine whether he or she is eligible for capital punishment. This is decidedly incorrect. In fact, the state of North Carolina had a law prohibiting the execution of mentally handicapped defendants some time before the Atkins decision, and has not modified it after the decision. Also, the North Carolina state statute states that, when deciding whether a defendant is qualified for a capital trial, the court must take into account whether that individual has ". . . *Significantly subaverage general intellectual functioning (defined as having an IQ of 70 or below), existing concurrently with significant limitations in adaptive functioning (defined as having significant limitations in two or more of the following adaptive skill areas: communication, self-care, home living, social skills, community use, self-direction, health and safety, functional academics, leisure skills and work skills) both of which were manifested before the age of 18"* (2001 N.C. Sess. Laws 346). I am quite happy to state, as a resident of North Carolina, that my state's basis for determining mental retardation is entirely in line with that of the American Psychiatric Association's *Diagnostic and Statistical Manual of Mental Disorders IV—Text Revision*—the "Bible," if you will, of mental disorder diagnoses.

While Asperger's syndrome has been recognized clinically since the mid-forties, it was not included in the American Psychiatric Association's *Diagnostic and Statistical Manual of Mental Disorders* until the early nineties.

Essentially, as Sidney Kingsley explained to Paula Paige in *The Unresolved Seventh,* it is a type of atypical autism. Specifically, Asperger's is considered to be part of a larger group of diagnoses called pervasive developmental disorders.

It is also considered to be in a class called "spectrum disorders," which means there are a wide variety of symptoms that are not exhibited uniformly in every client. There are many levels of severity, from virtually unrecognizable to incapacitating.

The primary criteria, however, are well documented. First, the Asperger's disorder client usually displays marked inabilities to interact with others in a socially prescribed manner. This means that they often scrupulously avoid eye contact, do not "read" body language or facial expressions, and depend entirely on verbal cues to know what other people are saying. They tend to have a very difficult time developing age-appropriate social—and sexual—relationships and, like many autistics, do not like strong physical contact. They tend to be very self-absorbed and not terribly interested in the opinions or feelings of others. Because of this, their approach to other people may be clinical and sterile, and they may need to be reminded when things they say hurt other people's feelings. They may seem insensitive to the kindness of others, and do not seem to feel the need to return favors.

A second primary diagnostic feature for Asperger's disorder is a keen awareness of details, adherence to fixed schedules and behavior patterns, and a seemingly unbounded ability to focus on certain tasks. As a result of this feature, Asperger's disorder clients tend to be extremely analytical. They want to know precisely how things work and fit together, and they tend to be fascinated by puzzles.

Of course, this is—after all—a *disorder*, which means that these diagnostic features must pose some sort of hardship or impairment for the individuals who have them. In fact, for most Asperger's disorder clients, the hardship tends to be felt by others who are around them. These clients tend not to see themselves as impaired, and in fact have developed a word for those people who do not have Asperger's—"neurotypicals." Despite the fact that they display a diagnosable mental illness, many people with Asperger's disorder would not be like neurotypicals if they were given the opportunity. They prefer their view of the world and tend to see it as much more honest and straightforward. Because they disregard subtext and nonverbal cues in others, they believe that people without Asperger's are confusing, indirect, frequently mistaken about the motives of others, and generally inefficient.

Despite these earlier features, and unlike many autistics, people with Asperger's often display extremely strong language skills, wide vocabularies, and above-average intelligence. They may tend to lecture when they speak, a feature that led Hans Asperger to refer to his clients with the disorder as "little professors."

People with Asperger's disorder are very much like the fictional Vulcan Science Officer Mr. Spock in the old television show *Star Trek*. They avoid emotion, dote on analysis, avoid lies and jokes, and strongly believe that the humans around them are more to be pitied than admired. In fact, one fairly famous website maintained by people with Asperger's disorder is entitled "Oops, Wrong Planet! Syndrome." This is the way the website designers see themselves, as if they had landed on some strange planet on which they just didn't fit comfortably and where their presence clearly discomfited others.

I should also note that the Asperger's syndrome diagnosis may have a fairly short shelf-life. The American Psychiatric Association is proposing doing away with the diagnosis in the upcoming *DSM-V* by folding it into a larger category of spectrum disorder, which will include a number of subcategories that are now clustered into autism, pervasive developmental disorder, Asperger's, and others. There is a strong movement in the Asperger's community to prevent this and preserve the autonomy of Asperger's disorder as a distinct and separate symptom cluster deserving of its own diagnostic category, but whether they will be successful is impossible to know at the time I write this.

In writing *The Unresolved Seventh,* I attempted to present a picture of a relatively high-functioning person with Asperger's disorder in Ben Long. Readers who would like to see a picture of a slightly more impaired (but certainly not helpless) person with the disorder may want to read *The Curious Incident of the Dog in the Nighttime* by Mark Haddon.

More than anything else, however, I wanted to write a good mystery featuring a sleuth who doesn't see the world the way you or I do.

Well, the way *you* do, at least . . .

Weddington, NC
February 21, 2010

ABOUT THE AUTHOR

Richard Helms retired from a career as a forensic psychologist to become a college professor in Charlotte, North Carolina. He has been nominated three times for the Private Eye Writers of America Shamus Award, and is the only author ever to win two Short Mystery Fiction Society Derringer Awards in the same year. An amateur astronomer, gourmet cook, and avid woodworker, Helms lives—as he refers to it—"back in the trees" in a small North Carolina town with his wife Elaine and an ever-changing number of cats.